Rescuing SIENNA'S HEART

RUBY JAMES

To every person living with any form of mental illness.
You aren't alone. Find your tribe and someone to talk to.
National Menal Health Hotline (United States) 866-903-3787

Contents

Chapter 1

Sienna Parker wouldn't take the thick, dark gray clouds as a sign she shouldn't move to Oak Mountain, Maryland. It *was* summer in the Mid-Atlantic region after all. Random storms pop up out of nowhere. It was sunny four hours ago when she left her parents' home in Philadelphia. Where she said goodbye to her husband's tombstone, gunned down in the line of duty.

As her therapist used to say, positive energy.

The rain washed away her old life, clearing the path for a new beginning. It was something she would have to play on a loop in her mind as fat drops bounced off her windshield.

Sienna glanced in the rearview mirror and smiled. Kai, her nine-year-old son, read to his turtle, Scooter. Her sweet baby lost himself in books or building Legos. Bright hazel eyes he inherited from his father intently followed his finger as he read aloud. His light coloring showcased his mixed heritage. Sienna's black and Hispanic light tone and Dylan's fair skin. Scooter was his partner in crime and co-builder. Kai didn't understand that he couldn't build a habitat out of the colorful blocks for the turtle. He compromised and built obstacle courses for Scooter.

Sienna returned her eyes back to the road and eased off the gas as traffic slowed. She took deep breaths and used her thumb to spin her silver meditation ring gently, an act she hoped to do less often after the move. Traffic came to a stop. Sienna adjusted the scarf that held her thick twists away from her face and exhaled a deep breath.

In the distance, she saw a large brown animal dart across the road, barely missing a car coming the other way. *Would contending with wildlife be the norm?* She thought as traffic began to move. She used to love camping with Dylan. Kai had a membership with the Philadelphia Zoo that gave him extra perks. Given their love for animals, she looked forward to sharing these discoveries with him.

"Was that a deer, Mommy?" Kai hoisted himself as far as his belt would allow and peered out the back passenger window.

"Sure was, sweetie. Remember, Aunt Maya said there is a lot in this area."

"I can't wait to tell Poppy I saw one." Kai gave her a toothy grin before settling back in his seat.

Sienna couldn't help but smile. It reiterated why leaving Philadelphia and heading to Oak Mountain was the right decision.

Sienna closed herself off, grief overly consuming her. Giving up her job as a nurse was the first sign. Sienna met her husband ten years ago while he waited for his partner to get looked over. They went out for dinner the following day and were together until that fateful day.

After Dylan's death, the hospital became too noisy. She took a leave of absence from nursing after her second panic attack and got help. If she didn't, she wouldn't be any good to Kai.

That leave led to her leaving the field and getting a certificate as a medical biller and coder. It allowed her to work from home for a national billing company and be there for Kai. Sadly, it contributed to her seclusion from the rest of her life.

Sienna's sister, Maya, and her husband, Vince, moved to the small town of Oak Mountain three months ago to manage the property of an animal sanctuary and small farm. After almost fifteen years on a cattle farm, they were looking for something new. According to her sister, it was the perfect decision. It was how Maya talked Sienna into moving.

The city had become overwhelming, with its noise, crowds, and the wail of sirens. Sienna retreated to the safety of her home, venturing out only for quick errands and doctor appointments. But when she called her mother to talk her through picking up Kai from a friend's house, she realized she needed to make a change. The memory washed over her like a tidal wave.

Sienna was leaving a routine doctor's appointment. Kai went to his friend's home from school, and she volunteered to pick him up since it was on the way home. Four blocks from the boy's home, traffic came to a halt. The distinct sounds of sirens came closer. She reached for the volume on her car radio and turned up the meditative sounds from her satellite radio. The louder the sirens became, the faster her heart rate became in sync with the pattern of the blaring sound. Sienna glanced around and could see a corner where she could turn to go around but three cars prevented her from moving in that direction. The thought of jumping the sidewalk crossed her mind, but she opted to call her mother instead. Flora calmly talked her through a breathing exercise while giving encouragement of Kai counting on her. Once traffic was diverted and she could go around the accident, Sienna felt her pulse slow. Her mother switched to talking about mindless topics until Kai was in the car and they were headed home.

Sienna shook off the trip down memory lane and focused on the road. She wanted to be an active mother. She started therapy, sold her house and moved in with her parents in the suburbs of Philadelphia. It wasn't something she wanted to do at thirty-five, but you do what you need to do. Talking to Maya gave her the courage to leave the city and give the quiet of a small town a try. Maybe even open herself up to dating.

So here she was, taking a leap of faith. Thankfully, she could work anywhere.

As quickly as it started, the rain ended. Sienna turned off the wipers as the exit for Oak Mountain came into view. *They must be big enough to get an exit*, she thought. Sienna considered herself a city girl. How her sister fell in love with small towns fascinated Sienna. But she had to give it a shot. Following the GPS, she made a right at the end of the ramp.

"Why don't you pack up, sweetie?" Sienna said to the mirror. "We should be there in less than ten minutes."

"Are you sure they will bring my bed tomorrow?" Kai asked as he slipped his e-reader into his backpack.

"Yep, Poppy is going to make sure the movers get everything in your room."

When Sienna sold her house, she put everything in storage but their bedroom furniture. Her father volunteered to supervise the movers in getting her items from storage and her parents' house. Sienna didn't want to deal with moving late in the evening, and Maya suggested arriving a day early so she could show her around. The movers were arriving close to noon the next day.

"Did you tell Uncle Vince about Scooter? It's okay if we bring him inside?" Kai laid a small wedge of lettuce inside the tank before closing the lid.

"Yep. He said they have a table he can use." Sienna pressed the touchscreen on her dashboard to switch to the phone. "Call Maya."

The ringing echoed in the car. Her sister answered on the third ring.

"Hey! Are you here?" Maya said over a chorus of barks. Sienna swallowed a chuckle.

"GPS said five minutes. I'm on a mountain road."

"Okay. I will meet you near the entrance. Pull over past the greenhouse if you don't see me. Tell Little Man I want a big hug."

Sienna checked the rearview mirror to find a wide grin splitting Kai's face. They said their goodbyes. She saw the first sign for Hawkins Ridge a mile on the left. A huge wooden sign announced their destination. Sienna made a left and gasped. Three large greenhouses flanked her left. An in-ground field pushed against an apple orchard. Workers busied themselves tending the dirt and pushing wheelbarrows across the gravel driveway. People waved, causing Kai to giggle. He waved back and pointed out the sights for Scooter's benefit.

A small cabin-style building sat on a patch of land. An "Office" sign hung from a post. Before Sienna could pull over, a fast-moving ATV barreled from a pull-off to the left. She eased on the brakes. Thankfully, she wasn't going over five miles an hour. Maya pulled up beside her, a toothy smile on her face.

Sienna couldn't get her seat belt off fast enough to climb out and give her sister a smothering hug. Both laughed as they rocked each other. A few seconds later, they stepped back so Maya could wave to Kai.

"Follow me," she said over the motor and hung a U-turn. Sienna shook her head at her sister before climbing back into the car and putting it in drive.

"Will Auntie take me for a ride on that?" Kai asked, glancing through the seat opening.

"I'm sure you can get a ride. I'll even take you if they're busy." Sienna didn't know if Maya would let her drive the ATV. She hadn't been on one since the camping trip with Dylan. It was before Kai, but Sienna remembered how free it felt. Maybe this was a good idea.

They continued up the driveway, passing a goat farm on the left and a chicken coop and run on the right. They crested a small incline; a large farmhouse rose into view. Maya told her that the Beckett family lived on the property. Each son had his own home. Past the farmhouse, Maya flicked her turn signal. They drove through an open gate. Activity increased with a UTV trudging by. They waved at Maya and gave Sienna a smile as they drove by. Sienna would need a minute or two to get used to the friendliness.

A gravel clearing next to a building titled "Clinic" sat in the middle, connecting the farmhouse she passed and another large cabin. A grassy courtyard with benches screamed meeting space. Maya continued a few yards past the cabin and pulled over. Sienna followed suit and killed the engine.

The two were always close, still talking on the phone twice a week and doing a video call for Kai. Similar in height at just over five foot six, Maya's solid build spoke of her time working outdoors. Sienna's athletic frame turned to soft curves when she gave up nursing. She still did yoga with her mother, but the thirty pounds she put on since Dylan's death gave her a vintage pinup body.

The sisters always had each other's backs. It's why she listened to Maya when she encouraged Sienna to consider a small town. If the noise of a large metropolitan area was killing her quality of life, she needed to change for her and Kai's mental health. So she let Maya and Vince find her a place to rent. Sienna didn't want to commit to a mortgage yet. Just in case she wasn't small-town material.

Sienna clambered out just as her sister was pulling the door wider. It was Maya's turn to give her a squeeze. Tears welled in Sienna's eyes. She didn't know how much she needed her big sister until that moment.

"Everything is going to work out," Maya whispered in her ear. "You're taking the steps to get control of your life again."

Sienna could only nod as she ran her fingers across her eyes.

"Can I get out?" Kai's innocent voice called out. The two sisters laughed and took a step back.

"I'm coming, Little Man." Maya shook her head and hurried around the other side.

"You made good time," a familiar voice said from behind. Sienna whirled and came face to face with her brother-in-law. A baseball cap covered his dark locks. A simple T-shirt and jeans fit his swimmer body. Sienna threw her arms around Vince, causing him to laugh. "I miss you too, bits."

Sienna playfully slapped his arm. "I'm thirty-five. Bits only applied when I was in high school."

"You'll still be that teenage girl with pigtails." Vince wrapped his arm around her shoulder before turning her slightly. An older, dark-skinned man stood with a warm smile on his face. He had a few inches on Vince's six-foot height. Built like a retired linebacker, his laugh lines and the twinkle in his eyes softened what might otherwise be an intimidating presence.

"Owen, this is my sister-in-law, Sienna. This is Owen Garrison, the man whose position we took over." Vince motioned towards a wiggly Kai. "The laugh box is my nephew, Kai."

Sienna hoped her eyes weren't too puffy and stuck out her hand. "It's nice to meet you."

"Nice to meet you too, dear." Owen's deep, radio-friendly voice relaxed her.

Maya stopped tickling Kai long enough to lead him over. Owen squatted and held his hand out. "Aren't you a big boy? Welcome to Hawkins Ridge."

Kai glanced at Sienna, who gave a small nod. He shook Owen's hand with gusto. "Thank you, sir. My mom said I'm growing faster than weeds."

Owen chuckled. "Your mother is right. Let me help with your bags."

"Can you carry Scooter?" Kai turned and opened the back door. Sienna shook her head.

"Why don't we get our overnight bags first, then we'll set Scooter up for the night?"

Kai nibbled his bottom lip. "He may get lonely if we're gone too long."

Vince stepped forward and clapped Kai on the shoulder. "I think he'll be okay. Besides, you have to tell me if his spot on the table is good enough for him."

Kai contemplated the argument before agreeing. "You're right."

All the adults laughed as Sienna pointed out their two overnight bags and the box with Scooter's heat lamp and covering. Sienna wondered if Vince was still in training. Did Owen live on the property? Was he expected to move because of Vince and Maya?

Her sister led them to a nice size cabin across from where they parked. The cozy porch stretched the width of the front exterior. A swing she remembered from her visit to their home in Kentucky hung proudly from the beams.

"I can't believe this swing made the trip," Sienna said, nudging it with her hip.

"It didn't. We had to reinforce the sides," Vince commented. "We have two rockers for you to use on your balcony."

"My son and I made sure the balustrade was secured yesterday," Owen added as he placed the box on the couch.

To say Sienna loved her sister's home would be an understatement. A welcoming open floor plan greeted them. The space held Vince's dark recliner and a contrasting couch in a soft beige. Both faced a fireplace with a TV hanging from the wood planks. Stainless steel appliances, buffed to a shine, gave the area a bright and airy feel.

Sienna set her valise on the floor and faced Owen. "You didn't need to do anything for my apartment. Thank you."

Owen waved away her concern. "My ex-sister-in-law is your landlady, and she's always asking me and my son for repair help."

Sienna noticed a wedding band on the older gentleman's hand. She didn't know if she would still let her husband do work for anyone in his ex's family.

Maya rested a hand on Owen's arm. "He's a big marshmallow, is what he is. Owen didn't tell you Denise supplies him with a weekly centerpiece for any repairs."

"Sam loves her flowers. He plans Monday meals around the centerpiece." Owen shook his head. "I don't know what I'll do when Denise retires."

The name rang a bell. She spoke to Denise when Maya did a video call walk-through of the apartment. Her new home was above Denise's flower shop and the store next door. Twelve hundred square feet with a balcony that looked over Main Street. The rent was half her old mortgage. Sienna transferred her deposit the same day.

"Is Sam your son?" Sienna asked.

Owen cleared his throat. "Sam is my husband. Noah is my son."

Sienna noticed the cautious look on the older man's face. Was he worried she wouldn't approve of his being gay? She didn't care. Dylan's former partner was gay, and she has co-workers in the LGBTQ+ community. "Cool. I can't wait to meet them. My sister swears I'm going to be here every weekend."

"That's because you are." Maya pointed to a TV tray next to the front window. "Is that okay for Scooter?"

Kai tapped his chin and circled the table. "It'll do. Thanks."

Maya ruffled his curly hair. "Anything for you. Let's go grab him."

"I'm going to head home." Owen tugged a set of keys from his pocket. "Let me know if you need anything tomorrow. Noah and I both are free if there're any issues."

"Thank you again for making sure the railing is safe." Sienna didn't know whether she should pay him. She'd have to ask later.

"No need to thank me. I'm sure we'll see each other again soon. Welcome to Oak Mountain. Make sure Vince or Maya gives you mine and Noah's numbers, just in case."

"You're supposed to be retired," Maya said as she passed, carrying Scooter's five-gallon tank. His forty-gallon setup would arrive with the movers.

"I am." Owen gave Maya a wink. "Making sure your sister and nephew are settled and comfortable doesn't affect my retirement."

"Whatever." Maya chuckled and sat the tank on its temporary table. "We'll make sure she has everything."

They all waved as they watched Owen climb onto the ATV Maya dismounted from minutes ago. Sienna checked Vince and her sister to make sure they were seeing it.

"The ATV was his. He let Maya borrow it. They were finishing up feeding the pack," Vince offered as an explanation. "Why don't you unpack, then we'll run over to the apartment. Kai and I can get Scooter's tank set up for the night."

"Kai and I had hoped we could ride the ATV." Sienna picked up their bags. Maya pulled one from her hand and chuckled.

"We have one, but the workers are giving it a tune-up. We can take it out on Sunday if you're up for it."

"Please? Can we, Mom?" Kai pleaded. Sienna nodded.

"I think that's a good idea. We have to stay tomorrow at our new place, though."

"And you're positive my stuff will be delivered?" Kai put his hands on his tiny hips. Maya and Vince turned away, both silently laughing.

Sienna rested her hand on her son's shoulder. "I am almost positive. I have no control over accidents, but Poppy will make sure it's on the van."

The answer seemed to satisfy him. He turned his focus back to the tank. "We have to put his bowl in first before the other stuff."

Sienna left Kai and Vince to get the turtle set up. She followed her sister to the bedroom in the back. A bathroom stood between the rooms. It would give them privacy. She'd also have to figure out a good time for Kai to take his bath. The guest room continued the cabin feel. A queen-size bed anchored the room. A handmade quilt from their maternal grandmother dressed the mattress. Sienna had a matching one in storage. She would find a way to display it later. Two distressed nightstands flanked the bed painted in a cheery lilac. A matching chest of drawers pushed against the jamb of the closet. Everything screamed her sister.

"I wish I could put Gammy's quilt on my bed. But I have a kid who doesn't wash his hands."

Maya laughed. "He's just being a kid. I don't think we washed our hands that often at that age, either."

"You told me I didn't need to until Mom said otherwise."

"It didn't bother Dad." Maya placed Kai's backpack underneath the window. "How are you with everything?"

Sienna sighed and sat at the foot of the bed. It was a question she asked herself driving along Route seventy. She could be honest with her sister.

"Nervous. Excited. Scared. I have never lived outside of the Philly metro area. But I know I need to try at least. For mine and Kai's sake. "

"Girl, Oak Mountain is different. It was a change for Vince and me." Maya sat beside her sister and linked her arm. "People are nice. Not fake nice. People smile and wave."

"It seems diverse. I was worried about that with Kai."

Sienna didn't want her son to deal with people asking what he was like at his old school. When the teacher started speaking Spanish, Kai politely said he didn't speak the language and asked her to speak in English. It was not exactly the truth. Kai spoke some Spanish thanks to their mother. Proficient, he was not.

"I was worried about that when they offered the job. But the staff and residents are of all races, backgrounds, and orientations. You know I wouldn't have suggested you come here if I didn't think it would do you good."

"I know. Leaving Philly had to happen. I think everyone knew that, but it took me a minute to catch on." High pitch giggling brought a smile to her face. "Kai is happy to be near Vince."

"Deep down, he's happy to have him here. Vince loves having him around."

Sienna didn't miss the slight drop in her sister's expression. Maya and Vince wanted to settle on a ranch before adding children to the mix. A mass on Maya's ovary took the option of children away from them.

"So children are officially off the table for you two?" Sienna knew the two talked of adoption but hadn't mentioned it in a year.

Maya shrugged. "I'm not sure. We wanted to see what Hawkins Ridge and the town were like before we started talking again. Everything checks all the boxes except lodging. We have this place, which is great for us; not sure that, with the addition of an older child, there is enough space. We'd have to either talk to the Becketts about building a place or find a place in town and commute."

Sienna could see that. The house was adorable, but she couldn't imagine three people living here. Especially a child Kai's age or older. Sienna would offer whatever help they needed. It was the least she could do. She herself was giving Oak Mountain a year. If she and Kai thrived, then she'd look at buying. Sienna didn't want to think about the options if it didn't work out.

She'd have to make it work for her and Kai's mental health.

Sienna clapped her hands in an attempt to change the mood. "Kai and I can just live out of the suitcase for the night, so there's no real unpacking. Let's head over to the apartment. First, let me make sure he uses the restroom, and do you have anything to drink?"

"Oh my gosh, don't tell Mom I didn't offer you something to drink right away." Maya shook her head.

"You were too excited. It slipped your mind. I won't hold it against you. At least not today."

"Brat!"

The two crumpled in laughter. Sienna missed being herself. Maya would make sure Sienna was in the right environment to find herself.

She would keep her mind and heart open for whatever Oak Mountain had in store for her.

Chapter 2

The sun dipped behind the tops of the trees, giving a break to the summer heat. Noah Garrison sighed with relief. Their mountain town might not experience the same humidity level as the eastern side of the state, but ninety-three degrees is still hot.

He ran his fingers through Meadow, his tan Maine Coon cat's fur. His fifteen-pound girl watched the birds from her window hammock.

"I'll see if your grandfathers have treats for you. Keep an eye on the place." Noah smiled at the deep purr in response.

If he mentioned to his father that Meadow was out of tuna, Owen would send him home with several cans plus sardines for good measure. The fluff ball came to Hawkins Ridge as a rescue. Underweight with matted fur, Noah nursed her back to health. He wasn't looking for a pet but fell in love with her.

As part owner of Hawkins Ridge Animal Sanctuary and Farms, one of Noah's responsibilities is the goats, livestock dogs and crops. He and his friends, Jace, Logan and Caden Beckett, officially took over the business from their parents almost a year ago. Each had their area of expertise. Using the goat's milk to produce cheeses, soaps, and lotions was Noah's idea almost twelve years ago when he and Jace returned from college. It was an idea, and a life he wanted to share with his ex-wife, Robin. He was wrong.

Robin was a city girl he met in college who thought small-town living sounded fun. Nine months into their marriage, Robin admitted it wasn't for her when she didn't return from visiting her family in Brooklyn. Throwing himself into building their goat product business and expanding their organic produce helped him deal with the loss. Having Meadow was helpful, but seeing his best friend Jace find love had him questioning what he was doing with his life.

A rough lick against his close-cut beard brought Noah back to the present. He gave Meadow another scratch behind the ear and left her to watch the birds. He grabbed his keys and hurried out the door.

All the owners of Hawkins Ridge lived on the five hundred acres. Originally owned by Josie Beckett's grandfather, Noah's father purchased twenty of the acres when Josie and Thomas pulled him out of retirement to be part owner and take over the management of the day-to-day operations. Owen gifted five acres to Noah so he could build a house for him and Robin. When his marriage ended halfway through construction, he redesigned it to his liking.

Climbing into his UTV, he pointed it towards his father's home. It was a three-minute drive to his prefab modular home near the stables. Owen and Sam constructed the house after moving out of the suite in the main house. When Owen, Josie, and Thomas turned the business over, the house went to the oldest son, Logan. Though Logan extended the offer for them to stay in the mother-in-law suite, his father and husband wanted their own space. Logan was a newlywed after all.

Noah waved to a few workers walking the horses as they boarded back to the stables. He cut through a cluster of trees and slowed down when he hit the small clearing. His father stood on the patio near the grill. The outdoor misting fan cast a soft, foggy haze around them. Even beneath the thick canopy of trees, the summer heat was still palpable. The mist, however, made dining outdoors comfortably bearable.

No one could ever deny that Noah was Owen's clone. Medium brown complexion, both men stood close to six feet five inches. Owen's close-cut fade was now a shiny shade of gray. Where Noah had a thick, muscular build, his father's muscles had taken on a softer tone.

Noah smiled as he killed the engine. He was thankful for their close relationship. Noah had doubts when Owen came to terms with his orientation, therefore ending the marriage to his mother twenty years ago. Noah was sixteen at the time and endured bullying and whispers. He hated his father and didn't speak to him for a year. Counseling and the support of their friends helped them get over the rough patch.

"You didn't bring Meadow?" Owen asked as he lifted the lid on the grill. Noah grabbed a flavored sparkling water from the bucket of ice and took a seat at the outdoor table.

"She was too busy watching birds. I told her you may send something home with me."

"That can be arranged. Your mail is on the kitchen counter."

Noah nodded in thanks. He had a personal post office box in which his father had a spare key. They always picked up the other's mail if they knew either was going into town.

"You saved me a trip. I need to go to the grocery store tomorrow and planned on stopping." Noah took a sip of his drink. "Where's Sam?"

"His sister called about ten minutes ago. They moved her to the rehab facility today. She's telling him about her young physical therapist." Owen took the seat opposite his son. "Speaking of sisters, I met Maya's earlier. Her nephew is too adorable. I told Vince to make sure she had our numbers in case something needed to be fixed."

"I'll text Aunt Denise in the morning and let her know I'm free if anything comes up."

Owen studied his son for a moment. Noah attempted not to squirm under the scrutiny. Since he was a kid, his father could always tell when something was bothering him. Noah wouldn't try to keep anything from him. That wasn't the type of relationship they had. But he tried to always work through his thoughts because, without fail, Owen would ask him questions.

After a long moment, the older man spoke. "What's on your mind? You've been quieter than usual."

Before Noah could answer, Sam strolled out the back door carrying a tray. A warm smile graced the older light-skinned male. His stepfather was a kind soul with a caring heart. Sam was a few years younger than Owen's sixty-two years, slender with a shaved head. The two met when Sam took the job as Logan's vet tech seven years ago.

Noah hurried and took the tray from his hands so he could close the door. A glass container held marinated boneless, skinless chicken thighs. Skewers of seasoned summer squash and zucchini rested on a plate ready for the grill.

"Thank you. I'll bring the pasta salad out when this is done." Sam gave Noah a half-hug. "No Meadow?"

"Not tonight," Owen answered, taking the food from his son. "Noah was just about to tell us what's on his mind."

"Thanks, Pop." Noah didn't hide the sarcastic tone.

Sam looked at the two men. "If you two need to talk, I can handle dinner if you want to go inside."

Noah shook his head. "No, you don't need to leave. I'm not even sure what's bothering me." He did, but he didn't want to make a big thing out of it.

Sam handed Owen his drink and took a seat. Owen checked the temperature and carefully placed the thighs on the heated grill.

"What's going on?" Sam asked, taking a sip of his wine.

Noah blew out a breath and just went for it. "I'm in a rut. I didn't realize that until Vince and Maya came on board and improved how things are done here. Don't get me wrong. I like them a lot and love the work they're doing, but is it wrong that they freed up time for us?"

Owen and Sam chuckled. It was his father who spoke after he lowered the lid.

"No, it's not wrong. When Josie and Thomas pulled me out of retirement to organize the business, I streamlined a lot of procedures. When you boys took over, you improved on what we were doing."

"But it makes sense they had different ideas," Sam added. He turned to Owen. "Didn't you say Josie and Thomas quipped at some of your ideas?"

His father nodded. "She did what her father and grandfather taught her. When you boys had ideas on how to make Hawkins Ridge profitable, we bucked back a little."

Noah snorted. His father, Josie, and Thomas didn't think other businesses would be interested in their products. They were wrong. Expanding boarding to horses from the surrounding farms, tripling the vegetable gardens, adding products made from goats' milk and having a steady booth at farmer's markets doubled the profits.

Since Vince and Maya's arrival, they forced Noah, Jace, Caden, and Logan to expand the workforce and streamline duties. Noah couldn't deny it was for the best.

"When you say you're in a rut, what do you mean?" Sam asked. The question was out of concern.

Noah scratched his cheek. "I don't think rut is the right word. Basically, I have free time and don't know what to do. I have quality goat handlers. The supervisors have the crops looking great." He hated to admit the following words. "Everything I've done has been for Hawkins Ridge. I have nothing just for Noah Garrison."

"Ah." Owen used tongs to flip the meat. "Even though you're an owner, Hawkins Ridge is still seen as a Beckett business."

Noah opened up a can of worms and just let everything spill out. "Exactly. You had a successful business, Pop, and didn't need to work. You came out of retirement as a favor to your best friends. No one saw your position as a Beckett charity case."

"No, they saw it as friends who should have turned their backs on me. Not give me a chance to come to terms with my new reality," Owen said.

Noah knew all too well the snark his father went through when he admitted to himself who he really was. Growing up in Tuskegee, Alabama, the only son of two college professors, Owen could never be true to himself until after his grandparents died. Josie and Thomas Beckett stood by their college friend, who built a life in Oak Mountain.

Sam gave Owen's arm a squeeze. He turned his attention to Noah. "Everything you're feeling has merit. Things are changing here. Logan and Naomi are expecting. Jace is engaged. Until a year ago, it was the four of you fighting to get out of your parents' shadows. You all made this business yours and still kept it as a family business. You know the Becketts see you and Owen as family. It's why they made you partners."

"I know and I see them as brothers and second parents."

"But now that you have time to kill, you don't know what to do with yourself and you started questioning what pet project you can take on," Owen finished.

He pulled their dinner off the grill while Sam hurried back inside to grab the pasta salad. When he returned, their Bengal cat Whiskers was on his heels. A stray whose whiskers were singed, Owen and Sam nursed the large cat back to health.

Noah helped bring everything to the table. His hesitation to be open about what was on his mind now seemed silly. Usually, he and Jace were each other's sounding board. Now Jace had Claire. Noah was happy for his best friend. Claire was his true love and made him a better man.

Since his marriage, Noah hadn't pursued another relationship. He would have a date or two with a friend in Stark Valley, the county seat. That ended three years ago when she met her future husband. He thought he was content being a bachelor because the farm kept him busy. Now, seeing Jace and Logan find their loves, he wondered if maybe there was someone for him. First, he needed to find a passion project.

Once everyone settled with their plates, Owen returned to the conversation.

"Do you want to sell your stake in Hawkins Ridge?"

Noah immediately shook his head. "Definitely not. This is my home, and I love everything here."

"I didn't think so, but wanted to be sure." Owen forked a piece of squash. "Have you given any thought to what you want to do? You have resources and capital if you want to invest in something."

Owen had introduced Noah and the Beckett boys to the stock market early, letting them play with pretend money. When they turned twenty-one, his father and Thomas revealed that they had actually invested in the picks the boys had made. Since then, they'd continued to dabble in stocks, each building a comfortable nest egg. Noah, however, had no intention of pursuing it full time.

"I want to give back," Noah finally said. "I'd love to teach, but I don't have the time to spend in the classroom. Things come up here, and I need to be there when it does."

"There are ways you can teach that aren't classroom based," Owen said around a bite of chicken. Sam nodded in agreement.

"If you want to impart your knowledge, you can give a talk at the community college. Invite the local 4-H one Saturday a month since Fiona is now a part of it. You can even do a blog or podcast. All options will allow you to do it on your own time."

Noah hadn't thought of that. Fiona, Logan's teenage daughter from his first marriage, was the next generation of Hawkins Ridge. Being one of two goat farms in the county, Noah had the upper hand in sharing the advantage of raising goats.

Blogs and podcasts weren't something he'd thought about, but sparked in his mind as soon as Sam said the words. Heck, he could write a post about enclosures every day for a month. Not to mention proper diet, the correct livestock dogs and bedding.

Noah scratched his beard as his mind spun with ideas. For the first time in the past few months, excitement bubbled in his core. He had a direction to funnel his restlessness.

Whiskers climbed into his lap, bringing him out of his thoughts. He scratched the affectionate feline behind its ear and met his father and stepfather's knowing scrutiny.

"Are you itching to start a list?" Owen asked. He knew his son's need to organize his thoughts on paper.

"I can wait until I get home. Thanks for listening and giving me ideas."

"You know you can talk to us anytime," Sam stated. "Dating is also a possibility with the time you have."

"Not subtle at all." Owen chuckled, causing Sam to roll his eyes. "He's right, though. You've thrown yourself into work since Robin left. All you boys have when faced with heartache.

Now that the business is where you want it, maybe it's time to open yourself up to the possibility of another relationship. Logan and Jace have."

It was true. Everyone wanted Hawkins Ridge to remain small yet profitable. They'd done that. It was why he and his soul brothers were looking into pet projects. Logan wanted to expand the sanctuary pack. Jace was building a foster home network for rescue animals. Caden wanted to grow his support animal program. Now Noah had ideas to share his knowledge. Adding romance would be the logical next step.

They were all in their mid to late thirties and joked about staying bachelors until old age over a game of poker. In truth, they all wanted what their parents had. A loving, committed relationship. Settling wasn't an option. Been there and had no intention of doing it again.

Noah built his home for a family. Even after Robin left in the middle of construction, with the changes he made, he still wanted the space to be family friendly. Sharing a two thousand square foot home with Meadow still made for lonely nights. The problem was finding the right woman. He wouldn't expect any woman he met to work side by side with him, caring for the goats and overseeing the production of the products. Though it would be nice if she were interested in learning.

What he wanted was an independent woman with her own passions. Most importantly, someone who appreciated the slower pace of a small town. Even Stark Valley, with a population of close to sixty thousand, would be acceptable. Noah had his fill of large city life during college at the University of Pittsburgh. He learned it wasn't for him.

He and Jace drove home once a month to escape the noise. The love of small-town living was something Noah wouldn't compromise on.

"Sienna, Maya's sister, is quite the looker," Owen commented as he stacked the empty dishes.

Noah shook his head. "She's also a city girl."

"Who wants to leave the city behind," his father argued.

Noah nudged a sleeping Whiskers from his lap and took the dishes from Owen. The cat scowled before darting to the back door and waiting for someone to open it for him. Noah spoke while he loaded the tray with their dishes.

"I'm not opposed to dating. Ma's been itching to put together a list of single women for me. All I have to do is say the word." Noah held his father's gaze for a moment. The setting sun woke the night insects. "I loved Robin and believed her when she said she wanted to live here. She didn't make it a year. I know what I want and have no intention of settling."

"No one expects you to settle, son. That's not a relationship. Just don't close yourself off to a former city girl. I'm not talking about Sienna per se. But people can change," Owen said, his voice soft.

"It's true," Sam piped in. "I lived in Los Angeles most of my life. I didn't realize I craved a small town until I visited my friend in Stark Valley. What started as a two-week trip turned into me packing up my life out west and moving within a month. Best decision I made."

Owen and Sam smiled lovingly at each other. Noah met people who craved a slower pace, and he knew it was possible. Robin moved to be with Noah and wanted to try his lifestyle. But it wasn't in her heart. That was the difference. It was the desire for change that made the switch work. The realization hit him like a ton of bricks.

Moving to a small town because a person needed and wanted the change made it work. If he had known then what he knew now, Noah would have realized his marriage wouldn't work. Robin never wanted the small-town life, but loved him to at least try. It was too late to go over what-ifs.

Noah would have to keep an open mind if he told his mother he wanted to start dating. She lived in Stark Valley and knew several transplants because of her real estate career. He would have to think more on that after he researched the ideas Sam and his father gave him for some form of teaching.

Noah hefted the tray and headed towards the house. "Set up the dominoes. Maybe I can beat you two tonight."

"Doubtful, but maybe we'll go easy on you," Owen teased, opening the door for him.

Noah didn't plan on talking to his father about what was on his mind. He's thankful he did.

Chapter 3

Sienna watched people bustle along Main Street. Friendly chatter drifted up to her spot next to the open kitchen window. She smiled, looking down at Maya speaking with her landlady, Denise, against the large moving truck. They waved to a young family strolling past the building.

You're not in Philly anymore, she thought, turning away from the scene.

For the first time since Dylan died, Sienna slept without her white noise machine. Crickets, owls, and nocturnal rustling lulled her to a peaceful slumber. She could chalk it up to her sister being under the same roof, but even in her parents' suburban home, she still contended with sirens, engines, and light noise throughout the night. None of that existed at Hawkins Ridge. The only downfall was the four roosters who signaled the start of the day at the hint of the sunrise. Kai giggled at the sound, and it made being woken an hour before her alarm worth it.

Sienna spared a final glance outdoors when she heard heavy footsteps on the long staircase. Spacious was the best word to describe her loft-style apartment. Built in the 1950s, the building originally served as a boarding house. According to Denise, in 1975 the original owners converted the lower level into a women's dress shop and a small café. It still housed two apartments on the upper level for the owner. Denise and her husband took over ownership twenty years ago when the building went into foreclosure. It took them close to ten years to renovate the space for her flower shop below and turn the two apartments into one three-bedroom apartment. Denise's daughters occupied the space until four months ago when they moved to the town of Stark Valley for work.

Sienna loved the scuffed hardwood floors, exposed brick and natural light seeping in from the large pane windows. The wrought-iron balcony wrapped around the front corner of the building. It would be a perfect spot for morning coffee and watching the sunrise. She made a mental note to thank Owen for securing the decorative balustrade. The last thing she wanted was for her or Kai to have an accident.

"Ma'am, these are labeled bathroom, but don't say which one," the younger of the three movers said.

"You can put them in the hallway for now." Sienna and Kai shared a bathroom at her parents'. Now that they had their own, she'd have to decorate each.

The other two movers followed with her dining room table. Sienna sold most of the furniture she had purchased with Dylan a year after his death because she couldn't handle the memories. The dining room table was the only piece she kept. Seeing it now, she wondered if it was time to let it go. It was small for the space, and she didn't really like the design. They bought it because it was on sale and could fit into their narrow row home. Neither really loved it and always kept it covered with a tablecloth. Something she would tackle in the weeks ahead.

Laughter echoed in the stairwell before Maya and Denise stepped through the front door. Both hurried over to Sienna, who was busy moving a stack of empty boxes out of the way.

"Girl, Vince sent pictures of Kai on the four-wheeler. I didn't think the boy could smile that wide," Maya commented as she shoved her phone in Sienna's face.

"That boy is going to be a heartbreaker when he gets older," Denise added.

Sienna left Kai with Vince after breakfast. She and Maya wanted to do a little grocery shopping and meet the movers without the little one in the way. It also gave them time to open all the windows since they didn't want to run the air conditioning since both the door on the ground level and the door to her apartment would be open for the move.

Happiness bubbled in her heart as she scrolled through the photos of her baby. Dirt smudged his cherub cheeks, but he didn't care. His toothy grin lit up the screen as he grasped the handles. Another picture showed him holding a watermelon as large as his head between rows of the juicy fruit.

"You have to send these to me and the folks," Sienna said as she handed the phone back.

"Will do. Vince said they should be here in an hour. There are only a few more boxes and the dining room chairs left in the van." Maya tapped away before Sienna's phone buzzed in the pocket of her shorts.

"I'm going to leave you to it." Denise wrapped her arm around Sienna's shoulder and gave a squeeze. "If you need anything, call me. I'm a ten-minute drive away. Otherwise, I will check with you on Monday morning. I really think you'll like Oak Mountain."

Sienna silently agreed. "Thank you. Enjoy the rest of your weekend."

The older woman waved goodbye and followed the movers out the front door. Maya moved closer and linked her arm with her sister's.

"What were you thinking about so hard when we came in?"

Sienna chuckled. "The dining room table. I'll probably replace it in a few weeks. Before then, I thought about how the noise from the street didn't bother me. This is downtown on a Saturday afternoon, and the only reason I hear everything is because I have the windows open."

"It helps the speed limit in the downtown area is twenty miles an hour," Maya added.

Downtown was a three-block radius made up of shops, city hall and a block-wide park. Along with angled street parking, there was a lot at the end of her block for overflow parking. Luckily, Sienna had assigned parking in the back of the building next to Denise.

"This is the last of it," the moving supervisor said. His two workers placed the dining room chairs next to the table. "Once you look in the back of the van to confirm, I can get your signature."

Sienna scurried to the kitchen area and pulled her purse from one of the cabinets. She pulled out the cash tip and stuffed it in her pocket.

"Take some water and something to eat," she offered. "There's meat and cheese to make sandwiches."

"We'll take some water if you don't mind," the supervisor said as she passed them two bottled waters each. "We need to be back by seven, and will stop and get food on the way."

It was a little over four hours back to Philadelphia and just after two o'clock. Sienna and Maya followed the men out to the van and stared into the empty cargo space. After signing the order form, she passed them the tip, which they gratefully thanked her for.

After a last wave, Maya tugged Sienna away from the ground-level door. "We have to get our order from the bakery before Vince and Kai get here."

Sienna looked at the open door and her unguarded purse upstairs.

"Let me grab my—"

"Just close the door," Maya interrupted her before she could finish, "we'll be less than five minutes depending on if there is a line. I placed the order yesterday. It is the best lemon sour cream pound cake you've ever had. I'm including granny's in that statement."

Their paternal grandmother used to make the best cakes from scratch. She passed before she could teach them her secret. Even following the recipes she left behind, it always missed something no one could put their finger on.

Sienna nibbled her lip before trusting her sister and pulling the door closed. She saw the bakery and its line when they arrived that morning. She would have suggested stopping, but they were on a schedule and didn't want to be late meeting the movers. There were cute stores along the block Sienna wanted to check out in a few days. Unpacking took precedence. Maybe after taking Kai to see his new school and meet his teacher on Monday, they could explore.

Maya waved to a few people before stopping at the entrance to the bakery. Closing was still thirty minutes away, and only one customer lingered at the counter. When she thought of small-town quaint, this bakery was exactly what came to mind. A tall display case with rotating shelves showcased expertly decorated cakes and pies, though the selection was limited given the time of day. Shelves lined with rectangular paper doilies accented baskets of cellophane-wrapped breads. A smaller glass case held donuts, croissants, and Danishes. Every selection made her mouth water. A few multicolored tables with mismatched chairs lined against the windows gave customers a perfect view for people watching while indulging in their sweets.

"I was just about to call you," the woman behind the counter said to Maya. She placed two pink boxes on the counter. "I would have dropped them off."

"Please. I would never ask you to do that." Maya wrapped her arm around Sienna, pulling her closer. "This is my sister, Sienna. She just moved to Oak Mountain."

"Oh! Denise said she had someone moving in. I'm Taylor."

The blonde woman gave a warm smile when she stuck out her hand. "Sienna Parker. Everything looks amazing."

"You have my mother-in-law to thank for that. I can burn toast," the younger woman teased.

"Taylor is a gardener at Hawkins Ridge. She helps out here on Saturdays," Maya supplied.

"I take tending to the plants over the weekend rush here any day." Taylor placed the boxes in a plastic bag. "I hope you enjoy the cake. Welcome to Oak Mountain."

The sisters gave their thanks and headed back to the apartment. Pedestrians nodded in passings as they strolled down the street. They waved to the worker in the flower shop before going in through the unassuming door that led to her place.

"It's going to take a minute to get used to the friendliness," Sienna commented as they climbed the stairs. "Remind me to amend my stranger danger talk to Kai." Sienna knew they weren't gone long enough for anyone to come in and take anything, but she gave a cursory glance inside her purse. Maya placed the bag holding their treat on the counter.

"Like I said yesterday, Oak Mountain is different. The town we left in Kentucky was nice, but it took a while for them to accept me and Vince. I don't know if it's because we manage one of the oldest properties or what." Maya shrugged and handed Sienna a bottled water. "But I know this is where Vince and I are going to set roots. The Becketts are amazing people and already treat us like family. That's what we want."

"There *is* a family vibe here. I know Kai likes the property."

It was important to her. During breakfast, Kai asked a ton of questions about the animals and crops. Sienna couldn't remember the last time he was excited about being outdoors. Even the pungent aroma of the goats and chickens was preferable to the exhaust and smog from the large city. Even a summer Saturday afternoon in downtown Oak Mountain still offered fresh mountain air with a hint of outskirt farms.

But was it enough for Sienna? Would Kai like his new school? What if the population exploded, and she found herself back in the middle of an internal chaos? Sienna promised herself and Maya she would give Oak Mountain a year. Knowing Maya chose this bizarre friendly town as her forever home would make the year easier. At least she didn't have the roosters to wake her in the morning. Was there even a nightlife downtown? The thought of boisterous laughter and excessive traffic at two in the morning didn't appeal to her.

Before Sienna could ask her sister, her parents' ringtone echoed in the space. She walked to the couch and pressed the speaker.

"Hey Dad! Perfect timing, the movers just left."

"I was wondering," Gerald Wood's deep baritone voice said. "Your mother is with me."

"Hi Mama," Sienna and Maya said in unison.

Flora Wood's laugh could calm the strongest wind. "Both my babies. How did the move go? We got the pictures of Kai. He seems happy."

"It went okay. I left Kai with Vince so he wouldn't be underfoot. They should be here soon." Sienna took in the piles of boxes. "I'm sure I'll be unpacking for a week. I'm glad I took the time off."

She'd taken a few days off for that very reason. She also wanted to spend time with Kai exploring the area before they jump back into their school routine.

"I figured as much," Gerald commented. "Will you have space for all of your stuff?"

"More than enough. I'll even be able to display Kai's Lego structures."

"I'm sure we're going to have to go shopping for more shelves and maybe a couple of bookcases," Maya piped in.

Sienna agreed. She and Kai shared a bad habit of collecting things that required dusting. Toy dragons for him. Small decorative wood boxes for her. There were built-in bookcases at her old house, so she didn't have a problem. When they moved in with her parents, they put all their collectables in storage. Seeing the nine boxes labeled decorative and dragons stacked in the far corner told her the shopping trip may be sooner rather than later.

"You'll have to send pictures when you get everything placed," Flora commented.

"Once you get settled, your mother and I will come for a visit," Gerald added. "I hear the fall colors are stunning."

"There's a fall festival at the end of September," Maya commented. "The family I work for is involved in the planning. There's plenty of room."

"That sounds like a plan. We don't want to keep you from getting the basic done today. We'll check in with you early in the week," their mother said in closing.

They said their goodbyes, and Sienna shoved the phone back in her pocket. The last thing she wanted to was to lose her phone among the mess. She glanced at her sister and sighed.

"Any chance there's an unpack fairy that can hang the curtains and assemble the beds?"

Maya shook her head and pulled out her phone. "I wish. Let me text Vince to pack an overnight bag and we'll stay here tonight."

"You don't have to do that." Sienna mentally cheered.

Maya spoke while she typed. "Girl please. We'd end up staying here late and be too tired to drive back. Even though we have the weekends off, Vince would end up helping with something in the morning. It would be a welcome break."

Sienna rested her head on Maya's shoulder. "Thank you. For everything."

"That's what sisters do."

No matter the distance, they were always there for each other. It had been seventeen years since they lived in the same area. They visited each other a couple of times a year while Maya lived in Kentucky. They were so focused on building their careers and living life; the distance wasn't important.

Now, a ten-minute drive separated them.

"You know we have to get a tattoo to celebrate the move," Sienna said as she looked at their matching ying-yang symbols inked on their wrists.

"I already got a parlor recommendation from a vet tech at work, and Vince already sketched out an infinity symbol made of tiny roses." Maya nudged her thigh. "Figured we could check them out when we hit the second-hand stores."

"I love how your mind works."

Maybe the move wasn't a bad idea after all.

Chapter 4

Noah tapped his fingers against the steering wheel to old-school R&B as he turned into the sanctuary. His parents had him listening to the good stuff from infancy. Back when singers didn't need filters or curse words to sell a record. He mentally chuckled. *Man, I sound like Pops.*

He waved to the gardeners in the field turning the pumpkins. Noah still struggled with delegating tasks, but he would admit it was for the best. It allowed him to spend the morning researching the ideas he had talked to Owen and Sam the night before. From what he learned, blogging and hosting a podcast worked better with his schedule. It was something he could do in the evenings and on weekends. He had access to generational farmers. Besides, he'd been responsible for the goats and expanding the vegetables since graduation. So he settled on his back porch with his laptop and a spiral notebook and planned. The more he learned, the more excited he became.

He found his passion.

The only reason Noah wasn't still planning was his stomach growling. He stopped and went grocery shopping. There was always something to eat at Hawkins Ridge between the greenhouse, eggs from the chickens, and parents. But there were times you craved a bag of chips, steak, and ice cream. So Noah paid a visit to Ms. Ophelia at the butcher before swinging past the store for junk food staples. Now he could eat, review his notes and watch some baseball.

Before turning onto the dirt path that led to his house past the goat enclosure, he noticed a small boy standing by the chicken coop. Noah had never seen the child before. His gaze darted around for an adult but came up empty. He couldn't be any older than eight.

Noah pulled his truck off to the side and threw it into park. He spared another glance before climbing out. The last thing he wanted was to spook the kid. Noah was not a small man and wore his muscular two hundred and twenty pounds well. He stopped at the passenger side of the truck and crouched down. He kept his voice low.

"Hey buddy. Do you need help? Are you lost?"

The boy turned to look at him. He clutched something close to his chest and took a step back. He glared cautiously. "You're a stranger. My mommy said I shouldn't talk to strange people. Men especially."

Noah smiled. "Your mother's right. I am a stranger, but I also own a part of this land. Is your mom close? Should we call her?" He pulled out his cell phone to show him he wanted to help.

"I'm not lost. My uncle told me to stand here for a minute."

Okay, they were getting somewhere. Before he could ask the name of his uncle, Vince strolled from around the side of the chicken coop. The little guy hurried to him and stood behind his legs. Owen was right; the kid was stinking adorable.

"Hey Noah. I see you met Kai." Vince ruffled the boy's curly hair.

Noah stood, groaning when his knees protested and moved closer.

"Not officially. He did the right thing and told me I was a stranger and couldn't talk to me."

"He admitted he was a stranger," Kai said. Both men chuckled. Vince wrapped his arm around the boy's slender shoulders and pulled him to his side.

"Kai, meet Noah. I work for him, and you met his father yesterday. The man who helped bring Scooter's tank in."

Noah dropped to his knees and held his hand out. "Nice to meet you, Kai."

The boy glanced at his uncle, who gave a nod. When Kai moved closer, Noah noticed the box turtle pressed against him. He assumed this was Scooter. Noah melted when Kai slipped his tiny hand in his.

"Nice to meet you, sir."

"Are you having fun with your uncle?"

The wide smile transformed the small face. "We went four wheeling. It was so much fun. Uncle Vince said we can do it again."

"I like four-wheeling too," Noah said. "My friends and I race each other."

Kai's mouth dropped. "That would be so cool. Do you win?"

"Not as much as I want." Noah stood and smirked when Kai's head followed his progression. "I thought you were helping with the move."

"Sienna didn't want him underfoot. But the movers are gone, and we're heading over there now. We have a lot of boxes to unpack and furniture to put together." He nodded to the side of the coop he had just come from. "There was a bend in the chicken run. I texted a worker to look at it."

"No holes?"

Vince shook his head. "I think one of the dogs tried to play with them."

Noah was the only one of his friends who didn't have a dog. Jace had three, Logan six, and Caden two. All of them loved taunting the hens until the roosters came to the rescue.

"That sounds about right. Do you need help? I got nothing planned." His friends postponed their monthly poker game until the following Saturday. Secretly, he wanted to meet Sienna. After his father put the thought in his head about dating, he was curious. Kai's cuteness only piqued his interest.

Kai tugged his uncle's shorts. "Please, Uncle Vince? He's big and can probably lift Scooter's terrarium with one hand."

Noah turned to hide his smile. Vince gave a look of mock hurt.

"Don't you think I'm strong?"

When Kai shook his head, neither man could keep their laughter in. Vince wasn't as muscular as Noah, but he wasn't a slouch either.

"What can I say? Little Man wants you to help. Are you sure you don't mind?"

"Not at all. More hands make for a lighter load." Noah smiled at Kai. "Let me drop my groceries off and have Pop feed Meadow later. I'll meet you over there in about forty-five minutes."

Vince pulled a set of keys from his pocket. "Sounds good. Thanks."

"Thank you, Mr. Noah," Kai said, still holding Scooter. Boy, that kid was cute.

"You're welcome. See you in a bit." Noah tossed up a wave and jogged back to the truck.

Noah liked Vince and Maya a lot. They were down to earth, hardworking and still new to Oak Mountain. Helping was the neighborly thing to do. He continued to his house and pulled up next to the front door. Meadow dozed in her window hammock without a care in the world. He shot a quick text to Owen before climbing out. He shuffled his parcels to make one trip.

Owen responded "no problem" when he stepped in. Should he take a housewarming gift? He racked his brain for possibilities while he put away the food. Eventually deciding on a plant, he called his aunt's store to have them set aside something. Also, his parents, including the Becketts, would read him the riot act if he went with only his toolbox in his hands.

Noah left Meadow to her own devices, promising to be home later. As he made the short drive to the center of town, his mind went back to his decision to start a blog. He scratched his chin at a light and figured after coming up with a name, he would need to get it out in the world. How he wasn't sure. He wanted to share knowledge about backyard and small-scale farming with those eager to learn. Making a small profit would be nice, but it wasn't the driving force behind his decision—education was. The image of his mother popped into his mind. She used a virtual assistant for her real estate business, even though she was trying to retire. He wondered whether he could hire the same person. Noah would have to call her to plan a lunch during the week. He needed to go to Stark Valley to pick up supplies, anyway.

He'd wait to talk to her about getting into the dating pool. If he mentioned it when he invited her to lunch, there'd be additional dining guests.

Traffic was light on Main Street, and he found a parking spot across from the flower shop. After grabbing his toolbox, he jogged across the street. The manager met him at the door with a vibrant spider plant in a ceramic pot. The low-maintenance wandering plant would thrive in the apartment's natural light.

Noah thanked her and went a few steps to the red door that led upstairs. Someone left the door slightly ajar using a block. Whether that was for him or Vince, it worked to his advantage because his hands were full. Once inside, he set the plant down and closed the door fully, turning the lock. He would come down and unlock it if someone was outside.

A decorative umbrella stand stood on the top landing. It was a nice touch and practical. He smiled, seeing a superhero umbrella already took up residence. He pressed the doorbell and waited. His mouth went dry when the door opened and the most beautiful woman he'd ever seen greeted him with a smile.

Dressed in mid-thigh cut-offs and a Bob Marley T-shirt, she was a natural beauty. A red bandana tied a head full of twists at the top of her head. Colorful tattoos decorated her light brown skin. He almost stumbled back when he took in her bare feet and painted toenails. *Woah.*

"You must be Sienna. I'm Noah Garrison. It is a pleasure to meet you."

When Owen said he had a son, Sienna expected a college-age kid. Why, she didn't know. What she didn't expect was a man who could model in any fitness magazine. Noah Garrison was Hollywood fine.

Close-cut fade that tapered to a close-trim beard. Not a sparsely, speckle of hair. No, full and clean, with a hint of gray. A fitted white tee strained to contain developed muscles. Not steroid gym rat muscles. This was outdoor, lifting bales of hay muscles. At least that's what she could picture him doing. Khaki casual shorts highlighted his powerful thighs and calves.

Sienna could see jumping back in the dating pool if Noah was the water. Maybe small-town living wasn't so bad after all.

What was she thinking? There was no way this man was single. Maya would have mentioned something if he were. Maybe she didn't want to bring it up because she'd only been in town for less than thirty-six hours? Maybe Maya didn't think he was good enough for her? Perhaps Baby Mama drama?

Sienna mentally shook herself. She moved to Oak Mountain to heal mentally. Though she would be open to dating again, she hadn't committed to more than a year in the quaint town. Would it even be smart to start something she couldn't guarantee would last after the school year? Then she had to think about Kai. Getting attached to someone only for her to take him away the same way a bullet took away his father. Nope. She could appreciate Noah, but nothing else.

"Nice to meet you, too," she finally said, taking a step to the side to let him in. "Thank you for offering to help. You didn't need to."

"I had nothing really going on but watching baseball with the cat." Noah shook his head. "Wow. That sounded pathetic."

"I didn't want to say anything, boss," Maya yelled from behind her, causing them all to laugh.

"Don't listen to her," Sienna said, closing the door behind him. "Give me the Phillies, a tray of wings and an ice-cold beer. I am a happy camper."

"Switch out the Phillies for the Orioles and that sounds like the perfect afternoon." Noah pushed forward a blue and white pot with a plant she was sure she'd kill within a month. "This is for you. Welcome to Oak Mountain."

Before she could thank the man, Maya strolled over and took the pot. "I'll help her take care of this. It's gorgeous."

"It's true," Vince spoke up from the corner of the room. He held a level to even out the TV brackets. "Sienna has a brown thumb."

Horror washed over Noah's face. Would he take back the plant and replace it with a fake one? She couldn't argue with her family. She killed a cactus because she over-watered it. When she tried again, it died when she forgot to water it. Fresh flowers were more her speed.

Sienna took the plant back and bumped Maya with her hip. "Don't listen to them. Thank you. I'll look up the proper care and take care of it."

"I don't mind writing a few pointers," Noah offered.

Sienna wanted to shimmy. For years, she focused on raising Kai and getting past the grief of losing Dylan. Her non-existent dating life was because she didn't want to betray the vows she made to her husband. Dylan's brothers on the force would ask her out or volunteer to take Kai to a game. Sienna would kindly say no until they eventually stopped asking. Then the wives would stop checking on her. So it gave her the go-ahead to get lost in her mind. Her therapist reminded her it was okay to open up her heart again. Death was one of life's guarantees. It was something she couldn't avoid.

Dealing with the noise and hectic city life was its own issue.

"I would appreciate any guidance you could give to help keep this alive for over two months," Sienna finally said.

The bathroom door opened, and Kai ran to the group. His smile wide and bright.

"Hi, Mr. Noah."

"Hey, Kai. Do you like your new home?"

His angelic face beamed. "It's great. I have my own bathroom. I didn't when we stayed with Poppy and Nana. Scooter can see the park from his log. Best of all, I'll be able to see the TV from the kitchen."

Sienna ran her hand through his thick curls. "As you can see, he has his priorities straight."

Noah chuckled. "He's a kid who knows what he wants."

"Can I show Mr. Noah my room and Scooter's terrarium?" Kai brought out his pleading face. Noah spoke before she could respond.

"I'd love to see your room, but I'm supposed to be helping. Let's see what your mom wants me to do first."

Sienna didn't know if Noah was trying to impress her or not, but the way he showed an interest in Kai's request but understood she had the final say was a plus. Besides, she just met the man. Sending him into a room with her son unsupervised would raise her paranoia flag.

"Why don't we work out here for a little while?" she suggested. "We have to hang the curtains and put your games in the entertainment center. Then we can work in your room, putting your bed together and installing your shelves."

"Why don't you help me and hand me tools?" Vince suggested.

"Can I hammer a nail?" Kai asked, moving towards his uncle.

Vince's gaze met Sienna, who frantically shook her head. The last time her son had a hammer, her father almost lost a fingernail.

"I don't think we'll need to hammer anything, Little Man. There are a lot of screws." He handed Kai a yellow handle screwdriver. The two went into a discussion about what needed to be done.

"Did you have visions of a hole in the wall?" Noah chuckled, setting his tools down.

"Flashbacks of the last time he tried to help my father build something."

"One time, my friends and I called ourselves helping our parents build a shed. It turned into chasing each other around the property and seeing how many rocks we could crush." Noah shook his head. "We all ended up with either a broken finger or toe."

"Owen told us stories about you four," Maya said. She sat a pile of curtain rods on the sofa. "To look at these men now, you would expect them to be uncontrolled hooligans, Cleo."

"Hooligans is a strong word. As accurate as it is," Noah teased. "Is Cleo your nickname?"

Maya snorted and left them alone. Sienna playfully scowled behind her sister's back. "She gave me that nickname in protest of our mother naming me after a color. Maya wanted to name me Cleopatra."

"After the queen. That's fitting."

Sienna's cheeks warmed. Noah was smooth. Shame she had to burst his bubble. "Not the queen, but the character Tamara Dobson, played in the seventies movies. When Dad asked how she knew about the movie, Maya threw our grandmother under the bus. Said she watched it with her one time at her house."

"I found it educational," Maya quipped, causing everyone to laugh.

Sienna missed being with her sister. Laughing over the phone is one thing, but it wasn't anything like being in the same room. It was definitely a reason to stay past the year. She could see how this town appealed to her and Vince. Maya was developing a community that accepted her.

Why couldn't Sienna have the same thing?

Nothing held her in Philadelphia. Their parents wanted to move to Puerto Rico to be closer to their mother's side of the family. Sienna suspected they stayed because of her. They had their friends, but that was it. Maybe by the time they visit, Sienna will have decided.

When they visited the apartment the day before to sign the lease, Sienna had visions of walking Kai to the park. They saw children his age playing and riding their bikes around the lush green square. Parents sat on benches under the trees, sipping cold drinks. Then there was the sanctuary. Sienna saw herself making regular weekend visits. Everything was open and fresh. After meeting Noah, maybe he would want to do some of those things with her.

She spared a glance at Kai. In less than two days, he's seen a deer, ridden a four-wheeler and helped his aunt collect fresh eggs. The move was for both of their benefit. If she saw Kai thriving, Sienna would stay.

Then it hit her.

She had yet to see a building over three stories. Even the one apartment complex she saw during their quick tour was a two-story brick building that formed a U with a manicured courtyard in the middle. No gates or bars on the doors or windows. No high rises. Oak Mountain was spacious. With a population of around thirteen thousand, you didn't get the sense of crowdedness. Nothing blocked the view. Maya told her there were no national fast-food restaurants or the green coffeeshop on every corner. Seeing is believing.

"Sienna? You okay?" Noah's deep, soul-searing voice cut through her thoughts. She mentally shook herself and gave a genuine smile.

"Yep. Sorry, I was thinking about the park."

He held her gaze for a moment, then showed his pearly whites. "The kids play pick-up softball Sunday afternoon. Twelve and under. They even let the little ones under five hit off a tee. They don't play in the field, but they get excited to run the bases."

"I didn't know that," Maya said, handing them each a bottled water.

Noah gave a nod of thanks. "Fiona played a few times last year. Now that she's thirteen, she can join the softball team, but I think she is too focused on 4-H this year to think about sports."

Maybe there is baby mama drama, Sienna thought as she twisted the cap off her drink. "Is she your daughter?"

"Sort of niece."

"She's the daughter of the Beckett's oldest son," Maya said. "I'll introduce you before school starts. She'll be in the same building as Kai."

Maya's brows furrowed. "Isn't that middle school?"

"Kindergarten through eighth grade are in the same building, just different wings," Noah added. "There aren't enough students to justify a separate building. The high school is across the street."

"I thought it was a typo when they said Kai's class would be fifteen kids." Sienna had an appointment to meet his teacher on Monday.

Noah nodded. "That sounds about right. Each grade has two teachers. It makes for smaller class sizes and a better teacher/student ratio." He pointed to her black curtain rods. "Are those the ones you want here?"

Right. Noah was there to help. Though she appreciated his information about the school setup.

She handed him a rod and a ziplock bag of hardware. He knelt before his box and adjusted the bit on his wireless drill. Sienna would steam the hung curtains later.

She turned and found her sister watching her from the butcher-block kitchen cart. An open box of pots and pans in front of her. A knowing smile graced her lips. Sienna ignored her and moved to place the glasses in the dishwasher.

Getting herself and Kai settled in their new home, and healing was all Sienna had time for now. Adding the possibility of Noah, or any man, was not in the immediate future.

No matter how handsome and skilled with a drill he was.

Chapter 5

Pinks, oranges, and yellow painted the morning sky. Dressed in a baggy tee and sleep shorts, Sienna clutched her mug of coffee to her chest. The view from her balcony was breathtaking. She would have to set her alarm every morning and make this part of her routine.

Main Street was empty. In the fifteen minutes she's been outside, only a single police car drove down the hub of Oak Mountain. Morning birds and the rustle of leaves were her only sounds.

She could get used to this.

Could something so simple be the answer to moving on in life? It was a question she couldn't answer at the moment. One day, one morning, didn't hold the key. Sienna understood life. She saw it daily when she worked in the ER. She had to get a feel for the town. Something she hoped she and Maya could do later.

Movement at the corner caught her eye. A woman shuffled to the bakery and unlocked the door. She disappeared inside a moment later. Lights stayed dark, but she was sure it was the owner getting ready for the day. Sienna smiled, thinking of the sour cream cake they had for dessert the night before. Do you stay in a town just for the sweets?

Having Maya, Vince, and Noah help her unpack and get settled was a blast. Once her brother-in-law mounted the TV and connected to the Wi-Fi, they were able the pull up a music streaming service. Oldies and Latin music had everyone singing along and bobbing to the beat. Even Kai caught the energy of the adults and shimmied his narrow hips while he put away books.

Her son loved his Poppy and Nana, but he opened up more around Maya and Vince. It could be they were younger and able to keep up with him. Sienna didn't know, but it was a flash of how he used to be before she fell into her depression and moved in with her folks. How could she even think of taking him from this positive environment after a year? She didn't want her son's happiness dependent on Maya and Vince. It was up to her.

And she saw a glimpse of her former self as well.

Laughing and teasing each other, sharing stories around a simple meal of sandwiches, did wonders for her. It was another night where she fell asleep to crickets and nature's nocturnal symphony. Her mind wanted to blame it on the exhaustion, and part of it was. But deep down, she knew it was more.

Sienna could build a tribe here. People in Oak Mountain may know her as Maya's sister, but their smiles were welcoming. They didn't see the widow of a slain officer. The sad daughter who lost herself in grief. The mother left alone to raise a son. No. This was her fresh start. Noah's blinding smile popped into her mind.

The younger Garrison was a pleasant surprise. He stayed until close to seven, helping put together furniture, making sure all the curtains were hung and unpacking boxes. He shared stories of growing up in Oak Mountain and how Denise helped him develop his green thumb. Though technically he was Maya and Vince's boss, their use of the term "boss" was one of teasing.

Kai also took an interest in the big man. He asked how much he could lift and whether he could beat the Hulk in a fight. Noah didn't seem bothered by the litany of questions. He spoke to Kai as a person and not a silly child. It impressed Sienna. Noah was down to earth, funny and couldn't carry a tune, but still sang along with the music. Sienna wasn't expecting him to be interested in her romantically, but she hoped they could be friends.

One side of the balcony's French door slid open. Maya smiled and took the seat next to her. She clutched her own mug of joe. Her headscarf was slightly askew.

"I hope I didn't wake you," Sienna said before taking a sip.

Maya spoke after swallowing a gulp. "Nah. We're up at this time, anyway. Vince is on the couch, scrolling through his phone. Couldn't sleep?"

"I slept great. Usually, I log on to work at seven, so I'm up at six. My hours will change when school starts in two weeks because I don't have Mom to take Kai to school. I worked it so I can pick him up during break."

"You know Vince and I can pick him up. The morning is just hard for us." Maya's eyes said how sorry she was. Sienna gave her sister's arm a squeeze.

"Even if you could take him, I wouldn't ask unless it's an emergency. This move is for me getting back into life. That includes taking Kai to school."

Noah explained there are school buses, but mostly for the kids that live on the outskirts and farms. Kai's school was a five-minute drive or a fifteen-minute walk.

"I get that," Maya said after a beat. "But we're still here for you. Don't think you have to do this alone."

"I know and I appreciate you and Vince for that." Sienna sighed and focused on the dark silhouette of the mountains. "I will always be thankful to Mom and Dad for their help over the past couple of years. But I don't know if it helped me heal in the long run. Does that make sense?"

Her sister nodded. "It does. You knew they'd take care of everything because that's what they do. You were losing your independence."

"Exactly. I went back to being their baby." Sienna motioned towards the ink on her arm. "Comments about the tattoos, the length of Kai's hair, the anime shows he watched. The worst was their disapproval of giving up nursing."

Her parents didn't, couldn't, understand. She was on duty when they rolled Dylan into the ER. Hospital rules stated she couldn't be part of the team that worked on him. So she relied on her colleagues. She saw the wounds and understood it was a fruitless cause. But they tried. For months, Sienna couldn't get the image out of her mind. Every gunshot patient that came through the doors made it difficult. Instead of shutting down her ability to show empathy to her patients, she left the field.

"I didn't like the person I was becoming," Sienna said. "Mom and Dad would never say it, but I think they were a little happy I moved."

"Perhaps. They know you needed to do this." Maya held her sister's hand. "I saw the old Sienna last night."

She squeezed her sister's hand. "I was thinking the same thing. I'm a realist and know a change of scenery isn't going to make me better overnight. But I want this to work." She pointed to the rising sun. "This sight alone can spoil me."

"Wait until you see the first storm come through. You will be glued to the window."

Sienna smiled. When they were younger, they would sit on the bed, braid each other's hair and watch the rain. It started out as a way to calm three-year-old Sienna, but became their thing until Maya left for college. If she wasn't working or caring for Kai, Sienna still found peace in listening to the rain.

"Are we still going shopping for shelves?" Sienna wanted to change to a happier subject.

Maya nodded while taking a sip of her coffee. "Noah mentioned the storehouse on the property has shelves we can use if we can't find anything."

Sienna didn't want to mention the big man, but since she said his name. "Why didn't you tell me about Noah? He's married, right? Girlfriend? Boyfriend?"

Maya chuckled. "I really wasn't expecting him yesterday. I didn't mention him because I didn't want you to think I was asking you to move because I wanted to set you up with someone."

"So you want to set me up?" Sienna didn't know how she felt about the idea, but she surely wouldn't move because of a man.

"I wanted you to move because I know this area would be good for you. Outside of work and family dinners with the

Becketts, yesterday was the first time Vince and I spent extended time with Noah." Maya held up her hand when Sienna went to speak. "I knew he was nice and a true gentleman, but Vince and I spend more time hanging out with Owen and his husband. Noah is best friends with the Beckett brothers and does a lot of stuff with the youngest one, Jace."

"I remember him saying something about Jace."

"I know Noah was married. No kids. According to Owen, Noah threw himself into work after his marriage ended." Maya nudged Sienna with an elbow. "I saw him giving you the eye a lot yesterday."

"Whatever." Sienna felt heat rise to her cheeks and took a sip of her cooling coffee. "He was nice and respectful. Not bad looking, but I'm trying to get better, not hook up with a man."

"I can honestly say Noah is not the *'hooking up'* type. That was Jace and I'm not speaking out of turn. Everyone, including Jace, said he was not a relationship guy until he met Claire. Oh, she is someone you have to meet. I just love her. She lives in the house next to mine."

"Either way, for now, I want to get Kai settled with school and work on myself. My therapist gave me a name of someone in case I wanted to continue my sessions."

Maya tapped her chin. "I wasn't going to bring this up now, but since you mentioned it. Have you considered a support animal?"

"I have. That's what Scooter is for Kai." Sienna hadn't told anyone, but his counselor suggested it. She saw it helped him process his feelings and gave him something to focus on.

"Mom's allergic to anything with dander, so I didn't pursue it. Why?"

"Well, Caden, the middle brother, is expanding his support animal program. He has PTSD from the military and uses a dog. Like you said, in a few weeks, we can talk about it again."

A pet would be nice. As spacious as her apartment was, Sienna didn't think a dog would work. Maybe a cat. For now, she had other things to focus on and would keep her mind busy.

"Thank you. For everything." Sienna smiled at her sister.

"No need to thank me. I'll always have your back."

Before she could respond, the balcony door crept open and Kai's cautious face poked through the crack. Sienna motioned for him to step out. Still dressed in his lightweight pajamas, he had run a comb through his hair.

"Morning, Mommy and Aunt Maya."

"Morning. I'm going to make breakfast soon." She pulled him close and pointed to the horizon. "See how pretty the sky looks."

He gave a cursory glance before turning his attention back to his mother. "Can I watch cartoons?"

"Sure. We still have things to do today."

"Thanks!" Kai kissed her cheek before scampering back inside. Sienna watched the door close, shaking her head. She spared a last glance at the sky and sighed.

"Pancakes?"

Maya stood. "With bacon and eggs."

Sienna followed her sister inside, where Kai was already explaining his show to Vince. Her brother-in-law gave a soft smile and held up his mug. Though she had her parents back in Philadelphia, this was the family she missed and the ones that would help her heal.

Noah's spider plant sat prominently on the kitchen windowsill. True to his word, he jotted down tips for her on the care of the plant. As she pulled the pancake mix from the cabinet, she tried to think of an appropriate thank you gift for the man. Something to show her appreciation, but not flirtatious.

Maybe a little flirty.

Meadow nudged Noah's thigh before curling up beside him on the outside couch. His small screened-in porch allowed the cat to take in the morning birds while getting a breath of fresh air. He reached over and ran his fingers down her thick fur. She would hate it, but a bath was on the schedule for later in the day.

Noah took a sip of his morning coffee and watched the sun peek through the trees. He loved the quiet of the day before the organized chaos started on the property. Sunday had limited staff to those taking care of the animals. Even before turning the management over to Vince and Maya, they worked it so all employees had two days off. As owners, they were available twenty-four seven, but they always tried to take the weekend to reconnect as a family.

Usually, that meant breakfast and/or dinner at the main house. With Logan's wife, Naomi, confined to eighty percent bed rest because of her high-risk pregnancy, meals in the house were now limited to Sunday dinners. The energetic woman was eight months pregnant, and all were looking forward to the twins in the next month.

Changes were happening at Hawkins Ridge. For everyone. Noah narrowed down his list of names for his blog last night when he returned home from Sienna's. He still wanted to run the idea past his friends. They would support him no matter what. It's what brothers did.

Growing up with the Becketts gave him the siblings his parents couldn't. Before Owen accepted his orientation, Noah didn't understand why his parents only had the one child. When his parents' marriage ended, he didn't think he could have dealt with everything if it weren't for Jace, Logan, and Caden. They stood by him when the bullies in high school made comments. It cemented their bond for a lifetime. When his mother remarried ten years ago, he gained two adult step-sisters, but they weren't close.

He saw the same closeness with Sienna and Maya yesterday. He learned why she had moved to Oak Mountain. Sienna was a fighter. She may not see it, but he saw the fire in her eyes when she spoke of what she wanted from the move. Her determination to strengthen her relationship with Kai. Sienna had a lot on her plate.

And why Noah couldn't consider asking her out.

Sienna moved to Oak Mountain to reclaim herself. Same as Naomi and Claire. Completely different reasons, but all wanted a new start. He was sure romance wasn't on her mind.

Noah found everything about her attractive. It was more than her outer appearance. He watched her with Kai and her family. The woman had a huge heart, fiercely loyal to her sister and a wonderful mother. Watching her and Kai work together assembling his desk showed her patience. He'd just met her, but everything about her called to him to get to know her better.

Even recognizing the need for help. Noah himself battled depression when Owen came out and when his marriage ended. Thoughts of not being enough consumed him. Counseling helped him restore his relationship with his father. Tai chi helped him get over his failed marriage. Though he no longer needed counseling, he still practiced tai chi to help maintain his mental and physical balance. He wondered whether Sienna considered meditation.

Noah mentally shook his head. It wasn't his place to offer any advice or suggestions to Sienna. Besides, she was a city girl. Oak Mountain may help her heal, but there was no guarantee it would be enough to keep her here. He had one city girl and didn't think he could handle the heartache of another one.

Maybe he could handle a friendship.

Movement in his periphery had Noah turning his head to the left. Jace Beckett stepped from the cluster of trees that separated their homes, holding a covered container. He checked his phone and figured his friend was coming for breakfast. Meadow stood and stretched as she climbed down when Jace opened the screen door. His messy, dark blond hair brushed against his shoulders. Dressed in basketball shorts and a comfy tee, his friend greeted them both with a smile.

"Morning." Jace reached down and ran his hand along Meadow's back as she weaved between his legs. "You're going to have my dogs attack me if you keep marking me like that."

Noah stood and stretched his back. "Hey. Here for break-fast?"

"Yes, and to drop off leftover lasagna." He held up the container. "Claire is spending the day with her aunt and took the dogs with her. Said Rue was making a tater tot casserole."

"We should have gone with her," Noah teased…sorta. Claire's aunt moved to Oak Mountain almost five months ago. The woman could cook.

"I thought long and hard about it, but I really need to work in the yard. Now that I don't have to worry about the dogs, it's the best time."

Noah stepped inside, holding the door for his friend to follow. "I need to do the same thing and give Meadow a bath."

The cat gave him an evil eye as she darted past. She went to her cat tree that caught the early morning sun. Jace poured himself a cup of coffee and leaned against the counter.

"How did things go yesterday? Is Maya's sister cool? Logan met her son yesterday when Vince was showing him the pack."

Noah pulled the package of country ham and the rest of the ingredients for a western omelet. He thought of how to answer the questions as he handed Jace the peppers to dice. Noah could talk to his friends about everything, but Jace was the one he could honestly talk about women with. He set a large cast-iron skillet on the burner before grabbing a mixing bowl to crack the eggs.

"Her name is Sienna. She's attractive, and the kid's adorable."

Jace looked up from cutting and flashed a stupid grin. "At-tractive enough for you to ask out?"

Noah let the corners of his lips curl up. "Definitely, except she's a city girl and the sister of our property manager."

His friend scoffed. "Maya was a city girl with the same upbringing, and adjusted to small-town living. You can't immediately discount a woman because of Robin. Did Sienna give off metropolitan vibes?"

Noah turned his head. "What are metropolitan vibes?" His friend had the decency to shrug.

"I don't know. Did she make comments about not having a coffeehouse on every corner? Not getting food delivered at one a.m.? Stuff like that."

Noah stared at Jace for a long moment before laughing. "Everything you said is a stereotype. She didn't ask me if I ever ate possum or if my parents were second cousins. Why would you think that?"

"Fine. I was making a point, though. I meant, did she make rude comments about how small Oak Mountain was to Philadelphia?"

"No. She was pleasantly surprised at how quiet the town was and the size of her son's class. You know his last class had thirty-five kids in it?"

"Remember the reality check when we went to our freshman English class at Pitt?" Jace shook his head. "Almost twice the size of our county graduating class."

Noah shuddered. Their county had four high schools, with each having fewer than seventy-five kids in their respective graduating class. Stepping into the lecture hall was a shock for both of them.

He set the beaten eggs off to the side, then cut the country ham into cubes and went back to the original topic. "You're right. I can't pass judgment on Sienna based on my experience with Robin. I can, however, *not* pursue that option because of Vince and Maya. She also just moved here less than seventy-two hours ago."

Noah wasn't going to tell Jace why Sienna had moved. It wasn't something he needed to know. Even if she stayed, which he hoped she did, that would be her story to tell. Jace became enamored with Claire a week after she moved to Oak Mountain. It took almost a year for their friendship to turn into something more. Noah could handle a friendship with Sienna.

"Now the Vince and Maya excuse is legit," Jace said. "Besides the fact that it took us six months to find them, they're amazing. If things didn't work out with Sienna, we could lose them both."

Noah agreed. If he had a chance with Sienna and it didn't work out, he would volunteer to move off the property or sell his share in the business. Vince and Maya were that good. Given his restlessness, it could be the best solution.

But he wasn't dating Sienna, so it was a moot point. It did, however, give him a chance to change the subject.

"I'm thinking of starting a blog and eventually doing a podcast." Noah turned the heat under the skillet and added a tablespoon of butter. He side-eyed his friend, who silently nodded. Jace spoke after handing him the bowl with the chopped veggies.

"I'll come back to the Sienna subject down the road. Except for the city reason, you made good points." Jace continued as he pulled the basket from the coffeemaker. "I can see you writing a blog. You would be a great teacher. What would you write about?"

He planned to run the idea by Jace before mentioning it to the rest of the family. They worked well together, always hashing out business ideas before presenting them. Noah added the veggies to the sizzling pan.

"Small farming. Ideas of various crops or livestock. Maybe installing irrigation systems, things like that. I'd have interviews with the farmers and suppliers we work with. At least to start out with. Eventually, I'd build a database with input from my readers or listeners when I move to podcasting. Thoughts?"

Jace tapped his chin, a sign that he was working through his thoughts. Noah moved the veggies around, then added the eggs while his friend thought. When Jace pulled the whole wheat bread from the breadbox, he shared.

"I think that's a great idea. My only suggestion is to gear it towards people starting out and those that have backyard farms." He shoved four pieces of bread into the toaster, then finished. "The only reason I say that is because most small farms like you're thinking of are generational. Look at us. Even though your dad didn't grow up on a farm, he knew you liked agriculture and had you spend a lot of time here. Almost everything we learned before college was passed down from my grandparents and parents. There are more people growing their own vegetables, even in urban settings. You will find homes in the suburbs with chickens. The advantage you have is that you have connections." Jace slapped the counter. "Do an interview with Bas and show his backyard farm. How huge is his fan base?"

Bas Gilmour was a best-selling horror author who lived in Point Harbor, on the eastern shore of Maryland. He and his wife adopted dogs and chickens from Hawkins Ridge. Noah and Caden spent three days on his property helping him set up his chicken run and a mini greenhouse. Bas touched base monthly, or more if he had questions.

Another reason he wanted to talk to Jace was his brilliant marketing mind. He was the face of the business and had a way of finding avenues they could sell their products and still stay small.

Noah added the ham and shredded cheese before folding the eggs over. "So you think this is doable? No one will have a problem with me doing something on my own?"

Confusion marred his friend's face. "Why would we?"

"It will be separate from Hawkins Ridge. I mean, I would have a link to the wholesale goat products' site, but it would be just me."

Noah cringed at the passing hurt on his best friend's face. Jace dropped the pieces of toast onto their plates and slid them to Noah for the main dish with a little more force than necessary. "Okay. I still don't understand why you think we'd have a problem or try to stop you. Naomi's practice is separate from Hawkins Ridge. Yes, she put Logan's name on it, but that's because they're married. We have no say in her business."

Why didn't Noah remember that? Naomi had her practice before selling the land to the county because of a foundation issue. She moved onto the property when she and Logan started dating and because she wanted to help with the rescue.

She still paid rent on the practice space to Josie and Thomas, even though they were her in-laws.

Noah and Jace took their plates out to the porch and finished their conversation. "Thanks for the reminder," he said after taking a bite. "I still want to run it past Pops before I bring it up during poker next week."

"You know we've got your back. Whatever you need, just say the word."

Noah gave a nod of thanks. He didn't know why he stressed over having their support. The Beckett brothers were always there for him, and vice versa.

"I still think you should give Sienna a shot," Jace said around a mouthful of food. "Unlike Robin, who only had you, Sienna has family here. The same family that helped her get set up. At least approach it from a friend angle. Get to know her and then see if there's anything there."

"I'll think about it."

And he would.

Chapter 6

"We should put his travel tank on the balcony," Kai said. He held Scooter in his hand as he stepped back inside, closing the French door behind him.

Sienna looked up from folding the load of sheets. "Maybe on the weekends and for brief spurts."

It was later in the day. Vince and Maya left an hour ago, leaving Sienna and Kai to get a feel of their new place. They'd lived with her parents for close to two years, so this was an adjustment for them both. Kai worked on decorating his room and setting up his computer. Sienna took advantage of the stackable washer and dryer and washed the sheets and towels that were in storage. She put off going shopping with Maya until the following weekend. Sienna wanted to make a list of everything she needed and see if there was anything she could repurpose or donate.

Now that it was just the two of them, the move became real. Sienna didn't think it was a bad thing. She missed having her own space. Her first two nights in Oak Mountain, she had Maya and Vince. It was comforting and allowed her to get her bearings. Now Sienna wanted to reconnect with Kai without the fun aunt and uncle around.

Earlier, when she watched Kai and Vince, she decided to give Oak Mountain more than a year. She wanted Kai to finish elementary school, at least. Nine to twelve months wasn't long enough to fully appreciate her new life. If they both were flourishing, she would make this quaint town her home.

Kai padded to his room to return Scooter to his enclosure. Vince bought enough veggies yesterday to get the turtle through a few days. Sienna still needed to get insects. If they wanted to get a feel for Oak Mountain, they needed to get out.

"Do you want to go get Scooter his insects?" she called out, folding the last pillowcase.

Kai scurried back into the room. "Really?"

"Yes. Aunt Maya gave us the directions to the feed store, then we can check out the burger place at the end of the block for a late lunch."

"Heck, yeah!"

Sienna wanted to correct him, but she laughed instead. Her son was happy. What more could a mother want?

"Alright. Let's change our clothes and give Scooter some lettuce. Does he have enough water in his bowl to lie in?"

"Yep. Can we stop past the park to see the kids play softball?"

Sienna nibbled her lip. She wanted to try baby steps. That may be a bit too much for her.

"Maybe next weekend. If they're still playing when we're done with lunch, we can watch it up here. We also don't want to keep the bugs in the hot car for too long."

Kai seemed okay with the decision. "Okay. Scooter hasn't had crickets or worms in days." He darted to the kitchen and flung open the refrigerator door. They separated the turtle's food from theirs. Everything was pre-sliced and washed, so Kai could just grab something.

Sienna put away the linen and went to her room to change. Her queen-size bed sat in the middle of the space. She had a view of Main Street. Totes that held her winter clothing sat in the corner near the entrance to her decent-sized bathroom. There wasn't a tub, but a comfortable walk-in shower with a rainfall showerhead. If she wanted a soak, she would use Kai's bathroom.

She pinned her twists into an updo. Sienna's hair frizzed in the summer. She thanked her mother's thick curly hair and her father's kinky coils for the problem. It was easier to put them in twists weekly when she washed and deep conditioned her hair. She settled on a red short-sleeved T-shirt dress that stopped at her knees and a pair of red Converse. She slipped her crossbody bag on and met Kai by the couch. Her baby changed into a blue T-shirt and jean shorts.

"Ready to see the town?"

Kai nodded and led her to the door. Sienna said silent words of encouragement, pulled the directions to the feed store from her bag and headed on their first adventure.

The Gray County Feed Store was nothing like Sienna expected. She'd never been to one, but the term "feed store" had her envisioning shelves of various foods for animals, farm and otherwise. She was partially correct.

Kai was gobsmacked.

Displays of everything from saddles to horse blankets greeted them at the entrance. Farming tools, clothing, bins of parts for any sort of machinery imaginable. Sienna forced herself to walk past the selection of boots. Clothing for all ages temptingly hung from racks. Thankfully, a female staff member helped them navigate the massive structure.

When they finally made it to the "protein feed" section, Sienna fought the urge to shudder. Terrarium after terrarium of rich, dark soil housed every insect and creepy crawly imaginable. Everything from earthworms to slugs to roaches and everything in between. Her son was in heaven. Kai impressed the salesperson with his knowledge of the bugs Scooter liked and really wanted him to try mealworms.

Sienna grew up as a tomboy. She played sports, loved fishing, and didn't have a problem with spiders. When Kai let three slugs crawl on his tiny, perfect hand, she knew it was time to go. The salesperson laughed and helped him put them back in their enclosure. Sienna handed him a wet wipe to clean up as they walked to the register.

"That was so cool," Kai commented as he clutched his paper bag of creepy crawlies. "Scooter's going to be happy."

Sienna snapped her seat belt and started the car. "It was a fun place. Next time, we'll see if Aunt Maya wants to go."

"I think she'll like it."

She didn't have the heart to tell him Maya was a regular because of her job. Kai ran down his knowledge of the various substrates as they headed home. He wanted to be a herpetologist when he grew up. She hoped his future wife was okay with snakes and slugs in their home.

Sienna pulled into her spot behind the building. She figured they would walk to the burger place. After leaving his package just inside the street-level door, she headed to the restaurant on the next block.

"If I play softball next week, I wonder if I have to bring my own bat." Kai glanced to his right towards the park. He had a glove for when he went to Phillies games in case he caught a fly or foul ball.

"Let's find out if you need to bring your own equipment first. Then we'll look at getting you a bat." Sienna pulled the door open to the restaurant. She didn't know how she would find out the information. Maybe Maya knew of a parent who worked on the property.

The hypnotic aroma of grilled meat, roasted garlic, and sizzling onions hit Sienna when she stepped through the door. Her mouth instantly watered. Sienna was more of a poultry and seafood person. When she went for red meat, it was a greasy cheesesteak with the works or one of her father's burgers on the grill. If the burger tasted as good as it smelled, she'd have to add it to her monthly red meat allowance.

"Mr. Noah!" Kai shouted, causing the person in front of them to turn and smile. Sienna followed her son to the large man sitting on a wooden bench.

Noah's smile was genuine as he shook Kai's hand. He rose to his impressive height and greeted Sienna.

"Afternoon, you two. Out exploring our town?"

Before she could speak, Kai answered for them, "We went to a place called a feed store. Mommy thought it was just a bunch of food for animals. Wow, it was awesome. They had everything." Kai moved closer and lowered his voice. "Mommy didn't like the slugs."

Sienna rested her hands on her son's shoulder and moved him to her side. Noah chuckled silently.

"I don't have a problem with worms. Slugs are just slimy and sucky."

"They're supposed to be slimy," Kai responded. "It helps them avoid predators and move about."

"If it's to help them avoid predators, then why can Scooter eat them?" Sienna argued.

Kai sighed. "Nature meant for turtles to eat them, so they don't mind the mucus."

Sienna gagged, causing Noah to laugh out loud. "I think you may want to change the subject, Little Man. Your mom may lose her appetite."

"As good as it smells in here, I doubt that," Sienna said.

"Do you want to eat with us, Mr. Noah?"

Noah had the decency to glance towards Sienna. She nodded. "If you're busy, we understand."

He shook his head. "No. I was going to give my cat a bath. The longer I can put that off, the better. It's not pleasant for either of us, but it's necessary."

Kai wrinkled his nose. "I didn't know cats needed baths."

Noah motioned for them to walk to the counter. "I have a Maine Coon cat. She has a lot of fur that requires brushing and cleaning. Sometimes her grooming isn't enough, so she'll get a bath every other month."

As they moved to get in line, Sienna glanced around the space. It reminded her of an old-time diner. Black and white tiled flooring with booths along the wall. Oversized wooden chairs in primary colors accented the orderly placed tables in the middle of the dining area. A soda and condiment station sat to the side of the register. Sienna loved it.

Noah spoke to the cashier when it was their turn. "Peg, is it too late to make my order for here?"

The young woman nodded. "I was just getting ready to call you." She grabbed the bag from the stainless-steel counter behind her. "Do you want us to put it on a plate?"

"That's okay." He motioned to the handwritten board. "They make everything when you order and bring it to your table. The meat comes from local farms, so it's fresh."

No wonder it smells so good, Sienna thought. She hadn't really looked at the offerings. She opted for a bacon cheeseburger and a kid's size with a basket of fries. Sienna stopped Noah when he pulled out his wallet.

"I got it."

"Consider it a welcome gift." Noah reached for his card, but Sienna rested her hand on his. She gasped at the tingle in her fingers from the contact. She quickly recovered, shaking her head.

"Really, it's fine."

Noah gave a slight nod and put his card back in his wallet. Sienna wouldn't dare let him pay for their meal. He helped them unpack and bought her a plant. She still couldn't decide what to give him as a thank you gift. She barely knew him. If they had arrived at the same time, she would have bought his meal as a way of thanks. Would a simple card do? She tapped her card against the screen and took the little placard that had their number.

"Can we sit in a booth?" Kai asked. He held his small cup to his chest.

She glanced at the booths, thankful they were higher than normal, and nodded her head. Noah went ahead of them and selected a spot near a window that looked out onto Main Street. Sienna helped Kai with his glass of apple juice while she went with the raspberry iced tea. Noah had his meal out of the bag and was scrolling through his phone by the time they joined him. She nudged Kai to the side across from Noah and slid in beside him.

Sienna glanced around. "I was expecting more of a fast-food vibe."

Noah moved his fries to the middle of the table. "Have a few while you wait. The owner wanted to offer something for families that didn't want to deal with the diner and still wanted quality food. You picked the right time. Once the pickup game is finished, they head here."

His statement allowed her to ask. "Speaking of the game, do the children provide their own equipment?"

"Some do because they play T–ball, but there are parents with extra bats and mitts." Noah moved his food when the server arrived at the table. Sienna thanked her. "We have extra equipment on the property if you want to see if any works for him before next Sunday."

"Oh, Mom, can we? We can see the chickens and the dogs." Kai's eyes pleaded with hers.

Sienna thought for a moment while she set Kai's food in front of him. Her son enjoyed sports, but he never swung a bat. If they could take advantage of a used bat to see if he enjoyed playing, she would.

"Fine. Not until next weekend, though. Aunt Maya and Uncle Vince have work."

The three were silent while they tucked into their food. Sienna swallowed a moan when she bit into her juicy burger. The perfect amount of seasoning allowed the natural flavor to pop. The bacon wasn't thin and limp, but thick and crispy. Sienna reached for a fry and was surprised it wasn't overly greasy and not salty.

"This has become my favorite restaurant," Sienna announced.

Kai chuckled and swallowed his bite before speaking. "We've only been to this restaurant."

Sienna faced Noah. "Are there other burger places here?"

He shrugged while taking a sip of his soda. "You can get a burger at the diner, the bar, that place by the feed store, or even the steakhouse, but this is by far the best."

She believed him. Sienna wanted to get to know Noah and see if there was more to what she'd seen thus far. He was the only person she knew outside her family. Building relationships outside of her family was a suggestion her therapist made when she told her they were moving.

"How long have you had your cat?"

"Two years. She was a kitten when the sanctuary rescued her and her mother. Josie Beckett has her mother." Noah wiped his hands and picked up his phone. He handed it to her a few moments later. "You can see why she needs baths."

Sienna's mouth dropped. A tan and white mound of fur with pointed ears sat next to Noah on the couch in a selfie pose. Holy moly, Sienna didn't think it was a cat. Gorgeous creature. She wondered if her fur was as soft as it looked. Kai leaned over for a gander.

"Woah. She huge!"

Sienna handed Noah his phone and picked up her burger. "How often do you have to bathe her?"

"Not that often, about once every five weeks, because she's mostly indoors and has an oily fur. Daily grooming is more important. Do you like cats?"

"I do," Kai answered while scooping up a sizable dollop of ketchup. "Can we see your cat when we come next weekend? If I bring Scooter, will she eat it?"

Noah laughed. "She would think it's a toy, but there's a better chance Scooter would hide in its shell."

"And we aren't bringing him," Sienna said. Her voice left no room for argument. "To answer your question, I like cats. My mother is allergic to dog and cat dander, so we didn't have pets growing up. She would have to take prescription antihistamines when we visited my grandparents in Puerto Rico. She can handle an hour or two around them before her eyes water and break out in red blotches."

"This one time, we went to the zoo and Nana couldn't be near the wild dog exhibit," Kai added. "She made all of us take a shower as soon as we got home and wash our clothes."

Sienna smiled. She thought for sure her mother was going to take a rideshare home to avoid the possibility of leaving dander in the car. How she would handle visiting Hawkins Ridge was a mystery.

They finished their meal with Kai sharing his knowledge of reptiles. Noah paid attention, asked questions, and ignored his phone when it beeped. It gave Sienna a chance to observe the man. Looking at his rugged looks, you'd expect him to own a big, powerful dog with a chain collar. A huge, yet fluffy, cat was a surprise. She smiled mentally at the image of him brushing Meadow while muttering cooing noises. Maybe he could brush and twist her hair. Curiosity tugged at her to find out why his marriage ended. Did they talk? Was the divorce recent? Why did it matter? Sienna knew why.

She was interested in Noah.

He was kind, patient and easy on the eyes. He didn't think twice about offering to pay for their meal and even shared his fries while they waited. Noah could have turned them down when Kai asked him to join them. Maybe he was interested in her?

Sienna popped the last of her burger in her mouth and looked out the window. The move was to get back to life. She patted herself on the back for how well she had done that day. On the drive from Philadelphia, she said she was open to dating. How would she even approach the idea? At thirty-five, she didn't need her sister to pass notes to a man or be her spokesperson. Sienna just had to find the courage. Maybe next week when they went to the property.

"How about it, Mommy?" Kai's voice brought her back to the conversation. How long had she been inside her head? Her cheeks warmed at the concerned look on Noah's face.

"I'm sorry. I was thinking about where I put the directions to his school for tomorrow." It wasn't the truth, but it reminded her to go through her moving folder to make sure she had the address.

"Mr. Noah invited us to a cookout when we go to see the cat next weekend."

"I figured since you'll be there, I could toss a few chicken thighs and potatoes on the grill." Noah's gaze bore into hers. She smiled.

"I'd like that. I insist on bringing something."

"Great. You have my number. Just let me know what day you're coming out." He held her gaze a moment longer before turning to the mess on the table. "Let me get this."

They piled their trash onto a tray. Noah was out of the booth and carrying the mess to the drop-off area near the register. Sienna gave Kai a wipe for his fingers before climbing out herself.

"I like Mr. Noah," he commented.

She spared a glance at the man in question, who stood near the bench where they had found him talking to an older gentleman. He flashed a smile when he caught her looking. She rested her hand on Kai's shoulder.

"I like him too, baby."

Chapter 7

Noah passed the feed bucket to a worker and pulled off his gloves. He took a moment to observe the goats noshing on their grain pellets at the three different feeding troughs. They would bring in the alfalfa hay for dinner. He would need to check with the supervisor about their vegetable supply for the midday snack. Kai's angelic face popped into his mind.

Would he want to feed them when they came to the property? He pulled out his phone to text Sienna, then immediately shoved it back into his pocket. What was he thinking?

It hadn't even been twenty-four hours since they shared a meal. He still tried to wrap his head around asking her to a cookout. The words were out of his mouth before he could stop them. While he gave Meadow a bath, he tried to reason with himself that he was just being neighborly. Noah knew it was a lie.

He was interested in getting to know Sienna.

After his conversation with Jace at breakfast, he had every intention of perhaps settling for a friendship. When he saw them walk into the restaurant and her interaction with Kai, he had to stop kidding himself. When she refused him buying their meal, it solidified his decision.

Noah hadn't been interested in a relationship since his wife. Women in town either wanted someone to take care of them, had dated Jace, or figured Noah was hiding his orientation, like his father had. Since they didn't see him dating, more chose the latter. It wasn't worth it to prove them wrong. Noah and his family knew the truth.

Robin did a number on his self-esteem. Work was how he coped. He heard the negative small-town chatter when he was ready to move on. So he stuck with work, found a special friend in Stark Valley, and went about building something at Hawkins Ridge.

Then his friends found their special someone, and he would admit, life was passing him by. He could easily chalk up his interest in Sienna to not wanting to be left out of finding someone. But something about her spoke to him. Seeing her with Kai, her decision to move to Oak Mountain, and the smile that lit up her face. Noah just knew the urge was something he couldn't ignore.

"I'm heading to the office," Noah called out. Three workers waved in acknowledgement.

He strolled through the cluster of trees and headed toward the greenhouse. Before Vince and Maya, the company didn't have an office. The brothers got together to talk, shared emails, and people knew to call Josie or his father. Each brother had his section and managed the workers within it. When Jace mentioned he needed an assistant months ago, they all realized it was a necessity for all of them. It was the first thing Vince and Maya took care of. They then converted an empty tiny home next to the greenhouse into an office.

The changes the couple made to the property in a short time proved invaluable.

It was why he had to talk to Maya. Losing them wasn't an option. If he pursued Sienna, he wanted to clear it with her big sister first. He understood they were adults, and that Sienna could make her own decision about whom to see. Except Maya scared him. Why lie?

Noah waved to a gardener as he walked up the stairs. He took a deep breath and pushed the door open. Cool air from the window unit brushed against his face. He quickly closed the door. Maya sat at the L-shaped desk she shared with Vince, clicking away on the computer. There were two guest chairs in front of the desk the assistant used. Noah chose the time because the assistant wasn't due for another thirty minutes and he saw Vince head to the stables.

"Morning, Noah. Just finishing payroll," Maya said. "There's fresh coffee and danishes on the counter."

"I'm good, thanks. You got a minute?"

Maya studied him for a moment before nodding. She motioned to Vince's chair. "What's up?"

Noah pulled off his cap and twisted the bill in his hand. "I wasn't sure if Sienna spoke to you or not, but I invited her and Kai to a cookout this weekend."

"She mentioned it last night when we talked. She said there's spare sporting equipment somewhere."

"Caden has them in a closet. The bats may be too big for Kai, but figured we could check, so she didn't have to spend money."

"Thank you." Maya leaned on the arm of the chair and crossed her legs. "What's really on your mind?"

Noah blew out a breath. "I would like to get to know Sienna. To be honest, I'm hesitant about pursuing her because I don't know if she plans on staying in Oak Mountain. After my ex and taking Kai's feelings into consideration, I don't want to try to start something that will end next summer."

"I can't tell Sienna who to see and not to see. If I could, I would have told her not to date Kai's father."

"Was he mean to her?" Noah knew he had died responding to a call. He'd hate to think he mistreated her or Kai.

Maya shook her head and stood, taking her travel mug to the coffeemaker. "Dylan was a good guy. At no time did I doubt his love for Sienna. But when they first started dating, he never made time for her."

Noah didn't understand that. If you care for someone, why wouldn't you try to spend as much time together as possible. Maya gave a small smile before continuing.

"By the look on your face, I see that is a foreign concept for you. I see the way every couple on the property is. Let me explain." She took a sip of her coffee. "Dylan was two years out of the academy when he met my sister. I know of four times he canceled plans because he picked up a shift. Not already on a call or anything, that's part of the job. But on his days off, he would call the chief to see if anyone called out. It started to get to her because she would always plan something then to have it fall through. Shortly before she called it off, she found out she was pregnant. That changed Dylan. He was more attentive. That's when they got married, bought a home. It looked like he changed. Then he missed Kai's first birthday party because he took a shift. Slowly, he started back doing the same thing. He had excuses that they needed him, and he wanted extra money to pay off bills. My gut told me the change wouldn't last. But she seemed happy so I let it go."

"Do you think he was cheating on her?"

Maya shrugged. "I don't know. I was in Kentucky so it's not like I could prove it. She was raising Kai almost on her own. A marriage where one person works eighteen hours, how can you keep that connection. Several times, Dylan would sleep at the station because of a schedule shift. He wanted to move up the ranks and work his way to detective before thirty. He volunteered to work overtime the night he was shot."

"Oh, man."

"It was hard to accept. Sienna kept thinking if he had kept his regular shift and came home, he might still be alive today." Maya leaned against the counter. "Back to the subject. You said, because of your ex. What happened if you don't mind me asking?"

Noah didn't mind. He would tell Sienna anyway if they got that far. "My wife wasn't cut out for this or small-town living. Robin was raised in Brooklyn. Loved the fast-paced environment of New York. But we loved each other. So, she followed me after college and wanted to give it a try. She lasted nine months."

"And you're concerned Sienna will realize this slow-paced lifestyle isn't all it's cracked up to be."

"In a nutshell." Noah hated putting Maya in the middle and powered on with his next concern. "I'm also worried if we went out and didn't work; you and Vince may consider leaving. That is something I don't want. You two are invaluable to Hawkins Ridge." He didn't want to bring up the possibility of him leaving the property.

Maya's shoulders slumped and blew out a breath. "Speaking as a big sister, this is the best place for Sienna and Kai. There's nothing for her in Philly. She's not the type that would move to another city unless she knew people. I think once our folks see she has made this work, they will move to Puerto Rico to be near my mom's family."

"What about Kai's other grandparents?"

She shook her head and returned to her seat. "Dylan was an only child, and his parents died in a car crash. Sienna may consider Stark Valley because it's bigger and a thirty-minute drive. I doubt it, though."

That was part of Noah's backup plan if it didn't work out, so they didn't lose Maya and Vince. Stark Valley had a population of sixty thousand. It was as big as he could handle. He had family there and could buy a nice piece of land on the outskirts. If things worked with Sienna, that was a compromise he could make. She could get a taste of city life, and he could still feel part of a small town. Maya continued.

"I think you would be good for Sienna and Kai. My suggestion is to be patient and not push her into a relationship. Just let it happen. Regarding Vince and me..." Maya rested her arms on her thighs. "We have every intention of making Oak Mountain our home. I've mentioned this to your father. Everyone here has welcomed us with open arms. In the near future, we'd like to discuss a bigger place, but we think we've finally found our place."

That meant a lot to Noah. If Vince and Maya weren't happy and looked at other opportunities with another farm, Sienna might go with them. The thought pierced his heart. Knowing

Maya and Vince were in for the long haul strengthened the chance of Sienna staying.

"I'm glad Oak Mountain feels like home. It's a special place." Noah stood when the front door opened. He nodded to the assistant. "The invitation was for you and Vince as well."

"I'll let him know. Good talking to you, Noah."

He gave her a knowing smile. "Thanks for listening."

He made quick work of an exit and took a deep breath as he stood on the porch. If Maya felt he was good for Sienna, he would just need to make sure the woman in question thought the same thing.

"Did you see the playground, Mommy?" Kai bounced on his toes, waiting for Sienna to meet him on his side of the car. "They had two slides and three swing sets."

"I know, baby. The jungle gym looked new." Sienna pressed the lock button and the fob and met her son at the front bumper.

The family was returning from Oak Mountain School. Kai was now a fourth grader when school started the following week. He met his teacher, Ms. Sara, and learned she was married to the cousin of the sanctuary's vet tech. It was the young woman's first year teaching the grade after handling pre-K and kindergarten the past four years. Sienna added the school to the list of items she wasn't expecting.

The brick building was the old town hall. It housed the elementary and middle school, with the higher grades stationed in the built-on addition with its own entrance, lunchroom, and office. The principal oversaw the school, with each section having its own vice-principal. It was a unique setup. Bright primary colors decorated the wall. Cubbies in every room and framed positive quotes throughout. The principal and teacher confirmed the smaller class size, easing Sienna's worries. It was a recipe for Kai's success.

"Do you think you're going to like your teacher?"

Kai nodded. "She seems nice. Are they really going to give me a buddy?"

"That's what they said." Sienna welcomed the school assigning a little friend to help Kai navigate his first few days with hopes it turns into a friendship. "Are you okay with that?"

Worry of suffocation momentarily rushed to Sienna's mind as they rounded the corner, stepping into the bustle of Main Street. Well, what Oak Mountain considered a bustle. Though more than she saw on Saturday, there wasn't a rush of people. Now, waves and greetings met them as people strolled to their destination. The knee-jerk expectation is why she made an appointment with her new therapist for the following week and planned to ask Maya to go with her.

Sienna understood that a move to a slower pace town alone wouldn't cure her anxiety. If it were that easy, more and more people would do it. She still practiced her exercises and made the appointment with the school after rush hour. She also had breakfast with Kai on the balcony to see what Main Street on a Monday would be like. Yes, there were more people, but nothing compared to the tens of thousands hurrying in downtown Philly.

As Kai continued to talk about the school, her mind drifted to Noah. Would he understand her need for mental pep talks before going into a busy store or area? Was it something she wanted to subject him to? Could she even start a relationship while healing? The grief of Dylan's death was the catalyst for her anxiety. Her parents confused her anxiety with grieving. She'd accepted Dylan's death a while ago. She *couldn't* accept how it led to a spiral.

Sienna mentally shook her head and took a deep breath. The world wasn't crowding her, and if there was something with Noah, if he couldn't accept all of her, then he wasn't the man for her.

Of course, Sienna needed to make sure he was interested in a relationship.

A display of colorful hibiscus caught Sienna's eye as they passed the flower shop. On a whim, she guided Kai and pulled the door. Denise stood behind the counter talking to another older African-American woman. Both greeted her with warm, welcoming smiles.

"Good morning, Sienna, Kai. I'm glad you stopped in. It saves me a trip going up the stairs."

"I saw my school today," Kai blurted as he ran to the counter. "I met my teacher and even picked out my cubby where I'll put my jacket and stuff."

Sienna chuckled and rested her hands on his shoulder. She glanced at the other woman with a short afro. The smell of something amazing drifted up her nose. She spotted a large plastic bag on the back counter.

"Ophelia Norris," the woman said, holding out her hand. Sienna shook her hand and encouraged Kai to do the same.

"Nice to meet you, ma'am."

"You're a handsome devil." Ophelia gave a grandmotherly wink before turning her attention back to Sienna. "I saw you the other day when you and Maya came into the butcher shop."

The memory came back of seeing her behind the swinging doors as they were leaving. "Yes. Sorry, I was still trying to wrap my head around everything."

Ophelia waved off her apology. "I get it, and you don't need to apologize."

Denise nodded. "Ophelia brought some fried chicken and pasta salad for you. I was just about to call you to see if we could bring it up. She makes the best fried chicken in town."

If that was what she was smelling, Sienna might have to agree with her. Denise sat the bag near the cash register, and her stomach let out an embarrassing growl. The yogurt for breakfast was long gone. Kai, of course, laughed.

"I am so sorry. Guess I'm hungrier than I thought."

"Then I timed it just right." Ophelia patted her hand.

Denise came around the counter. "Did you need something? Is everything okay with the apartment?"

Sienna took her mind off the food and focused on what she had come in for. "Everything's fine. I wondered if I could get a bouquet of the hibiscus and see if you had any that were wilted so we could give them to Kai's turtle."

"He really likes them," Kai added. "I told Mr. Noah at lunch yesterday how Mommy got creeped out with the slugs."

Heat rushed to Sienna's cheeks. The last thing she needed was for rumors to start about something that wasn't there.

"We ran into him at the burger place up the street," Sienna quickly added.

"Girl, I don't blame you one bit." Ophelia shuddered. "Every time I see them in my garden, I always get my husband to remove them."

"I told you to use them in your compost heap or spread some coffee grinds around the garden," Denise argued.

"I tell you they dig underneath all that and make it into my vegetables."

Denise rolled her eyes and turned her attention back to Sienna. "Don't pay her no mind. Give me about twenty minutes and I'll have that made up for you."

That would give Sienna time to help Kai clean Scooter's tank. "That sounds good. I'll come down. I don't want you dealing with the stairs." She turned to Ophelia. "Thank you for the chicken. How much do I owe you?"

"It's a welcome to Oak Mountain gift. I make this only about once a month and email our regulars the night before, so I know how much to make. Your sister is on that list."

If the chicken was good enough for Maya, it was good enough for her. "Add me to the list, too." Sienna grabbed a card from the counter and jotted her personal email. "My sister is a picky eater. If she swears by it and it tastes half as good as it smells, then I'm all in."

"Good enough." Ophelia slipped the card into her dress pocket. "I better get back to the shop. Nice to meet you two officially. Hope you like Oak Mountain."

Based on the food so far and the people, Sienna didn't see why she wouldn't.

Chapter 8

Deep shadows of the mature trees cast an eerie, yet comfortable image on the road to the sanctuary. Sienna didn't bother to hide her smile as she navigated the curves. She, Kai, and Scooter were spending the weekend.

In the days following the visit to the school, Sienna spent her time unpacking, decorating, back to school shopping, and spending time in the park. When Kai wasn't helping, he stayed busy reading, watching his favorite movies, and playing games. They made time to enjoy their breakfast and dinner on the patio. It gave them a chance to be together before adding school to the mix.

"Do you think I can pick eggs with Aunt Maya in the morning?" Kai asked, glancing at the sizable chicken coop and run as they turned onto the property.

"It will probably be Uncle Vince. Auntie and I are leaving early."

"But you'll be back to go on the four-wheeler?"

A soft smile creased her lips. "I'm sure we will."

Sienna scheduled her appointment with her new therapist for eight in the morning. It surprised her she had limited weekend hours, let alone an opening. The therapist explained the practice was attached to her home, and she didn't see patients on Mondays unless for an emergency.

She followed the curve through the gate that led to the residences, sanctuary, and stables. A group of men and roughly ten dogs stood in front of the clinic. Maya swore the vet, Logan, would see Scooter if he needed attention. Vince and Noah immediately caught her eye. All turned as she pulled the car behind her sister's. Maya sashayed down her front step and greeted them with a smile when Sienna opened the door.

"Perfect timing. I just put the salmon in the oven."

"Good, cause all I had for lunch was a PB&J and a small bag of chips. If I didn't have to make Kai lunch, I would have missed it." Sienna pulled their bag from out the back seat. "Who's that talking to Vince and Noah?"

Maya glanced across the street. "The Becketts. From left to right, Caden, Logan, and Jace. The dogs running around are theirs."

Kai batted his eyes. "Can I go say hi, Mommy?"

"Go ahead, but be polite and wait until they acknowledge you." She had to stop him when he went to take Scooter. She didn't want the turtle to meet its demise in the mouths of the dogs.

Sienna waved when the group of men did. Vince lovingly put his arm around Kai and began introductions. Noah's gaze lingered longer. Sienna felt her cheeks warm and ducked her head. Maya chuckled and tapped her on the shoulder.

"Come on. I need some AC. It's hot out here."

Sienna spared a last look and passed Scooter's box and the green salad to her sister. She received a text from Noah earlier stating that the pickup games had ended with school starting.

He kept the invitation open for a cookout the next day. Sienna tried not to read too much into the invitation. It was hard, though.

Cool air had Sienna sighing when she stepped through the door. Her tolerance for heat became less and less the older she became.

"We set up Scooter's tank in the guest room," Maya said, cutting into her respite. "The woman at the feed store gave us the basics."

"You didn't need to get a special habitat." Sienna followed Maya into the guest room. In the corner, next to the window, sat a new ten-gallon tank. It was small, but perfect for the weekend visits. They even remembered the heat lamp.

"Thank you for this."

Maya waved off the gratitude. "We don't mind. Vince eye-balled a lizard when we were there. Now that we're settling in, we've been thinking about pets. Reptiles weren't on the list until we met Scooter."

"It's more work than I thought, but worth it."

"We'd feel better about leaving a cat or reptile alone while we work." Maya sat on the edge of the bed while Sienna placed Scooter into the tank. "I see Noah couldn't take his eyes off you."

Sienna rolled her eyes. She ignored her sister's comment and pried open the plastic container, pulling out a piece of lettuce and a slice of cucumber, setting them next to the turtle's small bowl of water.

"You know he talked to me." Maya sucked her teeth. "Wanted to make sure I knew he invited you and Kai to a cookout."

Sienna turned to face her sister. "He invited you and Vince."

"That's what he said. Vince and I may be busy having a date."

"You really wouldn't go?" Sienna was a grown woman and didn't need her sister, but she'd be more comfortable if she went.

"If you want us to be there, we will, but I think it would be good for you and Kai to go alone."

She pushed her bag to the side and sat beside Maya. When the invitation was under the guise of sporting equipment, it was easier for her to say no. When Noah mentioned he still wanted her and Kai over, realization dawned that it could be something more.

"I've had passing thoughts about dating since Dylan," Sienna started. "Dad said a boy needs a man in his life."

Maya snorted. "Dad has a lot of old-fashioned views."

Gerald Wood served four years in the military to get the GI Bill. He was the first in his family to go to college. Though he was a retired lawyer who tackled human rights, he still fell back on his upbringing of the man being the breadwinner, boys needing fathers and girls needing husbands. His liberal, headstrong wife and daughters showed him how outdated his views were. Sienna continued with her thought.

"Anyway, after Dylan, I didn't want to go through the pain of losing a partner, let alone having Kai deal with it. Therapy helped me come to grips with how unrealistic that was." Sienna shrugged. "Since I was limiting my time out of the house to grocery shopping, the library, appointments and transporting Kai, I just figured I wouldn't meet anyone."

"And now?" Maya prodded.

"Now, I'm just scared."

"It's okay to feel that way. Especially with Kai in the picture." Maya squeezed her sister's hand. "Letting you in on a little secret, Noah's scared too."

Sienna's gaze met her sister's. "Why?"

Maya was already shaking her head. "Noah hasn't been in a relationship since his wife. Owen confirmed this but she left to return to the city. Noah didn't have a clue she wasn't happy until she told him she wasn't coming back when she went to visit family. Small town wasn't for her and Noah never really got over it. Since he has been focused on work, I suspect you both want a slow-burn relationship."

"True."

"Talk to each other. Maybe not tomorrow in front of Kai, but you should. I think Noah is good for you, and vice versa." Maya patted her sister's hand when she heard the screen door open. "You deserve to be happy again."

Kai barreled into the room. A large smile on his face. "Mommy, Mr. Caden said I can help brush the horses tomorrow if it's okay with you."

Vince chuckled, leaning on the doorjamb. "Most of the owners who board their horses here are scheduled to take them out tomorrow. They'll need a good brush-down when they're done. I'd be there with him."

That sounded like something Sienna would want to do as well. She and Maya wanted to hit a few consignment shops after her appointment, but figured they would make it back in time. She wrapped her arm around Kai and nodded.

"That sounds like fun. I'll even help when Auntie and I come back."

"Mr. Caden said we could feed them sugar cubes and apples, maybe. It all depends." Kai finally noticed the tank next to the window. "Wow. Scooter really likes his guest room. Thanks, guys."

Sienna hadn't thought of the tank that way, but she guessed it was. Her family went out of the way to make her and Kai feel at home. She hoped they would have a chance to show the same level of love to a needy child.

The buzz of the oven timer broke the family moment. Maya stood and ruffled Kai's curly hair. "Go wash up. Your mom and I will get everything ready."

Kai followed Vince out of the room, still talking about the horses and how he wanted Scooter to see the massive beasts. Sienna shook her head and grabbed the salad.

"Being here is good for him and his love of animals."

Maya nodded and led her to the kitchen area. "I know he has his heart set on being a herpetologist, but being around the animals may have him go into veterinary care."

Sienna washed her hands in the kitchen sink and thought of her short time in Oak Mountain. Spending time with her family exposed her son to animals he'd only seen at the zoo. Now she was considering dating again. She would have to agree; moving was probably the best decision she'd made.

Lightening bugs danced in the warm night air. Memories of visits to her paternal grandparents in Virginia filled Sienna's mind. She and Maya would snag their grandmother's canning jars and use them to light their camp outs in the backyard. It was an experience she wanted to share with Kai soon.

Sienna used her toe to start the wooden porch swing as she inhaled the fresh air. A joyful dinner ended two hours ago. Kai fell asleep on the couch as they watched a show. Maya and Vince turned in twenty minutes ago. Sienna wanted to take some time for herself and carried her e-reader and a cold beer to the front porch. She closed her eyes for a moment and listened to the wild nocturnal residents start their day. Before Oak Mountain, she enjoyed spending time in nature but considered herself a city girl. These past few days, she understood why her sister had converted to rural life.

Deep laughter drew her attention to the main house across the way. Noah, another man, and a German Shepherd strolled down the walkway towards a vintage truck. Seeing Noah in a pair of casual shorts and a fitted tee kept her attention. Sensing her presence, the dog stopped and stared in her direction. The conversation between the men abruptly ended as they followed the dog's gaze. Sienna awkwardly waved before reaching for her beer to quench the sudden dryness in her throat.

She sat straighter when the duo ambled closer—the dog leading the way. The lampposts highlighted their soft smiles. The gorgeous beast trotted onto the porch and sat beside her legs. With a gentle pant, his wagging tail meant he wanted some loving.

"He's friendly if you want to pet him," the man said, stepping onto the porch. Sienna remembered him being with the group from earlier. Now that he was closer, the man was handsome in a rugged way. A long scar ran down the left side of his face. Deep crinkles emphasized his bright blue eyes. The half-tattoo sleeve drew her attention, and it killed her not to ask where he had them done.

She let the dog sniff her hand before running her hand down his soft head. "You are too cute for words."

Noah squeezed past his friend to stand on the other side of her. The porch wasn't that big, and both men took up a lot of space.

"Sienna, this is Caden Beckett and his dog, Scout," Noah introduced.

Her mind connected once she heard the name. "You offered Kai a chance to brush the horses tomorrow." Maya also mentioned his connection to the therapy animal program. She wondered if Scout was one.

Caden nodded. "If that's okay. All the horses are gentle, and he'd be supervised the entire time."

"Thank you for easing my worries, but I already told him yes. I was hoping I could help when Maya and I return from our errand."

"I didn't know you liked horses," Noah said. He'd taken to leaning against the balustrade. Sienna shifted her gaze but continued to stroke Scout.

"My uncle in Puerto Rico has horses. He and my mother made sure Maya and I knew how to ride."

"Before Hawkins Ridge became what you see now, my great grandparents used to breed and train horses." Caden added. "About ten years before my grandpa died, we shifted completely to boarding and training."

"Kai has always loved animals. We went to the zoo so much, we got a membership." Sienna smiled at the thought.

"No zoos near here, but we have farms and sanctuaries with a variety of animals for him to get his fill," Noah said.

"That's for sure." Caden reached into his pocket and pulled out a set of keys. "It was nice to meet you. I hope Oak Mountain will feel like home soon."

It already does, she thought, but said, "Me too."

She gave Scout another deep scratch, then let him follow Caden down the walk and towards the truck. Once the engine came to life, Noah spoke.

"Mind if I sit unless you'd like to be alone?"

Sienna patted the cushion beside her. She could feel the happiness wafting off him as he settled beside her. That was enough to boost her confidence.

"No hot date?"

His deep chuckle vibrated the swing. "Not unless you consider playing poker a hot date."

"Not really," she snorted. "My date fell asleep on the couch."

Noah glanced through the open window. Kai slept in a starfish pose. One arm and leg dangled off the side.

"Now I know why he has a full-size bed."

"I'd hear him hit the floor at least five times a week when he was six. One night I watched him to see what was happening." Sienna shook her head, grinning. "Kid went to fling his arm and leg out and just toppled over. I was at the store the next day and got him a bigger bed."

Noah laughed along with her. It felt good to open up and enjoy the moment. She refused to kick herself for missing years inside of her self-imposed bubble. This was her time to take control of her happiness. For so long, it was easier to keep to herself to avoid the risk of hurt. Not anymore.

They sat for a few minutes, listening to nature's symphony. She'd taken to sitting on her balcony after Kai went to sleep, just soaking in the fresh air. Sienna made a mental note to ask Denise if she could use a small outdoor heater in the winter. Noah stretched his legs out, crossing them at the ankles. He cleared his throat casually.

"Did you mean what you said earlier to Caden?"

She furrowed her brow, wondering what she had said. "About the horses? Yeah, I think it would be great. It's hot, so I hope he's supplying cold water."

Noah chuckled. "They have a fridge in the stable stocked with cold drinks, so you're covered. I meant what you said about Oak Mountain wanting to feel like home."

"Oh." Sienna sighed not realizing she verbalized what she thought. She liked Noah. If Maya was right, and he was interested in her, she wanted to be honest.

"I meant it. In some ways, it already does."

"What do you mean?"

She wanted to look at him but kept her focus on the myriads of moths and lightning bugs. "Kai and I have a routine already. I know it will change slightly when he goes back to school, but I expected it would take time for that. I don't know if it's because we have our own space again or what. This is the first time in years I'm in a place where I can reclaim who I am. In Philly, it seemed I couldn't erase being the widow of a police officer or *'poor Flora and Gerald's daughter.'* Sienna shrugged and shifted in her seat. "I may be Maya's sister to some. Soon, I'll be known as Kai's mom, but I'm mostly just Sienna. That feels good. I finally feel like I belong."

Noah nodded, flashing an understanding smile. "Sometimes it takes a while to find your identity. Find out who you really are. I was a junior in high school when Dad came out, so I became the gay man's son. After college, when I became part owner of Hawkins Ridge, I became the Beckett's charity case. It didn't help my marriage ended."

"Did people actually have the nerve to say those things to you?" Sienna would not have been able to hold her tongue.

"To my face, no. Loud enough for me to hear it while standing in line at the store or snide comments to the Becketts, yes."

"You're a better person than me. I would have turned around and dare them to say something to my face."

Noah chuckled. "My family and friends didn't mince words when they heard something."

Sienna rested her hand on his forearm and gave a slight squeeze. "It seems like they accepted you and your dad."

"For the most part. There are some that don't and it's okay. Those that I care about do and that is what's important." He sighed. "No matter how others see you, it only matters how you see yourself. I'm sorry you felt like you couldn't be yourself back home."

Sienna glanced at the playful night insects chasing each other. "I probably could if I tried, but I didn't want to. Even before Dylan's death, deep down, I knew I needed a change. I have that now and am looking forward to building something here."

Sienna didn't know why she opened up to Noah. She shared some with Maya, but not everything. He was easy to talk to because he didn't know her past and couldn't judge her. He couldn't compare her to pre- and post-Dylan. To him, she was probably just Sienna, a single mother and the newest resident to Oak Mountain. She was okay with that.

"I'm glad you feel like you can build something here." Noah rubbed the back of his neck. Tiny beads of sweat suddenly dotted his brow. "Now that you mentioned building something, not in the way you were thinking…actually maybe, I don't know."

Was he nervous? Could Maya have been right? Sienna nibbled her bottom lip. Noah came across as a confident man. She doubted that being around her tied him up in knots. She held her tongue and gave him the time he needed. After a few pregnant beats, he continued.

"What I'm trying to say is I'm interested in getting to know you better. Romantically. I know you just came to town and are getting settled. The last thing I want is to mess up what you're trying to do here." He exhaled. "I just know that no other woman has made me want to give dating and a relationship another chance until you."

Sienna's cheeks warmed. "I haven't dated since Dylan. Like you, no one made me want to."

"And now?"

She gave him a solid look. Something about Noah spoke to her. Despite his small burst of nerves, he was a confident man. He was part of something good here with Hawkins Ridge. He liked baseball and tattoos. Not to mention, book-cover handsome.

"Now, I'd like to give dating another shot. I'd have to talk it over with Kai. He hasn't seen me with another man, so I want to go slow for his sake."

"I'm okay with you dating Mr. Noah!" A voice shouted behind them, causing them both to jump and turn. Kai stood a few inches from the window. A goofy grin decorated his adorable face.

"What did I tell you about eavesdropping? How long have you been up?" Sienna couldn't find it in herself to put any heat behind her words.

"I have to use the bathroom, and I saw you two outside. I didn't plan on listening, but when Mr. Noah said he wanted to date you, I wanted to see what you would say.

Noah silently chuckled when Sienna shook her head. "Thank you for your input. Go to the bathroom and then go to the bedroom. I'll be in shortly."

"You deserve to be happy, like Auntie Maya, Mom. I like Mr. Noah. If you want, I can have a man-to-man talk about his tentions for you?"

Sienna couldn't hold back her laughter. "I think you mean *intentions,* and we can discuss this in the morning. Go."

"Night, Mr. Noah." Kai scurried towards the back of the house. Sienna loved her son, and his comment helped ease the awkwardness of the moment.

"Sorry about that."

Noah waved away her apologies and stood. "It's fine. I'm glad Kai approved. It's getting late, and you said you have an early errand to run."

Sienna's jaw-cracking yawn agreed with his statement as she rose to her feet. She would tell him about her appointment later once she came to grips with dating. "Are we still on for the cookout tomorrow?"

"Most definitely. I'm sure I'll see you before then. Caden and I have to mark off a few acres of land near the stables." He softly brushed his hand against hers before bringing their joined hands to his lips. As soft as a whisper, he pressed his lips against her wrist. "Have a good night."

Sienna knew her mouth was open and didn't give a flying fig. Instant swoon.

"Night," she finally mumbled.

With a soul-stealing smile and straight posture, Noah strolled from the porch and towards a UTV parked across the road. Sienna willed her heart to settle and picked up her belongings and headed inside.

She would need to talk to Kai to see if he understood what dating meant. That would have to be in the morning. Now she had to get some sleep and come to terms with being back in the dating pool.

Chapter 9

Noah smiled as he weaved his way through town. The morning sun caused him to squint through his sunglasses. It was going to be a hot one that day. Hawkins Ridge invested in commercial ice makers a few years ago because of the animals. It was cheaper than using a supplier. Normally, Noah would be with the handlers filling buckets with ice for the goats and livestock dogs, but Vince had the workers operating efficiently.

Noah wanted to hate the husband and wife team for doing better than he and the Beckett boys did with managing. But he couldn't. Noah and his friends did well. The books proved it, but giving up control was hard for all of them. Three months into their tenure, Hawkins Ridge was where they wanted it to be.

It brought his mind back to his new project as he turned into the diner's parking lot. During the poker game the night before, he shared his idea with his friends. Everyone thought it was a great idea and offered to help anyway they could. Noah knew the brothers would have his back. That was never in doubt. But hearing their excitement and ideas for his blog made it real. He couldn't wait to tell Sienna later.

Noah parked near the back as his thoughts went to the beautiful, self-assured single mother he was now dating. Surprise would be an understatement about how easy it was to open up with her last night. He understood on a certain level what she was going through. Finding yourself after the pain and loss of a spouse was real. However, he couldn't imagine doing it while raising a child and helping that kid become who they wanted to be. Noah applauded Sienna for recognizing the need for change and taking action. He admired that about her and couldn't wait to see more of her strength show.

A ping showing a text had Noah scrambling out the door. How long had he been in Sienna-land? He hurried to the front door, stopped long enough to hold it for Mr. and Mrs. Applewood to exit, and stepped through.

Oak Mountain Diner was a town staple. Founded in the seventies, it kept the original owner until about fifteen years ago, when the family of one of Jace's old flings bought it. Hawkins Ridge supplied the eggs and goat cheese. They renovated it to bring it into the twenty-first century. Red leather booths ran along the large windows. Instead of the old Formica steel tables, now cheery wood tables brighten the space and complimented the stainless-steel counter. They kept most of the old menu, but added more heart-friendly, vegetarian and gluten-free options.

Noah scanned the busy dining area and broke out in a smile when he saw his breakfast date. Bev Johnson tapped her watch when she spotted him, but humor clouded the light brown eyes he inherited. The rose floral sleeveless dress popped against her light brown complexion. A short salt and pepper afro highlighted her round, perfectly made-up face.

He bent at the waist and gave her a hug. "Sorry I'm late, Mom. I had to make sure I looked good for you."

A throaty laugh accompanied the playful push of his shoulders. "Boy, please. You probably got caught up working."

Noah took his seat across from her and unwrapped the silverware. "It was work, but not what you think. You know I would have driven down."

His mother lived in Stark Valley, and if he didn't go to her house for breakfast, they met at a restaurant that made fluffy buttermilk biscuits and the best sausage gravy next to his father's.

"I am showing a house to a client here in an hour. Then I'm meeting Denise for some shopping." Bev tapped a packet of sugar into her coffee. "So tell me about this work that's not work."

"I'll tell you after we order."

As if on cue, a young server approached their table and turned over Noah's coffee cup. She always gave a little wiggle of her hips whenever she saw him. Though attractive, way too young for him.

"Good morning, Noah. Coffee and juice?"

Noah nodded. "Morning, Keisha. Orange juice, please. Can we also have a carafe of coffee?"

She jotted the information on the small pad. "Do you know what you want, or do you need a few minutes?"

Noah glanced at his mother, who placed the menu back in the holder on the table. "Egg white omelet with mushrooms, peppers, and goat cheese. Multigrain toast with butter on the side, and grapefruit juice."

"That has got to be the most boring breakfast," Noah teased. His mother tapped his hand. "I'll have the western omelet with the hash browns folded in. Wheat toast and the large fruit bowl."

"I like a man with a healthy appetite," Keisha commented with a wink before rushing off. Noah rolled his eyes and landed on his mother's knowing smirk.

"She's attractive."

"She's twenty-two, maybe. Way too young." Noah didn't want to bring up Sienna until they had an official date.

Bev fussed with the napkin in her lap. "Age is nothing but a number. You need someone young to give you little ones."

"Not that young." It was time to change the subject. Keisha returned with a four-cup coffee carafe and their juices. He waited until she was gone before speaking.

"I was late because I'm starting a blog. It's for small farms, gardens, and livestock. Different veggies that need little space, cities and suburbs that are zoned for a few chickens. I have a list of subjects that would easily fill up the first year." Noah twisted the lid of the carafe and poured a cup. "It's something for me, away from Hawkins Ridge."

Bev sipped her juice while she listened. When he finished, his mother set her glass down and met his eyes. "Smart. Really smart. There are a lot of podcasts, online videos, and blogs on the subject. What will make yours stand out is your years of experience and the network you already have."

Noah agreed. "That's what I'm thinking. I'm not expecting to make money from this —"

"Why not?" his mother interrupted. "Why are you doing it, then?"

Before he could answer, Keisha returned with their meals. Fluffy, cheesy goodness stuffed with chunks of country ham, onions, and peppers filled the plate. It was a lot, but he had a full morning after breakfast. He and Caden needed to plot out the perfect spot for the therapy dog training area and tiny homes for applicants to bond with their new animals. It was a project important to Caden, and everyone.

After a few bites and comments on the food, Noah answered his mother.

"The reason I'm doing the blog is because I have time now and I want something separate from Hawkins Ridge. Something with my name."

"More time could go towards finding a special person to spend time with. Besides that, it is great you decided to pursue this. Why again don't you think you'll make money?" Bev pointed her fork at him. "Advertisers are always looking for less expensive ways to promote. Blogs and podcasts are what they're doing now. The real estate office is always looking to sponsor events or entrepreneurs. You're a good-looking man speaking intelligently about a subject people are interested in with the high costs of produce now. Don't sell yourself short, baby."

Noah never doubted his parents would have his back. Both encouraged him to pursue his dreams. His father may have wanted him to follow in his footsteps in business manage-ment, or his mother may have thought of a mother/son real estate partnership. Sustainable agriculture spoke to him. He did minor in business management, though.

He focused on topping off their coffee while he processed his mother's compliment. "Thanks. Not sure what my looks have to do with this being successful or the blog's ability to make money."

Bev's fork, topped with a bite of her omelet, stopped midway to her mouth. "You're kidding, right? You have to post a picture of yourself so people will know you're legit and not AI. Advertisers will see the face I had a part in creating and want to toss money your way. TV shows will want to interview you. You could be the face of the latest soil mixture."

Noah stared at his mother for a long beat. "And now I'm doubting doing this."

"Why? Baby, I know you may not want the possibility of something more coming about because of your looks. You can't ignore it may have a play in it."

"I just want to share my knowledge. I don't have any interest in making this into a thing that requires more of my time than I have. What's wrong with a simple weekly blog and maybe a weekly or biweekly podcast?" Noah inhaled deeply, then slowly exhaled. "I get what you're saying. If I wanted this to be huge, I could. Now, I want to keep it small and with a goal of a few thousand subscribers."

Bev held her hands up in a faux surrender. "I'll leave it alone for now. Don't be surprised if people take notice."

"And if people do, I'll deal with it then. Now, tell me what else is going on? What do you and Denise have planned?"

Before she could answer, Keisha checked on them with a lingering look towards him. Noah wondered what Sienna would have to go through when it came out they were dating. Logan and Jace's significant others received looks when they were out. Would he need to prepare Sienna for the possibility of snide comments? Was he jumping the gun? They hadn't even had a date. The cookout that evening would be their first official time alone.

"Your aunt wants to get a few outfits for her vacation," Bev said, bringing the topic back. "She told me about her new tenant. Nice young lady with a cute little boy. Said you helped her the day she moved in."

And they were back to the dating thing. Something told him his mother would have said something earlier if he hadn't brought up the blog. Knowing his aunt, she put a bug in his mother's ear about Sienna being single and attractive.

His mother wanted grandkids before she was too old to enjoy them. She also felt Noah needed someone in his life to make him happy. He was happy with his life, but he would admit he missed spending time with a woman. Earlier, he didn't want to mention anything about Sienna. Now he would have to give her a piece of a nugget to end the topic and breakfast.

Noah waited until Keisha cleared their plates and brought a fresh carafe of coffee.

"I know you're fishing for information, and Denise put you up to this." He put his hand up when his mother protested but returned her smile. "Sienna is the first woman to interest me enough to consider getting into a relationship. I mentioned last night that I would like to get to know her. Since she's new and has a child to consider, we are going at her pace and starting with a cookout this evening. We'll go from there afterwards. Don't get your hopes up and tell everybody and their grandmother about this. Please?"

"I should be insulted that you think I am a gossiping woman, but you're right in this case." Bev's laughter lightened the mood. "I promise I won't say anything. If things progress, I would like to meet the young woman."

Noah gave his mother's hand a squeeze. "Of course."

He snatched the check before she could and gave a sly wink. She hated when he paid for meals. Bev still thought the parent should pay, even though she knew Noah was an adult and had the money.

They finished their coffee and then held her chair as she stood. He tossed enough for a decent tip and let her lead to the register near the front. After settling their bill and waving to neighbors, Noah walked his mother to her car. The blinding shine on her luxury SUV spoke of her visit to the detailer recently.

"Come to dinner this coming week and have fun tonight. I expect to hear details." Bev pressed a kiss to his cheek. "I'm proud of you. Let me know how I can help with your new endeavor."

"I will. Don't buy out the store."

Bev's response was a delightful cackle. The two women loved to shop and would head back to Stark Valley to hit the mall. Stores were having back to school sales, which they felt obligated to take advantage of.

Noah waited until she had pulled out of her spot before strolling to his truck. Now it was time to prepare his dinner after he finished with Caden.

"Do you really think Denise put Bev up to asking about Sienna?" Caden asked as they marked another tree with a red ribbon. "You know, Mom asked about you and Sienna during breakfast today."

"Did anyone say anything?"

"No." Caden shrugged. "There wasn't much to say, anyway."

Despite Caden's parents being best friends with Owen, they were still friends with his mother. Heck, Josie, and Denise were in the same gardening club. Noah still doubted her asking was because Denise said something. It was probably because she had heard a rumor or saw them on the bench last night. Their house was directly across the road from Vince and Maya.

"Thanks. To answer your last question, I don't think Denise put my mother up to anything. Bev is smart and was fishing in case she needed to remind me Sienna was single."

Noah tied his own ribbon around a dying tree. The Hawkins Ridge homestead was five hundred acres. Currently, buildings, including homes, stables, and riding trails, occupied a little over two hundred. For Caden's therapy animal project, they would need twenty of the unused acreage near the entrance for the stables. They were currently marking the trees that showed signs of dying. Those would turn into fireweed for all the residents of Hawkins Ridge. Once complete, they would use drones to see how to arrange the training building and lodging for clients.

"Did Josie leave it alone after no one gave her any gossip?" Noah flicked pieces of bark off another tree and examined the few bare branches.

"Logan mentioned Naomi felt queasy that morning, so she went off to check on her."

Noah jerked his gaze to Caden. "Did she really?"

Caden nodded. "He thinks she'll go into labor soon. If she could force it now, she would."

Logan's wife was pregnant with twins and spent the past month on bed rest. They scheduled her C-section in two weeks. Logan and Naomi both wanted to deliver before then.

"I can't believe there's going to be babies on the property." Noah loved Naomi like a sister. She brought a spark to their routine lives.

"Before checking on her, Mom's retreating comment was, 'Three down, one to go.' She wasn't even trying to hide the dig." Caden shook his head. "There is no one in Oak Mountain that could make me take a chance."

"We all felt the same way. Jace sort of ruined dating in town."

Caden chuckled. "Even before that, women saw Logan as the stable one. Jace was the challenge and felt if they could get him to commit, it would mean true love. Me, they're too afraid to say anything."

Noah stayed quiet. When Caden returned home after a medical discharge with partial hearing loss and a gash that ran the length of his face, the townsfolk didn't know what to say. The anxiety and PTSD led to the end of his engagement. His love of horses helped him heal. His therapy dog, Scout, helped him get back to living.

"You don't think she'll start setting you up?" Noah cringed at the thought. Caden shook his head vehemently.

"Nope. Mom knows I want to become a foster father or adopt once I get this program going. I don't need a woman to make either of those happen." Caden swept away fallen twigs with his foot. "Have you gotten over Sienna being a city girl?"

"Sort of. She seemed sincere when she said she was building a life here. It's just hard not to compare her to Robin."

"I get that, but they are two different people in two different circumstances." Caden held up his hand when Noah went to speak. "Let me finish. Robin was young and didn't know anyone here but you. Both families were dealing with their own issues. We didn't fully welcome her. Besides, she wanted you to decline the offer for ownership in Hawkins Ridge."

"I told her senior year I was returning home and taking the offer. It's why I majored in agriculture."

"I know. She thought she could change your mind. Sienna is different." Caden nailed the end of a ribbon to an old tree. "Besides having family settled here, she's mature and has a child to consider. If she is like Maya, she won't make rash decisions. I talked to her for three minutes, and I just didn't get that vibe."

Noah had shared his conversation with Sienna, including Kai's input, when they first started their task. After his break-fast, he wanted Caden's opinion. Jace may be his best friend, but the middle Beckett brother had wonderful insight.

"I agree. Sienna has her head on straight. She's starting over here."

"Just like Naomi and Claire."

"Maybe a single woman will move to Oak Mountain and fall head over heels for you."

Caden snorted. "Doubtful. I have a better chance of meeting someone that's part of this therapy program."

Noah hoped so. Maybe Sienna had a friend ready to move to a small town.

Chapter 10

Sienna gave a long once-over in the mirror of her outfit. When she agreed to the cookout, she assumed Maya and Vince would be with her and opted for a boho-style romper. It was summer in Maryland, after all. Now she wondered if it was too casual for a date.

Was this really a date?

Maya swore it was, but Sienna had her doubts. On the way to her therapist, she filled her sister in on her conversation with Noah, including Kai's input. Maya talked her off the ledge of overthinking. It was a simple cookout and meeting the cat. Noah said they would move at her pace, and her gut told her he meant it. He recognized Kai's role in any sort of relationship they may have, and she respected him for that.

She chuckled, thinking of her son. Sienna joined her son, brushing down and feeding the horses. It was the perfect time for them to chat. She wanted to make sure he understood what dating was and if he really was okay with her and Noah seeing each other. Kai expressed he wanted her to be happy and thought Noah would. He then told her, *"Daddy would want her to find another husband."* The last thing she wanted was to break out in tears in front of the horses and stable workers.

Knowing Kai seemed okay with her dating, a fresh set of nerves kicked in. What would she and Noah talk about? They both liked baseball and animals. What else? Of course, that was part of getting to know one another.

Deep breath in and slowly exhale. Don't make more of this than was necessary, she thought. This is new for her and Noah. Take one minute at a time.

Sienna admired her full figure. The romper camouflaged her stomach and was long enough to stop mid-thigh. It highlighted the tattoos that decorated her calves. She'd tightened her twists after her shower and pinned them high off her neck. Once the fall weather kicked in, she would go back to her natural wild spirals. No one wanted to see her frizzy do in the summer.

"Mommy? We're going to be late," Kai chastised from the other side of the closed door.

Sienna checked the digital clock on top of the dresser. He was right. She grabbed her crossbody bag and flung the door open. Kai leaned against the opposite wall, clutching the glass container that held the pasta salad she made earlier.

"Sorry. It takes a lot to look this good."

Kai laughed as she wanted. "You're always pretty. Mr. Noah will think so, too."

"He better or I'll have to slap him," Maya commented as she walked out of the kitchen and looked at her sister. "You've always had great legs."

"Cellulite and all," Sienna teased. She plucked the keys to the UTV from her sister's hands. "You sure there is enough gas? I'm not trying to break down in the middle of the woods."

Maya's hands landed on her hips. "Seriously, Cleo? It's a straight shot behind the house. If you squint, you'll be able to see my patio light from his front door."

Maya drove past Noah's house on their way to the stables. She wasn't kidding. It really was a straight shot. She would have walked, but sometimes there were predators trying to get to the goats and chickens after dark.

"You're sure you don't want to go?" Sienna flashed pleading eyes at her sister. It was her brother-in-law who answered.

"More every minute. We're going to dinner and a movie with Owen and Sam."

"Mommy." Kai looked again at the clock. Sienna had to stop stalling and go.

"Okay. Let's go. Have fun!" Sienna ran her hands down her outfit a final time and ushered Kai to the UTV parked next to the house.

"Do you think next time we can bring Scooter?"

Sienna wanted to get through the evening before planning the next time. She should reciprocate the invitation with dinner at her place. Maybe they could go for a walk or see a matinee first.

"We'll see. Perhaps we could invite Mr. Noah over for lunch or dinner. Let's see how tonight goes first."

That was good enough for him as he snapped the seat belt as they headed towards the worn path between the trees. They both giggled as they bounced over the uneven terrain. Sienna made a mental note to see if they could take the four-wheeler out the next day before they returned home.

The ride was over as quickly as it started when they cleared the trees and rolled onto Noah's gravel drive. The sprawling single-story brick home looked natural nestled in the copse of trees. Lush flowering bushes in soft blues and pinks highlighted the covered porch. She made a mental note to ask what kind they were.

Was Noah a flower-giving man? She wasn't the type of woman who liked roses. A home-cooked meal, her favorite candy, and a quiet night watching a movie were more her speed. Maybe even an addition to her decorative box collection. However, he gifted her with a plant, as do most people for housewarming presents. Sienna knew she was overthinking, but that was how her mind worked.

The unfastening of Kai's seat belt brought Sienna back to the present. She took two deep breaths to settle her nerves and followed her son and exited the UTV. By the time they closed the half door, Noah was coming from the back of the house. The man looked good in a pair of tan casual shorts and a fitted white tee. Sienna had to give it to the man. He wasn't the basketball shorts and loose tank top kind of man. For that, she was grateful.

"Hi, Mr. Noah," Kai said as he walked to meet the man. She chuckled as Kai attempted a fist bump while holding the pasta salad bowl. Sienna quickly relieved him before it hit the ground.

"I thought I heard you pull up." Noah slid an easy smile her way. "You look nice."

Sienna couldn't stop the heat that rose to her cheeks, even if she tried. "Thank you. You look good yourself." He cleaned up his fade and beard since the night before. *Maybe it is a date.*

Kai pointed to the bowl in her hand. "We made pasta salad. Mommy said we couldn't come empty-handed."

Now her cheeks heated for another reason. Noah chuckled and gently took possession of their contribution.

"You didn't have to bring anything. Thank you. I am looking forward to tasting it." Noah's hand softly brushed against her lower back. "Come. Let's put this in the fridge. Give you a tour and you can meet Meadow."

Sienna was dying to see if he had the typical bachelor pad. Her gut told her it wasn't.

"Does your cat go outside?" Kai asked as they stepped onto the porch.

"Only when she is with me and has her harness on. We have six outdoor cats that stay in the stables and barns. They patrol the property for rodents and help keep the hawks away and sometimes see Meadow as invading their territory." Noah turned the knob and allowed them to enter first. "Besides, she's too spoiled and loves the indoors."

As expected, Noah's home was warm, masculine and neat. An open-floor plan allowed a clear view into the back of the house and the modern kitchen. Paned windows allowed natural light to flow into the space. An L-shaped leather couch in a rich dark brown anchored the room and faced one of the largest TVs she'd seen outside of a magazine or showroom. Definitely bigger than her sixty-inch. Throw pillows and decorative pieces in buttery yellow, autumn orange and tan gave a cozy feel and softened the heavy furniture.

"Did you put these in for your cat? We should do something like this for Scooter." Kai pointed to the carpet-covered two-by-four fixed to the wall. Sienna's eyes followed the ramp to several alternating ledges, which gave perfect views of the outdoors.

Where the hallway met the last ledge, a fluffy tan and brown hulk of a cat leisurely draped. Her sharp, light green eyes studied, and possibly judged, Sienna and Kai. She was gorgeous.

"I'm not sure Scooter would use something like this," Sienna commented, resting her hand on his shoulders. "We'll figure out something else for him."

"If you need ideas, let me know." Noah ran his hands across the cat's head. Meadow leaned into the contact, drawing a smile from Sienna. "She's trying to butter me up for treats."

"I'm sure she doesn't have to try too hard," Sienna teased. She stepped closer and let the cat get a whiff of her hand. "How often do you brush her?"

"Two to three times a week. Any more would mess with her natural oils." Noah slid his gaze to Kai. "Do you want to pet her?"

Kai turned his pleading eyes to her. Sienna couldn't say no because it was killing her to run her fingers through the silky fur. When she nodded, Noah sat the bowl on the entertainment center and then lifted her son to the cat's eye level.

"Hi. I'm Kai. It's nice to meet you. Is it okay if I pet you?"

Sienna swallowed the lump in her throat. The pure innocence of the moment burned into her memory. Noah shared a glance with her as Kai tentatively reached his hand out for the cat to sniff. He held her son in such a way that if Meadow became aggressive, he could spin him out of the way quickly. When she butted Kai's hand with her head, the squeal of delight had them laughing. Her son had made a new friend.

Sienna ran her hand along the side. She wondered if Noah would let her brush Meadow once.

"We should get a cat, Mom," Kai said when Noah set him back on his feet.

"Maybe. We'll talk about it once we get more settled." She'd been thinking of the same thing, but wanted them to get a routine in place first.

Noah didn't comment on her statement, which she was happy. He gave her a wink over Kai's head and picked up the bowl. "I'm sure Meadow will make an appearance." He pointed down the hallway. "The first door on the left is the restroom. The remaining are bedrooms, an office and a linen closet, with the washer and dryer. Why don't we put this in the fridge until it's time to eat?"

Sienna and Kai followed Noah toward the kitchen. As they walked through the dining area, he mentioned the table and china hutch belonged to his paternal grandparents. The cherry wood pieces had nicks and scratches but shined to beauty. Sienna wondered if Noah had siblings or someone he could pass the heirloom to. A quick flash of him leaving it to Kai popped into her mind, and she forced it out. That was a path she wouldn't go down any time in the immediate future.

Stainless steel appliances gave the country kitchen a modern feel. Navy blue painted cabinets with brushed silver handles normally would have a dark, heavy feel. However, the windows allowed natural light in, brightening the space. Sienna loved it.

"I know you said you don't have red meat that often, so I figured we could do kabobs with baby potatoes." Noah slid her bowl into the refrigerator and pulled out a plastic container that held the kabobs and an iron skillet with chive-covered diced red potatoes. "If that doesn't work, I have a salmon filet I can grill."

Sienna was already shaking her head. "That sounds amazing. What can I do to help?"

"I wanna help, too," Kai piped in.

"You can help me carry this out to the grill. What can I get you to drink? Beer, iced tea, lemonade, or water. I don't drink sodas, sorry."

"Mom doesn't drink soda either." Kai accepted the grilling utensils.

"I gave up sodas before Kai was born. Too much sugar. We try hard to stay away from ultra-processed foods." Sienna sat her crossbody purse on the kitchen island. "If you tell me where the glasses are, I can get the drinks."

Noah pointed to the cabinet between the sink and refrigerator. "That's why I eat at home a lot to avoid the same thing. I ate so much junk in college and didn't think about it. When I came home and started working with the goats and expanding the garden, I became winded after two hours. Sodas and fast food were the first things I cut out, and I immediately felt the difference."

Sienna agreed as she poured tea into three glasses. "I did the same with nursing school. Late night studying and then doing clinical rotations, it was easier to grab something quick. During my first two weeks in the ER, I knew I had to change something."

"Nana tried to get Mommy to switch to tea in the morning," Kai added as they stepped through the door onto the screened-in porch and then out to the backyard.

"My mother lost that battle." Sienna mentally shook her head at the memory of her mother replacing her coffee pods with tea pods.

"My ex-wife tried that. I lasted three days on green tea before I craved coffee." Noah lifted the lid and checked the temperature of the grill. "Unless I'm sick, I need at least three cups in the morning."

Sienna took a seat at the table and sipped her tea. It wasn't overly sweet and had the perfect amount of lemon and mint. Kai spun in a circle, taking in the tall, mature trees. "I like it back here. Do you see a lot of wild animals?"

Noah spoke as he placed the items on the grill. "I do. Besides the typical squirrel and rabbit, I see a lot of deer in the morning when I'm doing tai chi."

"I know what that is." Kai proceeded to show something other than the slow, precise movements associated with the mindful exercise. Noah and Sienna shared a smile, but didn't laugh at his attempt. She always encouraged him to express himself.

"That's good, baby." She turned her attention to the man at the grill. "Have you always done tai chi? I've been meditating for about a year and have wanted to add tai chi or yoga."

"Is that how you got your muscles?" Kai asked, taking a seat next to his mother and picking up his glass of tea.

Noah chuckled. "No. The muscles come from the weights I have in my office. To answer your mother's question, I took up tai chi after my divorce. I told you I went through a bit of depression." Sienna nodded, remembering the brief conversation when he helped with the move. Noah continued.

"I needed something to help keep my mind in the moment so I didn't dwell on the end of my marriage. The therapist I saw suggested staying busy. I threw myself into work to where it became an obsession. Jace tried to get me into jogging. That was a major fail. Pops told me to research tai chi." He shrugged and rotated the food on the grill. "It worked. Been doing it for over ten years."

Sienna stayed quiet while Kai stood beside Noah and had a conversation about the proper way to grill. She let his confession sink in. She mentioned her being stuck in a holding pattern after Dylan. Even last night, the two opened up and shared about expectations and perceptions. It was apparent the two felt comfortable with one another. She could chalk it up to age or maybe finding a kindred spirit. Sienna didn't know.

What she knew was Noah Garrison was different, in a good way. How many men would remember she limited her red meat intake? Would admit they'd seen a therapist or not chastise her son for doing the exercise movements wrong? They had a way to go and a lot to learn about one another, but she looked forward to learning about the man with muscles.

And she thought of a wonderful first step.

"Maybe you could show me the basic movements in tai chi one morning."

Noah's gaze lingered on hers for a moment. A slow smile crept onto his lips. "I'd like that. How about tomorrow morning? Is five too early?"

"Not at all."

"I want to do it too," Kai piped in.

Her son was not an early-morning person. Seven-thirty was his sweet spot for waking up.

"If you can wake up without complaining and it's okay with Noah, you can join us."

Noah twirled a set of tongs around his finger before responding. "It's fine with me. Why don't we use Maya's backyard?"

"That sounds like a plan," she replied before finishing her tea. This way, she wouldn't feel guilty about letting him sleep in case it was too early for him.

"Perfect." Noah slipped the kabobs onto a platter and scooped the potatoes into a bowl. "I'm not sure if it's okay with you, but maybe we could eat indoors? The Phillies are playing the Pirates, if I'm not mistaken."

He wasn't mistaken. Sienna stood and gathered the glasses. "Mr. Garrison, I like the way you think."

"I figured you would." He flashed a wink before handing the potatoes to Kai to carry.

Her son eagerly took the platter and fell into step with her. "Things are going well, Mom. Maybe you can ask him about coming to dinner next week."

Sienna hoped for the ground to open up and swallow her. Noah's simple chuckle told her he heard Kai but thankfully didn't say anything.

Despite the generation rite of passage of children embarrassing their parents, all in all, maybe moving to a small town could rescue her heart and allow the possibility of finding love.

Chapter 11

Noah aimed the hose towards the line of water troughs in the temporary goat pen. Handlers ran around, setting up climbing obstacles and toys for their new arrivals.

Towards the end of his date with Sienna, he'd received a call from the state police. There were plans to raid an illegal petting zoo and breeding farm. Goats, llamas, and pigs needed a place to go. Lucky, they knew of a rescue for the llamas, and Noah provided the information. They would take the goats, while Ms. Ophelia would take the pigs. Now they had to get ready for ten new goats and isolate them from their herd.

Preparing for the arrival didn't stop him from meeting Sienna, though.

Noah enjoyed spending time with Sienna and Kai. When she mentioned being a baseball fan, he just thought she was a casual fan. No, she knew stats, pitches, and fan chants. He laughed at her and Kai's celebratory dance when a player hit a grand slam. It was a scene he thought he would share with Robin and had all but given up hope of having.

Now he had the possibility of having that family.

Yes, it was way too early to think about the future. But Sienna made it hard not to consider. It brought him back to a few hours before. She texted at four forty-five to see if they were still on for tai chi because he had to get ready for the new arrivals. There was no way he was going to pass up spending time with her.

When he cleared the trees, there she sat on Maya's back porch, dressed in a simple white T-shirt and black bike shorts. She still sported her sleep scarf, which spoke volumes about their comfort level over a short time. As expected, Kai was still sleeping.

For forty minutes, they faced each other while she mimicked his moves. He adjusted her form a few times, but Sienna was a natural. The silence added a sense of intimacy he wasn't expecting but welcomed. Something Noah could get used to. Vince flicked on the kitchen light and poked his head out of the window, bringing an end to their time.

Now Noah had to figure out a way to see her and Kai again.

"I think that's enough water, son." Owen's voice pulled Noah from his thoughts. The small troughs were overflowing and puddling around his feet.

He turned off the nozzle while shaking the mud from his work boots. "Sorry."

"No harm. Give the goats something to play in." Owen handed him the towel draped over his shoulder. "Thinking about your pre-dawn gallivanting?"

Noah chuckled at his father. "Pre-dawn gallivanting is something I hope to never hear you say again. I take it Vince told you?"

"Nope. Jace. Jogged past and saw you two swaying in the wind."

"Why is everything coming from your mouth sound scandalous?"

Owen's belly laugh had him choking on his water. He wiped his eyes and spoke when he got himself together. "That's not my intent, I swear. I'm just messing with ya. Good to see you out there doing something I can tease you about. So you and Maya's baby sister, uh?"

"I guess." Noah took a sip from his father's water bottle. "We're just talking now, taking it slow."

"Didn't look slow from my view," Vince commented, joining their group. "She was smiling a lot when she came in."

"I was just showing her some tai chi moves she could incorporate into her meditation."

Vince held his hands up in a faux surrender move. "Hey. I'm happy she's smiling again."

Noah realized his comment might have come across as defensive. "Sorry. I know you were just kidding. I'm just trying not to mess things up with her before it gets started. Rumors and gossip may give her second thoughts."

"No need to apologize. Sienna is stronger than you think. Town chatter won't influence her." Vince pulled a pocketknife from his belt to open a new bag of feed. "My sister-in-law wants this move to work. She wasn't happy with the person she was back in Philly. In the short time they've been here, she and Kai have opened up."

"You've even smiled more this week." Owen gave his son a side-eye. "People around here are going to tease out of love. You know from experience how this town is. They'll be whispers because it's new. Between Denise, Ophelia, and Josie squashing anything they hear, you won't be the topic of conversation for long."

His father was right. His aunt and her friends were the ladies who kept their fingers on the pulse. Descendants of the founding families of Oak Mountain. Denise already cared for her new tenant. Ophelia doesn't make fried chicken for just anyone. Josie was a second mother to him. Once she found out he was seeing Sienna, a family dinner would only be a matter of time.

What little Noah knew of Sienna, he would agree with Vince's opinion—she was stronger than people gave her credit. What he didn't want was people, i.e. family, making a big deal of his dating life. He understood they wanted the best for him, and Noah loved them for it. But he secretly hoped Naomi's baby and Jace's wedding would keep everyone's minds busy.

A cackle on their walkie-talkies drew their attention.

"State police SUV and trailer turning into the property," their gate security guard announced.

Vince unclipped his radio and replied as they hurried to the turnoff for the temporary shelter. Rare did the sanctuary receive rescue goats. Usually, the enclosure and open area housed goats they'd purchased from reputable farms, which still required quarantine. Not knowing the conditions of the animals or their temperament, they would require a two-week isolation from their herd. If not longer.

They arrived at the entrance to the dirt path just as the police vehicle cleared the gate. Sergeant Henderson led the task force, taking down smuggling, trafficking, and illegal businesses in their area. The sanctuary has housed animals from illegal dog and cockfighting, as well as dog breeding.

They directed the sergeant and the driver of the trailer down the path. Owen waved and moved out of the way for the trailer to back into the opening. By the time Noah and Vince jogged back to the pen, Henderson and the officer driving the trailer were climbing from behind the wheel. After a round of introductions and light joking, the men became serious.

"What were the conditions of the property?" Vince asked as they followed the other officer and the goat handler towards the back of the trailer.

"Bad." Sergeant Henderson raked his finger through his close-cut graying hair. "The group kept the animals in small enclosures. Everything was dirty, and the animals were clearly underweight. They would feed and clean the animals scheduled for buyers. It was how our office got the tip. Two llamas died within days of being on the new farm. The buyers had a connection to the governor."

"It helps to have friends in high places, at least in this case." Owen clapped Noah on the shoulder. "Are Logan and Claire going to wait until the animals had some time to decompress?"

He nodded. "Thomas and Josie are going to Ms. Ophelia to check out the pigs. She won't use them for meat, but figured they would be good for the 4-H troop."

They stayed quiet for a few minutes while the handler coaxed the goats out of the trailer with a trail of fruit and veggies. What Noah saw made him see red. They were a combination of mini Nubian and Pygmy goats. Given their small development, matted fur and obvious malnourishment, they were saved just in time. Noah hoped the so-called breeders received a long jail sentence.

"How small of an enclosure were they kept in?" Noah asked as he moved closer to the fence.

"The trailer is bigger than what they are used to," the officer commented as he closed the gate. "Barely enough bedding. They all cuddled together. The bigger ones were on the outside. They eagerly let us lead them in."

A string of curses left Noah, Owen, and Vince's mouths. The temporary enclosure the goats would bed in was eight hundred square feet set on four acres of open space. Quality pine shavings and a heating/cooling unit would make them comfortable. Noah hoped they would realize they were safe soon.

"I was thinking Hector would be good for them," Vince said, speaking of the senior Anatolian Shepherd. The dog was mellow and used to skittish animals. A rescue three years ago, he took to being a livestock guardian like a duck to water. Noah agreed with the decision.

"Good call. We'll bring him over with dinner. That will give Logan time to give them a quick once-over and a round of antibiotics."

The goats cautiously approached the water trough. After a healthy sniff, all ten drank eagerly. Noah didn't want to think of how long it had been since the little guys had fresh, clean water. They slowly made their way over to the pellets rich in vitamins.

"Let me get a statement from you regarding the condition they're in," Sergeant Henderson said, slipping his state police cap on his head.

Before anyone could speak, Sienna's car crept down the drive. He could see Maya in the front seat.

"I'll give him a statement," Owen offered. "You go say hi."

Vince fell into step with Noah. "Yep. Kai doesn't need to see them in this condition."

Noah gave a quick nod. "Maybe next weekend. Give them time to get cleaned up and an ounce or two of weight on them. We can let him name them."

Vince chuckled just as they reached the stopped car. "He'd like that a lot."

Three car doors flew open. Kai was the first one out, already talking. "Mom, let me hold the handlebars on the four-wheeler and steer!"

Sienna wiggled her hand back and forth, saying 'sort of.' Everyone smiled, not wanting to burst the boy's bubble. Vince mussed his nephew's hair.

"You'll be ready to drive your own in no time. At least four years from now." The beaming smile Kai gave them was priceless.

Noah turned his attention to Sienna. Dressed in simple jean shorts and a tank top, she still took his breath away.

"Sounds like he had a blast."

Sienna glanced at her son, who was busy filling his uncle in on their day. "I didn't realize I was raising a speed junkie. I've always loved rollercoasters and riding dirt bikes when I visited my family in Puerto Rico. Seems like Kai is going to take after me."

"Will you give him the car keys at sixteen?"

"Not my car," Sienna teased. She looked over her shoulder at the officer speaking to Owen. "How are the goats?"

"Bad, but I think we'll save them. They got here just in time. Vince and I were talking and thought it might not be good for Kai to see them now."

Sienna nodded in understanding. She opened her mouth to speak, but Kai's squeal filled the air.

"Mom! Uncle Vince said I could name the goats next week when they are feeling better. Is that true, Mr. Noah?"

"He was calling me mommy two weeks ago," Sienna quipped. Noah chuckled as he turned to the boy.

"It would help us out a great deal if you could. They just got here and still have to get used to their new home and get an examination. I'm sure next weekend they'll be ready for their new names." *Probably the first time with names*, Noah thought.

"Thanks, Uncle Vince and Mr. Noah."

"Why don't we do a quick trip to the other goat pen so Kai can learn the names of the other goats? We don't want duplicates," Maya said with her hand on Kai's shoulder, steering him towards the small clusters of trees separating the new arrivals from the resident herd. "Logan said he'll grab Claire in twenty minutes and head over to check them out."

"We stopped past the main house for canned apples," Sienna offered in explanation. "Logan was there double checking his bag for enough medication and making sure Naomi had everything."

Noah figured Maya suggested taking Kai to see the goats, to give them time alone. Sienna and Kai were heading home. After their lesson that morning, they hadn't talked. He wanted to ask her for another date.

"I'm glad you stopped by before leaving."

"I couldn't go without saying goodbye." Sienna shrugged. "It's why I volunteered to drop Maya off."

Noah reached for her hand. "You didn't need a reason to stop by, but I'm glad you care enough about your sister to make sure she arrived safely."

Sienna snorted. "Don't let her hear you say that. There's also another reason I stopped by."

Noah stiffened slightly. He hoped she hadn't changed her mind about them seeing each other. "Okay."

"I was wondering if you aren't busy Wednesday, you could join us for dinner. Kai has school half day—teacher conference or something. Anyway, that's our spaghetti night. If you're okay with ground turkey in the sauce, we'd love to have you over."

Noah wouldn't care if she used tofu. He'd still go. "And here I thought I could ask you on another date and you beat me to it."

"Don't let my invitation stop you from asking."

Noah laughed, squeezing her hand. "Fine. I would like to take you out on Friday night. Adult date, if that's okay."

"An adult date sounds great. Since he's naming goats and all next weekend, I'm sure Maya and Vince would babysit."

"We sure would," Vince called out. They stepped out from behind the same set of trees they disappeared into earlier. Kai held a shrink-wrapped block of cheese.

"Do I like goat cheese?" Kai scrunched his little face. "I thought cheese came from cows."

"And that is our cue to go. I'll explain the difference on the way home." Sienna ran her hand down Noah's arm. "I'll talk to you later this evening."

After saying goodbye to everyone, Sienna executed a three-point turn and headed toward the road leading out of the sanctuary. Kai waved through the back window. Noah was worried when he mentioned just the two of them for the date. He liked Kai a lot, but if he wanted to get to know Sienna, they needed alone time. Also, he figured she could use some adult time herself.

Noah turned to find Maya and Vince flashing cheesy grins. He playfully rolled his eyes and laughed. "Thanks for watching him."

"Anytime, boss man. Just make sure you have her back by curfew," Maya teased.

"And don't try that running out of gas trick either," Vince added. "Maya's father didn't buy it when I tried it, and I won't either."

The three doubled over in laughter. Noah worried when he first mentioned his interest in Sienna. Knowing he had Vince and Maya's blessings, he hoped they could start doing things together. The couple spent most of their down time with his father and Sam. Maybe they could do something as a group next weekend.

Noah mentally shook his head as they walked toward the goats, exploring the open area. It's been over ten years since he was part of a couple. Noah sent a silent thanks that he waited for the right person.

Chapter 12

"**M**rs. Sara said we're going on a trip to Uncle Vince and Mr. Noah's job to see them milk the goats next month," Kai said, gripping the handle on his backpack. "I raised my hand, and when she called on me, I told her my aunt and uncle worked there and my mom was dating one of the owners."

Sienna stumbled along the even sidewalk. She clearly misheard her son. Did he just out her relationship to his entire class? What possessed her son to share their business on the third day of class?

On the ride home from Hawkins Ridge, Sienna had another conversation about dating. She explained that sometimes she and Noah would go out or stay in to watch TV. Occasionally, Kai would join them, but a few times it would be adults only. Kai said he understood and didn't mind staying with Maya and Vince. Sienna didn't think she needed to tell him not to say anything.

She wasn't ashamed of seeing Noah. Far from it. But that night would only be their second date. Did a spaghetti dinner at home even count?

Over the past three days, Sienna and Kai began to develop a routine. With the school only a five-minute drive, she could take him before work and pick him up during her afternoon break. Kai focused on doing his homework or reading while she finished the rest of her workday. They both needed structure.

Sienna didn't need her new relationship to be fodder for gossip.

Sienna rested her hand on his shoulder, stopping him in front of the bakery. She purposely avoided looking at the mixed-berry pie she could see from the front window. "You told everyone I was dating one of the owner of Hawkins Ridge?"

Kai nodded. "Three of my classmates said their parents work there, and they liked Mr. Noah. They said he's really friendly and let them pick out an apple to take home."

Sienna could see Noah doing that. It didn't excuse her son's sharing, but she couldn't get upset. She didn't tell him not to mention anything. To him, it was innocent and a way to impress his new classmates. She met Kai's buddy, Adam, on his first day, and since then she has exchanged texts with the boy's mother. Sienna hoped Adam's mother didn't think she was fast. She'd been a resident of Oak Mountain for less than a month and already had a gentleman caller. Sienna giggled mentally at the term *gentleman caller* before sobering. She would have to tell Noah when he came for dinner.

She bent at the waist to be at eye level with Kai and gave a reassuring smile. "I'm glad you could share with the class about Maya and Vince. They really love their jobs and are proud to work there. However, maybe we should wait a little before we tell people about Noah and me. Maybe next time, ask me or Noah if it is okay before sharing something personal."

Worry clouded Kai's features. "You don't think he'll be mad at me, do you?" Sienna was quick to shake her head.

"Not at all. Remember when Nana had that visit to the doctor and came home with a pillow to sit on for a week?" Sienna and Kai snickered, remembering her mother's butt lift. "She asked us not to say anything to her friends. Over time, if things continue with Noah and me, it will be okay if everyone knows."

"I'm sorry, Mom."

Sienna pulled him in for a hug and kissed the top of his head. "No need to apologize. You didn't know. Now, how about we split a sandwich and a few cookies from the bakery before my lunch break is over?"

With Kai having a half day, it worked well with her schedule. She gave him another hug before pulling the door open for the bakery. The intoxicating aroma of cinnamon, vanilla, and nutmeg greeted them, causing Sienna to swallow a groan. It had been hours since her breakfast of granola, yogurt, and a pot of coffee. She waved to Denise, who stood a few feet in front of them. She motioned for them to join her. Sienna apologized to the woman they passed and gave Denise a hug. She kept her fingers crossed Kai wouldn't bring up Noah. Sienna didn't know if he had mentioned anything to his aunt about their relationship.

"What are you two doing out and about?"

"The teachers had a conference," Kai answered. "Can we get a croissant sandwich?"

"Sure. How about the turkey and avocado?" Kai nodded and stepped closer to the display case of scrumptious cookies. "I'm

glad I ran into you. The spider plant Noah gave me is dying."
There was a reason Sienna invested in quality artificial plants.

"If you have time, I can stop by after we get our order." Denise smiled at the worker and placed her order. When she added Sienna and Kai's, Denise shook her head when she tried to protest. "We have an arrangement. I supply the flowers, and I can get lunch a few times a week."

Sienna glanced at the floral display in the window and the single buds of various flowers on the few tables. She would have to do something special for Denise and made a mental note to ask Noah when he came for dinner.

"I'll let you take care of the sandwich, but I insist on buying our cookies." Sienna was firm. Denise gave the look mothers mastered for centuries when dealing with a stubborn child. She gave Sienna the win and nodded in agreement.

After Kai selected half a dozen cookies, the trio headed towards the apartment. She glanced at her watch and still had twenty minutes left on her lunch break. She was used to eating while she worked. Denise commented on the dollar store colorful artwork Sienna hung in the stairwell. There may be ample lighting, but the plain brick walls needed something. She and Maya hung them before returning to the property to help with the horses.

The quick shopping trip to the local dollar store gave the sisters time to discuss Sienna's appointment with her new therapist. Phoebe Monroe was friendly, understanding, and encouraging. The shopping trip was a test for her because Stark Valley was more populated than Oak Mountain. It gave Sienna a taste of a slower city life in case she left Oak Mountain. She didn't have an anxiety attack. The area they visited didn't have the noise of car horns, large buildings or crowds. She realized she didn't miss it. A visit was her speed now. Sienna was okay with that. She felt more present for Kai, and that was the ultimate goal.

"Go change your clothes while I get lunch onto plates," Sienna said as they stepped through the door.

"You've made this into a home," Denise said as she glanced around the open space.

Sienna wanted her place to feel lived in. She had a nine-year-old, for goodness' sake. Pillows still covered the couch from their movie the night before. Kai's slippers lay discarded near the front door. Their few breakfast dishes were still drying on the rack.

"Thank you," Sienna replied. She set the pink box, which held their sandwiches, on the small kitchen table and pulled out two paper plates. "I still need to go through my fall decorations. I haven't been in the box since I sold my house."

"Anything you don't want, you can sell at the indoor flea market during the fall festival. I always sign up for two extra tables in case my daughters or sister want to unload some things. The Becketts also have extra tables, so we've got you covered." Denise's gaze zoomed in on Sienna's plant near the French doors that led to her balcony. The tsking sound coupled with the shake of her head had Sienna chuckling.

"Maya told him I could kill a cactus."

"Bless your heart, child."

"That makes it even worse, Denise." Sienna laughed as she followed her to the plant. "Can it be saved?"

Denise set her package on the floor and felt the soil. "When was the last time you watered this?"

"Sunday when I came home from Hawkins Ridge."

"And the time before that?"

Sienna ducked her head. "Friday morning."

"These plants, you can get by with watering them about every ten to fourteen days. You've given it a month's worth of water in seventy-two hours."

"So I guess every other day is too much? I thought the soil was dry. It looked dry."

Denise barked out a laugh. "The surface will dry out because of the excellent sunlight, but you have to stick your finger in to see if underneath is dry."

Kai chose that moment to come back into the room. He'd change into a pair of basketball shorts and a tee a little too tight. She would need to put that into a bag for donations. He saddled up to Denise and watched carefully.

"What are you doing?"

Denise squeezed a few leaves before lifting the pot. "Making sure we can save the plant. I'm taking this with me so I can replant it and check the roots. Give me about an hour."

Sienna stopped her before she made it to the door. "I don't want you to walk back up those stairs. Call me, and I'll come down when it's ready. Please let me pay you for your time."

Denise leaned close and waited for Kai to rummage in the kitchen for glasses. "Putting a smile on my nephew's face is payment enough."

Before Sienna could form a response, Denise was through the door and walking down the stairs. Sienna couldn't help but smile. She closed the door when Denise was safely out of the entrance. Did she really put a smile on Noah's face? Did Owen mention something to his ex-wife? Had Noah said something to his mother over breakfast?

It was something Sienna didn't have time to dwell on. She had to get their lunch on plates and then back to work. Sienna had no intention of working late. She had a meal to prepare while planning a chat with Noah about Kai's declaration and his aunt's statement.

Not a problem for a single mother.

The mouthwatering aroma of onions, peppers, and garlic filled Sienna's apartment. She started her homemade sauce before taking Kai to school and had it on a low simmer all day. Leftover spaghetti was up there with cold fried chicken and pizza.

The afternoon flew by once she settled back into work. Denise repotted her plant and gave her a glass tube that would gradually water the plant. She promised to check its progress in a few days. She really wanted to do something nice for her and planned to ask Noah when he arrived in twenty minutes.

Sienna smiled as she lifted the pot filled with water to the burner. He insisted on bringing the garlic bread and dessert. She figured that trying to argue that he didn't need to bring anything was fruitless.

Her mind drifted back to Kai's class announcement and Denise's parting comment. Could she really have put a smile on Noah's face? They hadn't known each other for very long. Sienna would admit she enjoyed the excitement of starting a new relationship, which surprised her. It wasn't her goal when she moved, but she was open to the possibility. Just to find someone interesting in the first month was unexpected. She couldn't deny feeling something for the caring big man. They still had a way to go, and she was looking forward to the journey.

"Why are we using regular plates?" Kai wrinkled his nose as she stared at the stack of dishes on the dining room table. "Why can't we use paper plates?"

"Because we're having company."

"We use paper plates with Auntie Maya and—"

"It's different with family," Sienna cut him off. "Besides, spaghetti has some weight to it, and I don't want an accident." No way was she going to say she wanted to impress Noah.

Kai shrugged and went about setting the plates. "Do you think Nana and Poppy will like Mr. Noah?"

"I'm not sure, sweetie." Sienna's parents texted shortly after she logged off from work, saying they had made reservations to visit during the fall festival. The rooms in Oak Mountain were booked, but Maya found them a nice hotel in Stark Valley.

With good reason, Sienna hadn't thought about Noah and her parents. They would meet him simply because of Maya showing them Hawkins Ridge. If it seemed she and Noah would still be together, Sienna would let her parents know she was dating someone. Until then, mum's the word.

"Your grandparents will meet Noah and everyone else at Hawkins Ridge when they visit, but for now, I want to keep us dating to ourselves."

"I understand. Nana would get excited," Kai correctly concluded.

Sienna chuckled. "You're right."

Kai finished setting the table while Sienna turned the heat on under the water. They talked casually about what he wanted to do that weekend. Though he was spending Friday evening with his aunt and uncle, and naming the goats Saturday morning, they both wanted to hang out at home. It would also give Maya and Vince alone time. It was nice to have her family a ten-minute drive away, but Sienna wanted this move to work. That meant creating her own independence.

A rhythmic knock pulled her out of her thought. Since Noah had the key to the street entrance, he wouldn't need to use the intercom for a visit.

"I'll get it!" Kai yelled, putting the last fork on the table. Sienna shook her head and untied her apron. She stood five feet away and knew her son didn't have to yell.

"We will get it. You can't even see out the peephole."

Kai bounced on the balls of his feet as Sienna adjusted her knee-length T-shirt dress. It complemented her full figure while being cool and comfortable. After a quick peek to make sure it was Noah, she pulled open the door and stepped to the side.

"Hi, Mr. Noah." Kai beamed when Noah ruffled his curly hair.

"Hey, Kai." He shifted and pressed a kiss to Sienna's forehead. "Hi, beautiful. You look nice."

Sienna's cheeks warmed. Noah also kept his outfit casual in a pair of jean shorts and a fitted tee. "Thank you. Dinner is almost done. I just have to add the spaghetti."

She closed the door while sneaking a glance into the tote bag he carried. She saw a foil-wrapped loaf on top of a glass container.

"It smells amazing in here." Noah sniffed the air. "I've always loved the smell of garlic and onions."

Kai rubbed his flat tummy. "Mom's been cooking her sauce all day. It makes my tummy rumble. Sometimes we'll have it for breakfast the next morning."

"Please don't tell people that. It makes me seem like a bad mother because I'm not making you eggs or cereal."

"You're the best mom in the world." Kai wrapped his arms around her.

Sienna's heart melted. She had a good kid. "Thank you, sweetie."

"I've seen you with him. I must agree with the Little Man." Noah looked around her apartment. "You've done a lot with the place. I like it."

"You both are just buttering me up for an extra helping." Sienna chuckled as she walked past the two. "I have the oven heated for you. Can I get you anything to drink?"

"We have milk, lemonade, water, and tea," Kai supplied, running to the fridge.

Noah sat his bag on the counter and began removing the contents. "I'll take lemonade, please. I bought maple cookies for dessert. Pops made a big batch, and I figured it would be something light after a heavy meal."

"Does that have maple syrup?" Kai asked as he added ice into the cups. Noah nodded, unwrapping the foil.

"It's my grandma's recipe. My mother asked him to make a batch for a luncheon she is hosting tomorrow."

Sienna's mouth watered when she saw the French loaf and a thick smattering of garlic butter with tiny pieces of chives. She dropped two handfuls of spaghetti into the salted boiling water and handed Noah a cookie sheet.

"Is it weird for your parents to be friends?"

"Not really." Noah slipped the sheet into the oven then gently lifted the pitcher of lemonade from Kai's hands. "They didn't work everything out until I went to college. Denise and the Becketts helped bridge a way for them to be friendly. They'll never go on vacation together, but they get together for birthdays and help each other out, like with the cookies."

"It may help that they moved on and found new spouses."

Noah nodded as he passed Sienna her glass. "Most definitely. My mom and Malcolm, my stepfather, met on a blind date. They say it was love at first sight. Same with Pops and Sam."

"Is that how you feel about my mom?" Kai asked from out of nowhere. Sienna and Noah choked on their drinks and patted each other on the back while they got themselves under control. She handed a bamboo spoon to Noah and pointed towards the pasta. She kneeled in front of Kai and rested her hands on his shoulders.

"Sweetie, Noah and I just met. This is new for us—all of us." She moved her hand between the three of them. "When people say it was love at first sight, it's after they've dated for a while. They can look back and see instances when they felt a special way when they were together. Noah and I haven't even talked about our favorite colors or food."

"Favorite color is navy blue. Favorite food is Ms. Ophelia's fried chicken, followed closely by my pop's smoked brisket," Noah added as he opened the oven door to check on the bread.

"I've had her fried chicken. You're not wrong in making it a favorite. My favorite color is red." Sienna gave him a wink then returned her attention back to Kai. "I know you want everything to work between Noah and I, but it's going to take a little time while we get to know each other."

"So that's why I shouldn't have said anything to my class? You don't know if it's love at first sight yet?"

Sienna could only drop her head. She thought of how to bring up Kai's announcement during dinner. *I guess she didn't need to anymore.*

"What happened?" Noah turned around, his glass halfway to his lips.

Sienna groaned as she rose to her feet. It was time to check the sauce and figured she could talk while she stirred.

"Kai's teacher mentioned an upcoming field trip to Hawkins Ridge. He raised his hand and told the class his aunt and uncle work there, and I was dating one of the owners."

Noah laughed and choked on his lemonade again. Sienna shook her head and lifted the pot to drain the pasta. Once Noah could speak, he leaned against the opposite counter.

"First, I didn't know his teacher was Claire's cousin-in-law. She asked if she could bring her class before the scheduled trip for the fourth and fifth-grade classes." Noah took a sip and spared a glance at Sienna. "What did your mother say when you told her?"

Sienna appreciated Noah wanting to hear her stance on the matter before he spoke. She motioned for Kai to answer. He stood straight, not wavering in his eye contact.

"She said that you two are new and that I should have asked permission before sharing something personal. She wasn't mad, though."

Noah nodded. "I'm not mad either. I don't care who knows about your mother and me. It's a close-knit town, and people will find out, eventually. But your mom is new here. People are already naturally curious about you two. The last thing we want is to give them material to gossip about." He leaned in closer as to share a secret. Kai grinned. "But, Ms. Denise, my pop and Mrs. Beckett will put any tongue waggers in their place and tell them to mind their business."

Kai giggled. "He said, tongue waggers."

Sienna laughed as she added the pasta to the sauce. It was good to know there were people willing to stand up for their relationship. Sienna liked how Noah spoke to Kai with respect and explained what she had attempted to say earlier.

As he said, she wasn't ashamed of Noah. He was an attractive, successful man who she was sure had a list of women hoping for a chance. Plenty of questions will fly. Wondering what it was about her he found interesting enough to pursue. Sienna wondered also, but that was something to ponder later.

For now, she wanted to provide a tasty meal, nosedive into the maple cookies and get to know the man pulling the garlic bread out of the oven better.

Chapter 13

An upbeat old-school song had Noah tapping his fingers against the steering wheel. Despite the tiring forty-plus hours, he was in a good mood. It was Friday night, and he was on his way to pick up Sienna for their date. If the beautiful woman had her way, they would have postponed it until later in the weekend. She didn't think he'd be up for going out.

But she was wrong.

On his way home after a food coma meal with Sienna and Kai, he received a call that Naomi went into labor. He turned his truck around and headed to the hospital in Stark Valley. Since it was a high-risk pregnancy, Naomi's doctor insisted on her delivering at the larger hospital. Everyone agreed. After a successful cesarean, Jack and Cole Beckett entered the crazy world. Mother and babies returned home Friday morning, and Sienna thought Noah would want to be with the family.

He would, but everyone wanted to give the new family a night together. There would be plenty of time for visitors. That meant he could keep their date. Noah compromised and agreed to stay in Oak Mountain. His initial plan of taking her to his favorite restaurant in Stark Valley would have to wait a week. Instead, they were going to the Chinese restaurant three blocks from her apartment.

Noah looked forward to the date all day. He enjoyed Kai and began to care for the bright boy, but he wanted this time alone with the single mother. He understood that having a relationship with Naomi meant Kai would be a factor, and that was okay with him. However, they needed to see if there was more there without the Kai buffer.

The sun was low in the sky when he pulled in front of Naomi's building. He shook his head when he saw the woman in question standing outside her building scrolling on her phone. Dressed in a pair of navy capris and a white sleeveless tunic, the casual outfit didn't take away from her beauty.

She smiled and headed towards his truck. Noah scrambled to meet her at the passenger door. They greeted each other with a hug.

"You look beautiful. I wanted to pick you up at the door."

"Thank you. Technically, you are picking me up at the door," Naomi teased. "You look nice yourself."

Noah decided on a pair of dressy black jeans and a light blue short-sleeve button-down linen shirt. He had his father clean up his fade and close-cut beard. He understood that after that night, tongues would start wagging. No need to make his physical appearance part of the conversation.

He opened the door of the truck and helped her in.

"I thought we were walking?" she asked, clicking her seat belt. "It's just down the street."

Noah shook his head, opting for honesty. "Between Kai's declaration in class and our date, this relationship will be all over town by Sunday night. The last thing we need is for people to say I wasn't a gentleman and made you walk in the heat. We'd be a sweaty mess by the time we got to the restaurant. I would then get a call from Mom asking what's wrong with me and how could I let you walk because that wasn't how she raised me. Then she'd get Pops to sit me down and have a talk." Noah used air quotes, then continued, "He would need to remind me how to court a person. Ms. Ophelia would drop me from her fried chicken notification email list, meaning I'd have to pay someone to sneak me some." Noah leaned forward and kissed her on the temple. "It's a slippery slope, and one I'm not willing to walk when I can just drive the three blocks."

Sienna blinked, then blinked again before barking out a laugh. "Wow. You thought that through for a minute."

"I know the people in this town. Mom may live in Stark Valley, but too many people still have her on speed dial, and if they don't, they have Aunt Denise and Pops." Noah closed the door and hurried to the driver's side. "I was serious about Ms. Ophelia. Jace got kicked off when he went on a date with her daughter after we returned home from college. Even though they both admitted it was a friendly date, she banned him from her chicken for two months. Gave me, Logan, and Caden the stink eye when we picked up our order because she knew we would share with him."

Sienna shook her head, chuckling. "That means I need to stay on her good side."

"That's best."

Noah put the truck in drive and headed towards the restaurant. It warmed his heart as she laughed at his take on Oak Mountain gossip and relationships. He went for comedic effect, but it was still the truth. As they rolled into the parking lot a minute later, Sienna spoke.

"Were you serious about people knowing about our relationship by the end of the weekend?"

Noah sighed and put the truck in park. He left the air on while they sat.

"The timeline may have been an exaggeration, but I believe it will be by next week. Workers have asked Caden if he was dating, and he is all too happy to point them my way. A little will be because you're new. Mostly, people will either have confirmation I'm not like Pops, or they'll still be waiting to see if I do to you what he did to Mom."

Sienna shifted in her seat to look at him. "You mean being in the closet when they married?"

He nodded. "When Robin asked for a divorce, people assumed she found out I was hiding my orientation. Even when my father was honest with himself, people never factor in that a black man, the size of a linebacker who grew up in the South during the seventies and eighties, had to stay in the closet for his own safety."

"I can't even imagine what he went through."

"He still waited until my grandparents had passed. If their neighbors had known, it would have reflected badly on them. It's why I have no relationship with anyone on his side of the family."

Sienna placed her hand on his and gave it a supportive squeeze. "People are going to talk and form their own opinions no matter what. It was my first initial reaction when Kai told me about his class. New resident jumping into a relationship with one of the town's most eligible bachelors. But then your aunt thanked me for putting a smile on your face." She shrugged. "Then my worry moved from other people to what *you* would think about what she said. Same with tonight. I want this date to be about us, though your reason for not walking is valid."

Noah laughed, lightening the mood. "I'm glad you support my argument." He brought their joined hands to his mouth and pressed a kiss. "People's opinions don't bother me. I think I was more worried that the stares would bother you. In the end, none of it matters as long as we're happy."

It was Sienna's turn to sigh. "When I went back to work after Dylan's death, my co-workers walked on eggshells around me, whispered behind my back. It fed into my depression. Though I still struggle with anxiety, whispers no longer bother me."

"I'm glad." Noah killed the engine. "Come on. I'm craving a plate of spring rolls."

Sienna waited until he opened her door and helped her out of the truck. Head held high and hand in hand, they strolled to the entrance. They nodded to customers entering and leaving and wished them a wonderful evening.

Noah's fear that the gossip would scare Sienna off was unfounded. She confidently met any gazes thrown her way. It justified pursuing Sienna was the right call. He spoke the truth about their relationship being the talk of the town the following week. He just made a mental note to call his mother first thing. Having her find out about his date from a third party would still get him reamed out.

Sienna dropped her napkin on her empty plate and leaned back in her seat. It took all she had not to moan her contentment. When Noah suggested Chinese food for dinner, she didn't know what to expect. The perfectly seasoned Szechuan chicken with fluffy brown rice was a surprise. She contemplated getting a to-go order of the spring rolls for dinner tomorrow with Kai, but figured they would be better fresh.

"I take it you liked dinner?" Noah's smirk caused her to roll her eyes.

"I haven't eaten out much since I've been here, but every meal has been amazing."

"Oak Mountain is big on family-run restaurants."

Sienna could see that. The best places to eat back home were mom-and-pop restaurants. She would have to ask Maya if there was a good cheesesteak place near. Her sister could be a snob when it came to the Philly sandwich. If she recommended a place, Sienna was sure she would like it.

"Noah? Is that you?" An older, well-dressed couple moseyed up to their table. The light-skinned woman sported a stylish salt afro and wore a white, wrapped blouse and matching linen pants. Dressed in a white-button down and brown dress pants, the bald, dark-skinned man shook his head at his wife and mouthed 'sorry' to Noah. The woman spared Sienna a quick glance when Noah stood and greeted them with a hug. She spoke as she stepped back.

"I thought for sure you'd be fighting for time to hold the new babies."

"I'm sure I will this weekend. We wanted to give Logan, Naomi, and Fiona the night with the twins." He gave an apologetic look to Sienna. "What are you doing here?"

The woman gave a warm smile to Sienna. "We had a showing and stopped by Denise's to get the flowers for our open house tomorrow. We placed a to-go order. You know they make the best beef and broccoli." The woman gave her full attention to Sienna. "Hi. I'm Bev Johnson, Noah's mother. This is my husband, Malcolm."

Sienna didn't believe in coincidences. The look on Noah's face said he didn't either. Denise was still at the flower shop when Noah picked up Kai. She took the outstretched hand. The reason his parents were in Oak Mountain was legit. Stopping past the restaurant, when you could see Noah's truck from the street, was suspect. Especially the exasperated look on Malcolm's face.

Sienna matched the woman's warm smile and held out her hand. Something told her Bev knew who she was.

"Sienna Parker, Noah's date." She motioned to the empty chairs. "Why don't you join us while you wait for your order?"

Noah coughed, causing Malcolm to chuckle. "Thank you for the invitation. I'm sure we would've made ourselves comfortable even if you hadn't offered."

The look Bev shot at her husband spoke volumes. Noah hid his smirk and stacked their dishes. A server immediately gathered the dishes and left a fresh pot of green tea. Malcolm let the server know they were waiting for their order and asked if he could bring it over. The server snagged two empty cups from the table next to them and set them in front of Noah's parents. Bev didn't waste any time. She reminded Sienna of her mother.

"So, Sienna. How do you like Oak Mountain? I'm sure it's an adjustment coming from a big city."

"Ma." Noah dropped his head forward. Sienna tried not to laugh at his embarrassment.

"I like the town a lot. People have been welcoming, and my son already loves his new school."

"Have you ever lived in a small town? You know we are a more slow-paced than a metropolitan area." Bev poured herself some tea, ignoring the looks from her son and husband.

Sienna gave Noah a subtle head shake when he went to say something. His mother wanted to feel her out and make sure she was committed to staying in the small town if things progressed between her and Noah. Sienna understood as a mother, you wanted the best for your children, no matter how old they were. Bev wanted to make sure there wouldn't be a repeat of Noah's ex-wife. Sienna guaranteed she'd be the same way if Kai found himself in the same boat. It was time to show Noah, and anyone else, that she was committed to seeing where this relationship would go.

Sienna shifted to face Bev head-on and crossed her legs. She gave her best welcoming smile.

"It's funny you mentioned slow-pace compared to a metropolitan area. I'm thirty-five and ready to slow down. After my husband was killed in the line of duty, that same noisy big city crippled me to where I became a homebound introvert."

Bev had the decency to look abashed. "I'm sorry. I didn't know." Sienna was already waving away her apology.

"It's fine. You didn't know, and I didn't say that to make you feel bad. You want to make sure I don't have the same feeling about small towns as Noah's ex. No need to feel bad about that. I would do the same if it were my son." Sienna sighed. "Mrs. Johnson, yes, living in a town with a population smaller than the suburbs I grew up in is something I am getting used to. But Oak Mountain already feels like home. I'm sure as time goes on, I will miss certain aspects of a larger town. My son enjoys zoos and seeing live baseball games. We don't have that here. However, Oak Mountain has his aunt and uncle who work on a property with a bunch of animals. We also have people willing to incorporate watching a baseball game when they invite you to a cookout."

Noah reached across the table and took her hand. Sienna appreciated the sentiment and didn't miss the look of approval on his parents' faces. Sienna continued.

"My point is, I have nothing pulling me back to Philadelphia. The concern that I will up and leave because I don't have access to my favorite tattoo artist isn't warranted. I have family here. My son and I are enjoying building a life here. I also met an incredible man whom I'd like to see where things go." Sienna removed her hand from Noah's and rested it on Bev's wrist. "I'm a mother. I get it. But you have to trust your son. I don't think he would have asked me out if he thought I would take the first opportunity to jump ship."

"She's right, Mom," Noah said, drawing Bev's attention. "We've already talked about living in a small town and what Robin did. Sienna is the first woman since the divorce I have wanted a relationship with. I get you're looking out and hoping to get some juicy tidbits you can share with the family." Malcolm snorted, but quickly took a sip of his tea when Bev glared lovingly.

The server brought his parents' order and set the check for her and Noah's meal on the table. Bev gave a quick nod and grasped her purse handle.

"Thank you for understanding and respecting my concerns. Noah seems happy, and that's all a mother wants. Maybe we can get together for brunch in the coming weeks."

"I'd like that."

Malcom grabbed the bag and stood. They said good night and watched his mother and stepfather leave hand-in-hand. Sienna met Noah's admiring gaze and smiled.

"Sorry about that. You handled it like a champ, though."

Sienna chuckled. "I spoke to her as a mother. I would do the same thing with anyone Kai brought home."

Noah fished his wallet out and pulled out his card. Sienna had a crisp twenty-dollar bill for the tip and set it under the condiment holder. Noah smartly opted to keep his mouth shut.

They walked to the entrance in silence, stopping briefly for Noah to take care of the bill. When they stepped out into the warm evening air, Noah took her hand.

"Night is still young. Can I talk you into an ice cream cone?"

Sienna had a better idea, and one that would take them out of the public eye. "Rumor has it the Orioles are on a west coast stand. How about some popcorn, a cold beer, and watching a couple of innings?"

He swooped in and pressed his lips to hers. For just a moment, the evening sounds in their quiet town melted away. Kissing Noah didn't bring guilt for kissing a man that wasn't Dylan. It brought a glimpse into a future she didn't know she wanted.

Noah's toothy grin when they separated had Sienna smirking. "Cleo, I couldn't ask for a better offer."

Laughter bubbled forth at his use of Maya's nickname for her. Noah held the passenger door for her as she climbed in. Sienna didn't know where things would go with Noah, but she looked forward to finding out.

Chapter 14

"I still can't believe you haven't told them." Maya flipped down her visor and met Sienna's glare in the back seat. "You've been seeing Noah for a month. You know, if they ask me if I knew, I'm throwing you under the bus."

Sienna kicked the back of the seat. "What happened to my big sister having my back?"

"I always have it, unless it means I have to deal with Mom's judgmental look of disappointment."

Vince snickered from his spot in the driver's seat. Kai had the decency to just smile at his aunt. Sienna rolled her eyes and brushed the invisible fuzz off her dark jeans.

"Your comment about Mom should answer your question about why I haven't said anything." But Sienna couldn't avoid having the conversation any longer.

Their parents had arrived in Stark Valley two hours ago, and they were headed to meet them for dinner. With plans for her parents to spend the weekend at Hawkins Ridge, there was no way Sienna could keep her dating life a secret any longer. Not that Sienna was embarrassed about her relationship. Far from it. Flora Wood would make it into something bigger than what it was—a fledgling new relationship.

Sienna caught herself smiling as they entered Stark Valley's city limits. Being with Noah was easy. He was easy to talk to, and they spent a lot of time discussing books, sports, and playing board games. They were also silly together, much to Kai's enjoyment. One of their favorite games was playing keep-away in socks. Sienna and Noah both had hardwood floors and open floor plans. She was sure he let her and Kai win, but hearing her baby's fits of giggles was worth it.

Her son had blossomed over the past few weeks. Kai expressed himself better and took Scooter to show and tell the week before and even had a playdate with his friend Adam. His friend's mother, Dawn, was a single mother who was the dispatcher for emergency services. The two had a lot in common, with plans to meet up during the Fall Festival.

Sienna could confidently say Oak Mountain was home.

"What if Nana asks me if I knew about you and Noah? Should I say what Auntie said?" Kai swung his legs and studied his mother. Sienna immediately shook her head.

"No. I want you to be honest."

"I doubt they would ask you," Maya added. "If anything, they'll ask if you met and like him. Poppy may ask if you've seen them kissing."

"Maya!" Sienna felt her cheeks heat. Vince's guffaw didn't help the situation, but she grinned. Kai walked in on them sharing a kiss the night before when Noah had come over for dinner. Her son gave them a thumbs up before asking if the chicken tenders were done.

"I can see your grandfather asking that," Vince said as he pulled into the parking lot for the hotel.

The Orchid Inn was a converted Victorian Queen Anne–style mansion nestled on the edge of the historic section of Stark Valley. Painted in a classic peach and bay blue with white trim, the house used to belong to one of the founding families of the area. Sienna's eagerness to check out the decor of the interior was crushed when she spotted the distinguished couple posing for selfies in front of a collection of mums.

"You know they're going to post pictures of their meals," Maya mumbled, causing the rest of the car to snicker.

Gerald and Flora Wood began posting pictures of various hidden gems in and around Philadelphia on social media after they retired. They had a few thousand followers. Nothing that would label them influencers, but it made them happy to share how they spent their retirement.

Sienna checked her appearance in the passenger window after she climbed out. Kai was already running full speed towards his grandparents. He knew better than to run in a parking lot, but they were mere feet from the sidewalk.

Their parents had coordinated their outfits, something they've done since she and Maya were young. Tonight, their mother wore a white sweater set with mini red polka dots and dark jeans, which complemented her curvy frame. Gerald opted for a white button-down, dark jeans, and a navy-blue blazer with a red pocket square. Flora drew the line at matching tracksuits. *"I will not be one of those couples,"* she told her friends once. Sienna and Maya placed bets they would.

"There's my girls," Gerald called out as they came closer. He pulled them both in for a group hug before stepping aside so their mother could get in on the action. They greeted Vince with the same smothering hug.

"How was your trip? Do you like your room?" Sienna asked. Her parents were to stay with her Friday night after spending most of that day at Hawkins Ridge. They had plans to attend the opening event that evening and hit the festivities early Saturday morning. If they didn't like their room, Sienna would put them up for their week-long visit. The beaming smile on her mother's face eased her worry.

"I love it. It has a bed-and-breakfast vibe but clearly is a high-end hotel. It's charming, and the staff is very accommodating."

Maya sighed. "Please tell me you didn't ask for anything outrageous. They're one of our customers and gave us an amazing rate."

Flora rolled her eyes, causing Sienna to laugh. She and Maya perfected their eye rolls from their mother. "*Mija*, asking for an extra pillow is not outrageous."

"The room is wonderful," Gerald spoke up, dropping his arm around his wife's shoulder. "After we checked in and settled, the staff directed us to a lovely coffee shop. We have plans to take a tour of a winery tomorrow."

Sienna looked at her sister. "There's a winery? Why haven't we gone?"

Vince and Sienna shrugged. It was her brother-in-law who answered. "We didn't know there was one."

"You three don't even drink wine," Flora teased. She turned her attention to Sienna. "Maybe we can go again while we're here. It's good to know various things about wine for when you meet someone."

Sienna looked everywhere but at her mother. Noah was not a wine drinker. She, Maya, and Vince weren't either. Now, if there were a brewery that gave tours, they would be there. Sienna met her sister's glare. Telling the folks about her dating life in front of their hotel was not the right time.

"Are you ready for dinner?" Sienna asked, nudging Kai to start walking.

"Do you want me to drive?" Gerald had his keys in his hands. Vince shook his head.

"The restaurant is on the next block. Figured we could walk."

It was the middle of September, and the temperature was a comfortable sixty degrees. The walk would help Sienna gather her nerves to tell them she was dating.

Vince and Maya took the lead. Kai held his grandparents' hands as they followed closely behind. Sienna pulled up the rear and took in her family. She missed her parents. For two years she saw them daily, but leaving was the best for everyone. Her parents seemed lighter and could enjoy their retirement without having to worry about their adult daughter and helping to raise their grandson.

Sienna also would not have met Noah.

Nestled between a bookstore and a consignment clothing store stood the seafood restaurant. She and Maya had lunch after their tattoo appointment two weeks prior. After the meal, they knew their parents would love it.

Vince pulled the door open and let everyone enter. Subtle lighting and dimmed wall sconces highlighted the dark wood walls and tables. Breathtaking photos of underwater shots decorated the entrance along with a built-in aquarium that ran behind the hostess area. Flora commented on the decor as they made their way to the table. Once they placed their drink and appetizer order, the conversation turned to catching up.

"Have you met any of the parents?" Flora directed the question to Sienna. She waited until the server set their drinks and a basket of cheddar biscuits before answering.

"I have. I've had lunch with Kai's friend's mother and spent a little time with my landlady, Denise."

"Maybe they could introduce you to some nice men." Gerald used the plastic tongs to set a biscuit on his and Flora's saucers. Maya again gave her a look and knew this was the time to speak.

Sienna took a fortifying gulp of her beer before sitting straight and clearing her throat.

"I've actually been seeing someone for the past month."

Simultaneous mouth drops had Maya and Vince giggling. It was her mother who gained control first.

"That was fast. How did you meet him? Please tell me he wasn't the first man you met and just agreed to go on a date with him."

"His father was the first man I met." Sienna gave a toothy smile.

"He's a child? What was wrong with his father?"

Sienna and Maya both rolled their eyes. "First, his father is your age and gay. He is the man who held the position Vince and Maya took over. His son, Noah, is thirty-five—"

"And our boss," Maya interrupted. Sienna's look promised retribution later. Gerald finally found his voice.

"Do you think that's wise, dating the man responsible for your sister's employment?"

"And mine," Vince said. He tipped his head towards the server, who timed their appetizers perfectly. Everyone waited until she left the order of fried oysters, calamari, and Old Bay seasoning hush puppies before returning to the conversation. Maya took control of the moment while everyone filled their plates.

"Noah spoke with me before even asking Sienna out. He wanted to see if I was okay and clearly stated our jobs were not in jeopardy if things didn't work out between them."

"From what we've seen, Noah is a good man," Vince said seriously. "He treats Sienna with respect and adores Kai. They're good for each other. Maya would not have given her blessings if she didn't think it would work."

It touched Sienna that Maya and Vince had her back and supported her relationship. She expected nothing less from Maya, but hearing Vince share his thoughts as someone who interacted with Noah daily meant a lot. It gave her the needed push to finish her reasoning with the folks.

"Even though I didn't need my sister's blessings." Sienna stuck her tongue out at Maya, who returned the gesture. Both immediately laughed before Sienna sobered. "When I moved here, getting into a relationship was low on the list of priorities. We both were cautious and talked before our first date. This is the first relationship for both of us in a long time. I wanted to be sure there was something there before mentioning him to you, but I really like him."

The next voice drew everyone's attention. "I like Noah," Kai said. Hush puppy crumbs dotted the corner of his mouth. "He's also super cool and let me name a bunch of goats. He also makes Mom happy, and she should be cause she's the best,"

Kai finished with a shrug and shoved another hush puppy in his mouth.

Sienna leaned over and gave her son a one-arm hug and kissed the top of his head. "Thank you, sweetie."

Vince reached over and took the three fluffy fried breads from Kai's plate. "Since you didn't mention me in why your mom is happy, I'm eating these."

Leave it to her brother-in-law to lighten the mood. Everyone laughed just as the two servers returned with their meals. Kai's eyes widened when they set his plate of popcorn shrimp, fries, and green beans in front of him. Sienna knew there would be leftovers based on the number of hush puppies he ate and the large grilled trout the server set before her. With her roasted potatoes and asparagus, there was no way she'd be able to finish. The rest of the table also commented on the amount of food. Her father looked at Flora, expressing his gratitude for the mini-fridge and microwave. Sienna didn't think the hotel would be happy they reheated fish in the room, but that was something her parents would have to deal with. After a few minutes of everyone digging into and enjoying the succulent flavors of their food, Sienna thought the conversation about her relationship was over.

She was wrong.

"So this young man, what's his name? Noah?" Flora started as she cut into her blackened salmon. "You said it's been a while since he's been in a relationship. Why is that? Has he ever been married? Children?" She then turned to Maya and Vince, who had their forks in each other's dinner. "If you could let her answer the question, I would appreciate it."

Sienna and her father shared a look before snickering. Her brother-in-law and sister shrugged and continued to eat. Sienna took a sip of her beer and debated how much to share. With Kai at the table, she wanted to keep some of it from his knowledge. She slightly tilted her head towards Kai, elbow deep in ketchup and shrimp, to say what she said would be limited.

"Noah was married for almost a year to his college sweetheart. Small-town living wasn't for her. Between building the business, helping his friends get through the end of their marriages and slim pickings his age, no one caught his eye."

"I've been telling you how great of a catch you were." Gerald finished his statement with a wink. "Boy already shows signs of a man with a solid head on his shoulder. I take it we will meet him during our trip."

It wasn't a question.

"I already planned on it, Dad." Sienna planned on having Noah over for appetizers Saturday since he and the Becketts were helping with last-minute prep for the festival. Noah had the crazy idea of getting both sets of parents for dinner the night before her parents headed home.

There wasn't enough whiskey to deal with Flora and Bev so early in their relationship.

"Are you going to give her parents a gift?" Jace said as he placed two gourds into a bushel.

Noah almost dropped the pumpkin he was carrying and snapped his head to his father, going through a basket of apples.

"Do I really need to get them a gift? I'm just meeting them for snacks and drinks."

Owen chuckled as he tossed a couple of bruised apples into a bucket. Those would be used for applesauce or in the dog treats they made.

"It wouldn't hurt to show up with flowers and maybe a bottle of her father's favorite spirit."

Noah groaned but made a mental note to ask Sienna what her father drank when they talked before bed. Thinking of the feisty single mother put a smile on his face.

Being with Sienna was more than Noah expected. She was caring, funny, an amazing cook, and easy to be around. She found herself still baffled by small-town living, but she loved the sense of community. That eased the fear he had.

Noah was falling in love.

He didn't want to give his heart if he felt she still had doubts about staying in Oak Mountain. That didn't seem to be the case. Sienna befriended Adam's mother, meaning she wanted to expand her connection with the town. Noah saw firsthand during the field trip to Hawkins Ridge, Kai was popular in his class. Denise even told him Sienna had asked about painting her apartment. He may be overthinking it, but in his mind, that was a good sign. Of course, he'd let her decorate his entire house if they ever came to that point.

Something he hoped they would get to one day.

Sienna was nothing like Robin. It could be because they were older, or both had experienced life. It didn't matter.

Being from a large city is where the similarities ended. It was easy to picture a future with Sienna and Kai.

"When are her parents coming to the property?" Caden asked as he pulled the tractor to a stop. "You lucked out. Mom is too busy with the festival and the twins to think about a family dinner."

Josie Beckett was the unofficial hostess of any and everyone that came in contact with Hawkins Ridge. She subjected Sienna to lunch when she came to bring a gift to Naomi and Logan for the twins. She probably wouldn't escape when the holidays rolled around.

"I am thankful for that. Maya said they would stop for a quick visit Saturday, but I am thinking of having her folks meet Dad and Mom." Noah turned to Owen. "Even though Sam's out-of-town taking care of his sister, I thought maybe you, Mom, Malcolm, and her folks could come over for a cookout. I'm not sure when they will be back in the area. Sienna mentioned they were going to Puerto Rico for a month."

"I'm sure your mother will love that. You know she'll probably want it at her place, especially when she finds out Sienna's parents are staying two miles from her house." Jace climbed onto the trailer hitched to the tractor and took the basket of apples from Owen.

"That's why I want it to be Sunday. Mom said she planned on coming up to support Denise in the fall arrangements contest. We would have it at Sienna's or my place. Her dining room table seats eight."

Owen nodded. "I think that's a good idea. If it were at your mother's, she would control everything and make it formal.

This way, everyone will be relaxed because of the festival. We could do something in a slow cooker, so you only have to worry about salad and bread when you return home."

Noah hadn't thought about that, but it was a great idea. Chili or a hearty soup in a bread bowl popped into his mind. The forecast for the final weekend of the event showed a drop in temperature.

"Not to change the subject, but I see your blog has fifty replies already," Jace said, shaking his phone. "I told you it was a good idea."

Noah posted the debut issue of his blog over four hours ago. Though he wanted it to be separate from Hawkins Ridge, Jace included a link on the social media account and sent an email blast. The response was better than he had expected. He believed highlighting the rescue goats helped. The new arrivals were adorable and thriving in their new home. Kai took his job of naming the goats seriously. He had a list of thirty choices and spent an hour observing them before assigning an appropriate name.

"I've received two emails from farms offering to foster any rescues we have in the future." Noah leaned against the wheel of the tractor and flipped the top on his water bottle. "I figured we could reach out to them tomorrow to see where they're located and if they are open to helping the sanctuary with dogs."

Jace nodded. "That's a good idea. It's another way we can help small farms get the recognition they deserve."

"Have you thought about selling advertisement space?" Owen grabbed Noah's water bottle and took a swig.

"I have down the road. I just don't want this to get bigger than I can handle. It goes back to why we've taken a pause on new customers for the produce and cheeses." Noah met each man's eyes. "This is and always will be a family business. We have plans in place in case the next generation wants to do something other than Hawkins Ridge. It's going to be the same with the blog and eventual podcast. I won't have it sponsored by some large corporation. I'd give it up before that happens."

When their parents turned over the reins to Noah and the Beckett brothers, they increased produce and cheese contracts with local and regional businesses faster than they expected. Factoring in the boom in the online market for their goat's milk soaps and lotions, they accomplished in a year what they set out to do. To avoid being on a large distributor's radar for their produce or buyers harassing them to sell, they paused signing new customers. Another reason they added Maya and Vince to the fold. Noah and his friends recognized the need for experienced managers. The efficiency the couple brought to the business while still turning a nice profit had the families considering offering the couple a small stake in the business next year.

Jace tossed his work gloves onto the dashboard of the tractor and stretched his back. "I need to head home. Claire is planning a nice dinner, and I want to make sure the dogs don't eat it all."

"I better run too. The guys are grilling, and I have to finish my pieces for the festival." Caden created leather bracelets and necklaces, which he burned designs into the material. The three older stable hands who lived on the property always took grilling to the next level.

Noah waved as Caden and Jace headed towards the greenhouse with their load. He ambled over to Owen and the UTV parked on the road.

"I have leftover chicken if you want to stay for dinner," Noah offered as he climbed into the passenger seat.

"Sounds good. I'm sure Whiskers would like a little more time with Meadow." Owen eased on the gas and headed towards his son's home. Their cats were having a playdate while they worked in the orchard. "When you talked earlier about the next generation, did you include Kai with your statement?"

Noah chuckled. "It's still early, Pops, to talk like that."

"I knew Sam was the one after two weeks. Logan knew Naomi was his better half after one weekend. Heck Jace swears he fell in love with Claire after she smiled." Owen raised his hand when Noah went to argue. "I'm not saying get married next week. You both are still too cautious, and you have Kai to think about. I'm just saying, you spend a lot of time together. You're talking about hosting a family dinner. Don't say you haven't thought about it."

Noah sighed. "I have thought about it. What I feel for Sienna is stronger than what I felt for Robin. That bothers me because it makes me wonder if I ever loved Robin or if what I feel for Sienna is a strong infatuation."

They turned onto the stretch of grass that ran along Maya and Vince's home and slowed to handle the bumpy ruts. "You loved Robin," Owen said. "She was your first long-term girlfriend. You've matured, settled down. I don't know what

Sienna's dating history is, but you both have loved and lost. I don't think she would have Kai involved if she didn't think there was a possibility."

Noah agreed. Sienna was an exceptional mother. The way they met is the only reason Kai was part of their relationship. Sienna wouldn't let just any man around her son. But they have dinner at her place during the week and at his on the weekends. They still found time to have adult dates. Being with Sienna felt like home. It scared and excited him. Noah didn't want to make another mistake. There was still a small part of him that feared she would leave Oak Mountain. He couldn't give in to that feeling. He had to trust that she felt at home in his small town.

As they pulled to the back of Noah's home, he found his voice. "I care deeply for Sienna and Kai, and we're taking this relationship one day at a time. No one has sparked even a passing glance until her. For now, I want to get through meeting her parents. Then we can talk more about where we see this going."

"Fair enough." Owen killed the engine and climbed out. "Let me know if you need help with this dinner and keeping your mother in check."

Noah would have to take his father up on the offer.

Chapter 15

Orange and red hues colored the early evening sky. Sienna inhaled a deep breath and slowly exhaled. She loved this time of the day. It soothed her after a long day of analyzing medical notes for correct codes for billing. It was her few minutes to decompress so she could be present for her after-work life with Kai, Noah, and friends.

Except that evening, she used the time to settle her nerves.

She snuck out onto her balcony to glance down on Main Street. Barriers blocked her street for the weekend events scheduled for the festival. As a resident, she didn't have to worry about losing her assigned parking spot behind the building. Of course, she had no intention of moving her car until Monday, when she took Kai to school.

A few citizens of Oak Mountain strolled down the road carrying blankets and folding chairs, animatedly greeting each other. The festival's kick off events were scheduled to start in two hours. Sienna quickly learned the town loved any excuse to gather and socialize. The agenda for that evening included a welcome address by the town's mayor, a concert from the fifty-five and over choir, a re-enactment of the founding of the town put on by the middle school drama club, and a pie-eating contest. Numerous activities were also planned to keep the kids entertained.

First, she had to get through her parents meeting Noah.

Maya and Vince dropped their parents off at her place when they picked up Kai to help with any last-minute tasks for the Hawkins Ridge booth. It took Sienna ten minutes to convince her parents to take her bed instead of sleeping on the pull-out sofa in her office. Since Flora and Gerald were staying the night, she wanted them to be comfortable. They were due to meet up with everyone in an hour. Sienna wanted the quiet of her home for the introduction instead of among hundreds of strangers.

"You want me to take the dip out?" Flora said from the open French doors.

Sienna spared one final look up and down the sidewalk, looking for Noah before turning to her mother. "I want you to relax, Mama."

"I relaxed already. Now I want to help."

Sienna chuckled and linked her arm with her mother's. Her father sat on the couch looking for a music station on the TV. Her parents entertained a lot. They believed in setting the mood for the situation with music. Since this was the meeting of a suitor, Sienna guessed her father was trying to find contemporary jazz. When the piano notes of Jon Batiste echoed in the room, she smiled.

"Good choice."

Gerald ambled over to the kitchen area where Sienna and her mother were putting together the serving tray.

"You have amazing views. Will the shops be open tomorrow? I'd love to peek in before we go to the festival." Gerald plucked a cherry tomato from the decorative dish. "What time is your young man supposed to be here?"

Sienna checked the clock. "Any minute. I'm not sure where he'll park. To answer your other question, yes, they will be open. Most are having sales."

"I'm glad we bought an extra suitcase," Flora commented.

A quick rap at the door had Sienna smoothing the imaginary wrinkles on her long sleeve tee. She shook her head when her parents stood mere inches behind her. After a deep breath, she opened the door. Noah's smile lit up his face. Freshly trimmed fade and beard highlighted the sparkle in his eyes. Dressed in a fitted Hawkins Ridge button-down and comfy jeans, he looked amazing.

"Sorry I'm late." He pressed a kiss on her temple before handing her a covered container. "I had to walk from the plaza."

"You're right on time." Sienna closed the door and motioned with her hand towards her parents. "I want you to meet my parents, Gerald and Flora Wood. Guys, this is Noah Garrison."

"Sir. Ma'am. It's nice to meet you. This is for you. It's from one of the local vineyards." Noah handed over a wine gift bag after shaking their hands.

"I thought Kai was exaggerating when he said you were big." Flora gave Noah a once-over. "I think he was being kind."

"Mama," Sienna hissed. Noah was thick and muscular. Not gym muscles. He lifted a lot of goats, bags of feed and shavings, not to mention his work in the greenhouse. He kept his two hundred twenty pounds in shape.

Noah laughed off the comment. "It's okay. When Kai first met me, he asked if I could beat the Hulk."

Gerald had taken the bottle of wine out of the bag, examining the label. "We planned on visiting this vineyard on Monday."

"My parents have turned their visit into a wine tasting and antique shopping one." Sienna lifted the lid and groaned. "You didn't have to go all out."

Flora looked into the container and grabbed a crab and artichoke topped toast points. She mimicked Sienna's sound earlier. "Oh my word, this is good."

"Noah is an amazing cook." Sienna gave him a wink.

"Well, I'm curious now." Gerald popped one into his mouth and nodded with approval. "That is good. Why don't we open the wine and get to know each other?"

Sienna led everyone to the kitchen area. She handed her father the corkscrew while her mother placed two wine glasses in front of him. Noah went to the sink and washed his hands.

"Does the festival have events during the day when people are at work?" Gerald asked as he sniffed the open bottle.

Noah shook his head, helping Sienna by pulling out saucers and utensils. "From eleven to two this week, they have a farmers' market in the plaza. On Friday, they'll create a small pumpkin patch in the plaza for the elementary school kids. The older kids will visit a farm for mazes, make candy apples and cider."

"I love the community here. We've been here for almost two days and can see why Sienna and Maya love it." Flora thanked her husband for her glass. "You grew up here, right?"

"Yes, ma'am. Went to college at Pitt, but always returned home every chance I could."

"City life never appealed to you?" Gerald asked, leaning against the counter. Noah shook his head.

"Like your wife said. It's the community here. They have a different kind in Pittsburgh, but I will always be a small-town guy."

Sienna knew that. It's what led to his marriage ending. Staying in Oak Mountain, or even Stark Valley, was important in their relationship. The town made a lasting impression on her, and she couldn't see herself leaving. If things didn't work out between her and Noah, it would be awkward around town. Something she didn't want to put Kai through, but her son was resilient.

So was she.

Sienna and Noah kept up their end of the small talk while they put together the tray of appetizers. Once everything was set, Noah carried the offerings to the coffee table, while she pulled up the rear with two bottles of beer and napkins. Her parents gushed over the wine and spoke of the lunch they enjoyed earlier. Once everyone had snacks on their plates, Gerald became serious.

"Sienna tells us you're an owner of the business Maya and Vince work for. This budding relationship can affect both our girls. Sienna moved to this town for a fresh start. The last thing we want is for her and Kai to deal with the fallout if things don't work out. Would that affect Maya's employment?" Though she and Maya told their parents it wouldn't, she guessed they wanted to hear it from the horse's mouth.

Noah wiped his mouth and leaned slightly forward. "Let me answer those concerns in reverse order. I'm not worried. Maya and Vince are the best things to happen to Hawkins Ridge. I recognize that, as well as the other owners. There wouldn't be a problem with my stepping back from day-to-day operations or moving from the property if it came to that."

"They would never want you to do that," Sienna argued. Maya and Vince were talking about buying a home, but she wasn't sure if they'd mentioned anything to anyone. Noah placed his hand on Sienna's arm and smiled.

"I know they wouldn't want me to, but if tensions prevented them from doing their job or if the business suffered, it wouldn't be a problem for me to move. That's a bridge I hope we never have to cross."

"That makes two of us."

Noah brought her hand to his mouth and pressed his lips to her wrist. "Regarding blowback to Sienna and Kai, yes, this is a small town where people know everyone's business, but if we don't work out, then it wouldn't affect her or Kai as residents. My aunt won't kick them out nor will Kai become an outcast at school. If I thought that any of that was possible, I wouldn't have expressed my interest in her."

Sienna swooned. She held Noah's gaze before giving his hand a squeeze. Gerald cleared his throat, causing heat to rush to her cheeks. Flora pushed her husband's wine glass towards them before crossing her legs and addressing the couple.

"I understand you were married before? Why did it end? Have you been in a long-term relationship since? You're a good-looking man with a promising future. I can't imagine no other woman in town hadn't tried to snatch you up."

Sienna rolled her eyes but kept her mouth shut. Noah's past was his to tell. He didn't miss a beat and spoke with confidence.

"I married my college girlfriend a year after graduation. It didn't last as long as the engagement. She didn't like the slow pace of small-town life. I considered moving to New York City when she returned home, but knew I wouldn't be happy." Noah shrugged and took a sip of his beer. "While my marriage was ending, so were the marriages of my friends. Besides all of us being shell shock about another relationship, Jace, my best friend and one of the owners, opted to go the playboy route. Dating one of his flings just seemed wrong. They also weren't relationship material or were only interested in a man to take care of them.

"Building the business and proving to our parents we were ready to lead took priority," Noah continued. "Until my father bought into the business, it was family ran, so I put more pressure on showing I could contribute to the Beckett family legacy, while cementing one for myself. I didn't have time for a relationship."

"But you saw something in my baby girl that made you find time?" Gerald held Noah's gaze, daring him to answer correctly. Noah didn't miss a beat.

"Maya and Vince were the ones who gave me the time. Also, seeing two of my friends find the love of their lives gave me hope. Maybe I could find someone looking for the same thing I was."

"Which is?"

Noah glanced at Sienna and smiled. "A future. A mature person who believed in family. Someone independent and not looking for a meal ticket. It doesn't hurt your daughter is drop-dead gorgeous."

Sienna dipped her head to his shoulder, causing him to kiss the crown of her head. Noah never hesitated to show and express his feelings for her. A simple linking of their pinkies, his hand brushing the small of her back when they worked together preparing dinner, or complimenting her even when she still wore her sleep scarf Sunday mornings for breakfast. She hoped her actions showed him how much he meant to her.

"You got it bad, son," Gerald said, lifting his glass to Noah. "I'll admit you said the right words, and I've seen some of the small things you've done since you walked through the door. I'm looking forward to getting to know you better while we're in town."

Noah gave a quick nod. "Thank you, sir."

"Enough with that 'ma'am' and 'sir.' Flora and Gerald." Her mother finished her last of her wine and stood. "We'd better get going. We have to meet everyone in twenty minutes."

Sienna looked at the oversized wall clock. The plaza was two blocks away and wouldn't take any time to walk. Everyone hurried putting away the food and making last-minute stops to the restroom. They were out the door fifteen minutes later. Maya texted while Sienna locked her door, saying they would meet them at the corner entrance to the plaza.

"Are you going to be okay with the crowd?" Noah whispered in her ear. "If you feel any sort of anxiety, we can go home."

She rolled to her tiptoes and gave him a soft kiss. "Thank you for checking. I should be okay if we stay along the fringes. I'll let you know otherwise."

Noah studied her eyes for a moment before flashing a grin. He linked their fingers together and led the foursome down the sidewalk. The greetings from the residents no longer surprised Sienna. People knew she and Noah were dating. But more important is people knew who she was. Something Sienna wanted with the move.

Five minutes later, she saw Maya and Kai standing on the corner. Her son pointed and hurried over to meet them.

"Mom! I helped set up the booth, and Mr. Owen paid me five dollars." Kai dug into his pocket and showed her the money. It was the same as his allowance. "Can I buy something with it? Do you think we should take something back for Scooter?"

She rested her hands on his shoulder and grinned. "We'll see if there is anything you can take back for him. You know Poppy may not let you spend your money."

"That's right," her father said, moseying up to them. "Grandparents are supposed to spoil their grandkids. Maybe if you see a gift for your mother, we can use your money."

Kai's eager nod had them laughing. He slipped his hand into his grandfather's and led him away. Flora joined them. Noah gave Sienna's hand a squeeze.

"I'm going to go see if they need any help. I'll meet you near that tree in ten minutes?" He pointed to a large oak at the edge of the walkway. It was behind the residents, setting up their chairs and blankets.

Maya strolled over and linked her arm with Sienna's. "Vince and I have our stuff near there. Your dad is watching everything."

They looked in the same direction and saw Kai introducing Gerald and Flora to Owen. Noah said he would meet them there instead and promised to bring snacks and drinks. He pressed a kiss to her temple before jogging towards the booths set up at the end of the plaza. Maya pulled her to a stop and leaned close.

"What do they think of Noah?"

Sienna rolled her eyes before giving her a rundown of the meeting. Maya chuckled when she was finished. "So they acted the same way when I brought Vince home?"

"Pretty much, but I think they like him."

"What's not to like? He's intelligent, gainfully employed, and handsome. He cares for you and Kai, which is always a plus."

Heat rose to Sienna's cheeks. "That he is. I am trying to take it one day at a time."

"Smart. Now, let's go to the blanket. Owen has a cooler full of stuff."

By the time the sisters made it to their setup, Owen, Gerald, and Flora sat in stadium chairs, each holding a plastic cup of wine and passing around a container of cheese. Owen rose to his feet and gave Sienna a hug.

"Good to see you again. I made maple cookies for you."

Sienna stepped out of the embrace, grinning. "You know my weakness."

Flora held up a wedge of cheese and her wine. "I love this town."

"I'm going to be so embarrassed if Mama gets drunk," Maya hissed in Sienna's ear.

"Well, she had a glass at my place." She tapped her chin. "Or was it two?"

"You aren't helping."

Sienna laughed. "Sorry. They seem to be having fun, though."

The sisters watched their parents joking with Owen and Kai. Her son ate up all the attention. Sienna wanted her parents to like Oak Mountain and see why she and Maya immediately fell in love with their new home. They hoped it led to more visits.

"Are you bringing them back to the property tomorrow? Thought we could go horseback riding or four-wheeling."

Sienna settled on the blanket, tugging Maya with her. "They saw the shops and wanted to look around. I thought we could have a family breakfast."

Maya nodded. "That's a great idea. I know the folks would love it. Vince won't mind if I spend the night, and you have something I can wear."

Her sister was a size smaller than Sienna's eighteen, but they could put together something for her to sleep in. She had a washer and dryer for any undergarments.

"Have you told the Becketts you are looking for a house?" Sienna asked. With Maya and Vince wanting to adopt, they needed their own space.

"We mentioned something to Owen to gauge their reaction. He said they would be supportive and would still keep a small house there in case we needed to spend the night or an emergency comes up. We want to be as close to the property as possible." Maya slid the cooler closer. "Would you want to live on the property if things between you and Noah go that far?"

Sienna sighed. She loved Noah's home. There was enough room for her to have an office for work. Kai would be over the moon if they lived there. She leaned back on her elbows.

"I think I would like it. The Becketts are nice. I know Noah talked of doing his own thing separate from the family. Whether that included finding his own plot of land, I don't know." Sienna shrugged. "It's something we'd have to talk about down the road."

Sienna grabbed a bottled water from the cooler and handed it to Kai. He nibbled on a cream cheese and veggie pinwheel while looking around the square, waving to some of his classmates. Sienna scrambled to her feet when she saw Noah weighed down with a drink holder and box. She took the drinks while he set the box on the blanket. Vince, only a few seconds behind him, set his own box on the blanket.

"What's all this?" Sienna asked, lifting the tea towel and foil.

"Fried chicken, corn on the cob, potato salad, and rolls." Noah sat beside her. "It's not the same as Ms. Ophelia's, but close."

Sienna glanced at Owen. "Did you do all this?"

"I just helped with the potato salad. This is all his idea." Owen nodded to Noah.

"We bought the drinks," Vince added as he passed out individual compartment containers holding a serving.

Sienna leaned closer to the man who stole her heart. "Why did you do all this? You didn't have to."

"This is the first of many festivals for you and your family. I wanted to make it memorable."

"Having you here make it memorable enough." She leaned forward and pressed her lips to his. "Thank you."

"You're welcome."

Sienna nibbled on her food while watching those she cared about get to know each other. They listened to the mayor give opening remarks before watching the middle school kids give the history of the town. To learn Josie Beckett's great-great-grandfather was part of the group that founded Oak Mountain impressed her. Then, to know they sold part of their land to some of the first black farmers in the area made her love the Becketts even more. The night finished with the senior choir singing show tunes.

Everyone helped pack up and made plans for the next day. As everyone said their goodnights, Noah pulled Sienna off to the side and rested his arm on her hips.

"I hope your folks like me."

"You gave them wine and food. They love you." She wrapped her arms around his waist. "Are you sure about this dinner? My parents will visit again."

Noah chuckled. "No, I'm not sure, but I already mentioned it to my mother."

"Bev is going to go overboard even though she isn't cooking."

Sienna and Noah had lunch with his mother two weeks prior because they were in Stark Valley running errands. They'd left Kai with Maya under the guise that he was helping brush the horses. The parents meet dinner was taking place at

Sienna's since everyone would be in town on Sunday. Noah bent over and pressed his forehead to hers.

"I told her this is just a casual dinner. Just a chance to meet your folks, since we didn't know when they would be back in town."

"My parents are thinking of spending the holidays in Puerto Rico, so I guess you have a point."

Noah studied her for a moment. "We don't have to do this if you have concerns."

Before Sienna could answer, Maya called out from the sidewalk. "We'll meet you back at your place."

Kai was struggling to stand on his feet, and Flora leaned heavily on Gerald's arm. Since Maya had a key, they'd be able to get in. They waved them on and turned back to each other. Sienna wanted to be honest in the relationship, and he'd given her the opening she wanted.

"It's not that I don't want our folks to meet. They love Owen already. Heck, I love your dad." Sienna met his eyes. "Casual introduction when your mother comes up for the Sunday event is one thing. Dinner is too much, too soon."

Noah sighed. "Yeah, I can see how it would be stressful. When I came up with the idea, I didn't see the big picture."

"My parents will be back. I'd like to think we'll still be together when they do."

Noah pressed his lips to hers, settling her worries. "I know we will be because I want to build a future with you. There will be plenty of opportunities for our mothers to bond over wine and cheese."

Sienna rolled her eyes, shaking her head. "That's scary enough to keep them apart until Kai graduates high school."

Noah chuckled and gently tugged her towards her place. "How about we still make dinner, but it's just the three of us?"

"That sounds like a great idea."

Spending a quiet evening with her two guys was indeed a perfect evening.

Chapter 16

Noah scowled at Caden and Jace as they each slipped pieces of cornbread into their mouths.

"Why didn't we think of this idea before now?" Jace said around a bite.

"Because we were too busy worrying about the chili and crumbling up the cornbread. Making a bowl out of it was brilliant." Caden held up the top of one of the bowls in salute. "Kudos."

Noah shook his head as he chopped the onions. He dropped the chili in the slow cooker off at Sienna first thing so it could cook while they went about their day. He came up with the idea of baking the cornbread in large ramekins. They could then cut a hole and spoon chili into the opening. It was just the right size for Kai and would give extra pieces of cornbread for him and Sienna. Provided his friends didn't eat all the extras.

Noah moved the dishes away from his friends and set them inside a tote. "Make a mental note to do this next month for poker night."

"How did your mother take postponing the dinner?" Caden popped a piece of cheddar into his mouth. "Is she blaming Sienna?"

"If she is, she wisely kept it to herself. She said she understood and said when Flora and Gerald come visit again, she'd throw something at her house."

Noah called his mother the next morning after his talk with Sienna to let her know they were holding off on the dinner. Bev tapped into protective mother mode. Wondering if it was due to her parents not liking him or if there was something wrong in the relationship. Since he didn't want to share Sienna's battle with anxiety, it took him five minutes to assure her it was just a lot for the weekend.

There was a bit of truth to the statement.

Noah, Jace, Caden, Vince, and Owen took turns manning the Hawkins Ridge booth both days. Keeping her parents busy fell to Sienna and Maya. Stress can trigger anxiety attacks. Why hadn't he considered that when he mentioned the dinner? Between her folks' visit, preparing for the increase in crowds, introducing him, as well as getting ready for another work and school week, he should have been more preceptive. Luckily, they had that evening to just be together and decompress.

"Have you talked to Vince?" Jace asked before picking up his bottled water. Noah had a feeling he knew where his best friend was going. When neither he nor Caden said anything, Jace continued.

"He and Maya want to move off property. Get their own place."

Noah came clean as he snapped the lid on the cut onions. "He mentioned something yesterday. Wanted to see if their job would be in jeopardy if they found a place. I told him it didn't bother me, but they would need to talk to you all."

Caden ran his fingers through Meadow's fur when she hopped up on his lap. "He said something this morning, but I didn't want to say anything. I told him to go for it. The rest of us live on site. If there is an emergency, they can still make it here in under twenty minutes, no matter where they end up."

Noah nodded. "I think they want to find a place between here and Sienna."

"What about when Sienna moves here?" Jace's sly grin had Noah rolling his eyes.

"We aren't anywhere near that."

"Perhaps." Jace shrugged. "I'm just saying the way things are going, you'll be having the conversation sooner rather than later."

"Instead of having that conversation, how about the conversation about her staying in Oak Mountain?" Caden met Noah's gaze. "Have you talked about it?"

Noah sighed and took a seat at the kitchen island. He would need to leave in twenty minutes for Sienna's. He'd hoped to avoid deep conversation.

"How did we give from Vince and Maya moving off Hawkins Ridge to me and Sienna?"

"We're nosey," Jace quipped.

"And subtlety is not a Beckett trait," Caden added, causing all three to chuckle.

Noah told himself he would take his relationship with Sienna one day at a time. He wouldn't think about a year down the road, not even six months, but it was hard. He cared deeply for her and Kai. When he saw the future, they were front and center. The thought of them not happy with Oak Mountain or missing Philadelphia to the point they went back didn't sit well with him. He even wrestled with the possibility of following them if they wanted some place larger than Stark Valley.

His gut told him they were happy. Seeing her smile during the festival and Kai introducing his friends to everyone said they were laying roots. Something Robin never did.

Noah stood and began placing items in his tote while he answered his friend.

"Of course, anything can change. Right now, she and Kai seem happy."

Jace agreed. "According to Sara, he's popular at school."

Kai's teacher was Claire's cousin-in-law. Jace spent more personal time with her than Noah ever would. It made him wonder why they asked him? Was there something else they were wondering? Had they heard something in the town's gossip mill? Noah stopped packing the bag and studied his friends.

"Why all the questions?"

They looked at each other than back at Noah. Caden spoke for them.

"We just wanted you to know we always have your back. If you and Sienna get to the living together or marriage talk, we'd understand if you wanted to leave Hawkins Ridge."

"We aren't saying you have to," Jace quickly added.

Caden emphatically shook his head. "Definitely not."

Noah blew out a breath. He understood what they were saying. If Sienna didn't want to live at Hawkins Ridge, they were okay with him looking to build someplace else. Especially with Maya and Vince looking off the property. They had a similar discussion when Owen and Sam moved from the mother-in-law suite in the main house.

"I appreciate that," Noah started. "But we are nowhere near that conversation. When I think we are at that point, I'll talk to her and Kai. No need to bring up anything now and scare her off."

Noah never doubted his friends having his back. They'd support him in whatever decision he and Sienna made. Deep down, he wanted to stay in his home and do a remodel. Give them a larger suite and add a bath to the room Kai would take over. But that was at least a year or two away.

For now, he wanted to do everything he could to keep Sienna and Kai happy in Oak Mountain.

"Scooter is going to love these," Kai said as he slipped the apple peels into a plastic bag. "Do we have any hibiscus petals left?"

Sienna wondered how the turtle became so spoiled. Denise dropped off wilted hibiscus flowers the day before. She planned on using them in the floral arrangement competition. When her landlady didn't think they would hold up, she gave them to Scooter.

"I think he's had enough for today, sweetie." Sienna slid the cookie sheet that held individual apple tarts into the oven. It was her contribution to the dinner. "Can you clean off the coffee table, please?"

"We aren't using the dining room table?"

"No, we're keeping it casual tonight." Sienna set the timer and placed the mixing bowl into the sink. "Do you want to eat at the table?"

Kai shook his head as he stacked the papers left by his grandparents. "I like when we eat in front of the TV."

They had a view of the TV from the kitchen and dining area, but she didn't want to correct him. Sienna, too, looked forward to having just a laid-back meal. It wasn't like her parents required a formal setting. But she felt obligated to eat at the dining room table, even with the pizza they had the night before. She didn't know how many more meals she would share with her folks after their announcement during breakfast that morning.

Her parents were selling their house in Philadelphia and moving to Puerto Rico. According to Flora, part of their visit was to see if Sienna and Kai were happy. If they had an inkling their daughters would move back to Philly, her parents would hold off a year or two. Sienna didn't want that, and guilt weighed on her.

They waited because of what she went through after Dylan's death. Her parents saw how happy she was and felt the need to move forward with their plans. Since Sienna and Maya were staying in Oak Mountain, they would visit a few times out of the year. Kai took it to mean they would spend summers on the beach. It was another reason Maya and Vince wanted their own home with land. They figured they could put a small modular on their property or build an addition for when Flora and Gerald visited.

"Do you want to go back to living with Nana and Poppy?" Kai asked from his spot on the corner of the couch.

Sienna looked up from stirring the chili. Why was he asking this? Was he not happy in Oak Mountain?

She placed the lid on the slow cooker. He needed her full attention to find out the root of his question. The last thing she wanted was for him to think he couldn't talk to her. Once she settled beside him and lowered the volume on the TV, she turned to face him.

"Why do you think I want to live with your grandparents?"

Kai shrugged and focused on his bare toes. "Since they are moving someplace else. I thought you'd want to go with them."

Sienna loved the area where her mother's family lived—to visit. She rested her hand on Kai's, drawing his attention.

"I don't want to live with Nana and Poppy. Not in Philly or Puerto Rico." She girded herself for the next question. "Do you want to go back to living with them?"

Kai shook his head. "I like it here. My friends are cool. Auntie and Uncle are fun to hang out with. Plus, you have Mr. Noah. If we move, you won't have him anymore, and you'll go back to being sad."

Ah, now they were getting to the core of the question. Sienna gave a warm smile. "I like it here too. Oak Mountain has welcomed us, and we're making friends. Your grandparents gave us a place to live when I was sad about losing your father. I'm not sad anymore."

"What about Mr. Noah? What if you two stop liking each other? Would we move?"

Sienna shook her head. "Even if Mr. Noah and I decided we didn't want to date anymore, we would still stay here. Oak Mountain is our home now. Are you okay with that?"

Kai's answer was a hug, knocking Sienna back slightly. She laughed and kissed her son's forehead. He shuffled back and grinned. "Does this mean we can get a pet now?"

"Scooter's a pet."

He started to roll his eyes but thought better of it. "I mean like a cat or dog."

"Oh." The buzzer dinged, causing her to stand. "A cat would be better for us. Except for lunch, I wouldn't have time to walk a dog while I work. Why don't we ask Noah if the sanctuary has cats available for adoption?"

"Okay. I'm going to go feed Scooter." Kai snatched the plastic bag from the counter and scurried towards his room.

Sienna lovingly shook her head and pulled the tarts from the oven, setting the sheet on the cooling rack. Getting a cat was something she'd considered recently. Spending time at Noah's, she and Meadow bonded. The fluffy Maine Coon cuddled with Sienna on the couch and always looked for tummy scratches. Getting her feline fix outside of Noah's home appealed to her.

A rapid knock at the door had Kai sprinting from his room. He slid the red stool so he could see out the peephole. He flung the door open after sliding it out of the way.

"Hey, Kai."

"Hi, Mr. Noah. Are you going to Puerto Rico with us when we visit my grandparents?"

Noah's gaze met Sienna's, who flashed a grin. "Why don't you let him put his things down first?"

She took the tote, giving him time to toe off his shoes. He padded to the kitchen area and pressed a kiss on her temple.

"Puerto Rico?"

"My folks are selling their home in Philly and moving there. They told us today. I think they are looking for a place when they go during the holidays." Sienna pulled out the pitcher of sweet tea. "Kai is looking forward to visiting so he can go to the beach."

"We aren't moving with them. Mom and I like it here too much to go with them," Kai added.

A look crossed Noah's face. Sienna recognized the brief flash of panic. The last thing she wanted was for him to think that had even been a topic of discussion at some point. She stood on the balls of her feet and pressed her lips to his.

"We aren't going anywhere."

Noah snuck his arm around her waist and pulled her closer. "I *hear* you."

"Good." She gave him a kiss and took a step back. "I am ready to eat, though. This chili has made my place smell good all day. What else do we need?"

Noah washed his hands while Kai gave him a rundown of their day. He pulled out a tray, and she gasped when she saw the bread bowls.

"Not once had I thought of doing cornbread as a bowl. That's brilliant."

Kai frowned as he studied the ramekin. "I don't understand. Can we eat it?"

Noah plopped one out and sat it in a bowl. He lifted off the pre-cut top and set it to the side. "The best thing about chili is cornbread. By using this as a bowl, you get the best of both. The top you can eat while you're at the beginning. By the time you're halfway through, the bread is soaked, so you can scoop some of the bread with your bite of chili. Any bread left, you can use to sop up the yummy juices that leaked out."

Kai grinned at his mother. "That sounds fun!"

"It does," Sienna agreed. "And sleep-inducing."

Noah chuckled as he pinched off a piece of the bread and passed it to Kai. "I never denied that it wouldn't make you sleepy."

"Another reason I'm glad it's just the three of us. I'd hate to snore in front of company." Sienna finished taking the small containers of chopped onions and shredded cheese. "Why don't you take the napkins and silverware to the coffee table and then clean up, sweetie?"

"Okay." Kai grabbed a stack of napkins and scooped three soup spoons from the drawer before running to the living area.

"So how do you want to do this?" Noah rested his hands on his hips, looking at the ingredients. "Put together the servings and have the toppings on the table?"

"Sounds like a plan." Sienna turned the slow cooker to warm and handed the ladle to Noah. She set the bowls on a tray before focusing on the drinks.

"Mom texted that she met your folks."

Sienna shook her head. "In two minutes, our mothers hit it off. They complimented each other on their outfits and found out they shop at the same online store. Then your mother told them of two restaurants in Stark Valley that have exceptional wine tasting before they exchanged contact information. Oh, and Bev gave her card to Maya and Vince for when they are ready to look at homes." She placed glasses of ice on the counter. "Poor Dad and Malcolm just smiled and nodded."

Noah snorted. "I can see that. Did Denise win?"

"Second place. I think it was rigged."

Sienna thought Noah's aunt should have won the floral arrangement contest. A young woman from Stark Valley won with a cascading rose display. It was large, but that was about it. Denise used a variety of fall flowers and arranged as a centerpiece. To Sienna's untrained eye, Denise's looked more appealing and fitted within the fall theme.

Noah focused on dishing out the chili while he spoke. "My aunt always places in the top three and has won the past three years. I'm sure she didn't mind second place."

"Perhaps. I just think hers looked more appealing and festive." She poured sweet tea into each glass and placed them on the tray. "Kai asked about getting a pet today. I told him we'd talk to you about a cat."

"Scooter and the rescue goats aren't enough for him," Noah quipped.

"Please don't let him hear you say the goats are his pets."

Both laughed as she carried their meal to the living area. Kai skipped from his room. He'd changed his shirt, and Sienna figured he'd either splashed himself with water while washing his hands or he'd played with the turtle and had paw prints on his shirt. Either way, she didn't mind.

Once they settled with their meal, Kai using the table, Noah answered her question.

"I am sure Josie has kittens and two senior cats ready for adoption." Noah glanced at Kai. "Your mom said you want a pet."

Chili dotted the corner of her son's mouth. He used a napkin before answering. "Since Mom and I are staying here, we don't have to worry about Nana's allergies. So now we can get a pet. She said that it would be hard with a dog because she didn't have time to walk it during the day because she works and I'm at school. A cat uses the bathroom inside, so it's a better choice."

Noah nodded, and the two talked about what Kai wanted in a cat. Sienna loved her son's explanation, and didn't miss the uptick of Noah's lips when Kai mentioned them staying. It solidified her statement earlier.

They were here to stay.

Chapter 17

Sienna fought the urge to stare out the window in her office. It was a perfect fall day, and she would love to go for a drive with the windows down, singing silly songs with Kai or doing tai chi with Noah.

Instead, she kept her eyes glued to her computer screen as her boss droned on and on during their weekly meeting. Numbers weren't her friend. Listening to the quarterly projections, the number of new clients signed, and how many claims they billed had her reaching for the iced coffee she purchased from the bakery during lunch. It didn't help that it was Friday afternoon. Thankfully, Maya offered to pick Kai up from school.

As her boss flipped to another slide, Sienna's mind drifted to the past week. Her parents went home three days ago. She loved their visit, but trying to keep them busy was a chore, especially when she and Maya had to work. Sienna hoped during their next visit she'd be able to take the time off. That wouldn't be until after the holidays.

Instead of selling their home, her parents decided to use a management company and keep it as a rental. It would give them the peace of mind that a reputable company would find the right tenant and handle any problems that arise. Sienna and Maya agreed to take a long weekend next month to help them clean. Sienna had her eyes on some of her mother's tchotchkes and hoped they'd find a way back to Oak Mountain. Maya wanted furniture for her new place.

Though Noah and the Beckett brothers didn't have a problem with Vince and Maya living off the property, they still wanted to clear it with Josie and Thomas Beckett. Hawkins Ridge was a family business, and even though they gave full control to the guys, Noah and the others still ran things past their parents.

Josie immediately offered to give them two acres on the edge of the property for them to build. As generous an offer as it was, Maya and Vince decided to see if there was anything else close to Hawkins Ridge first. Everyone understood and made sure they knew the offer was there. It would be the first time her sister and brother-in-law would own their own home. For close to twenty years, they've always lived on the ranches and farms they managed. They wanted their own roots and something they could pass on to the children they adopted.

The introduction of the COO brought Sienna back to the meeting. The medical billing company she worked for handled the billing for small and rural practices throughout the country. Based out of Philadelphia, they allowed the coders and billers to work remotely. They paid well and supported her when she moved to Oak Mountain. For the COO to grace a lowly staff meeting with her presence, it was important.

"I want to thank you all for making this past quarter a huge success." The middle-aged woman gave a round of applause with everyone returning virtual claps. Once the last emoji disappeared, she continued, "That being said, we have a bittersweet announcement. The city has contracted us to help with the billing of its workers' compensation claims."

Sienna's eyes widened. That was a huge bump for their company and spoke volumes about the quality of work they did. When it registered the COO said bittersweet, a sense of dredge washed over Sienna.

"With this new contract, we will need to add to our billing team. It also means we will go to a hybrid working environment. Employees will need to be in the office two days a week. Your team leads will put together a schedule so that everyone will have a remote Monday and Friday twice a month."

Sienna tuned out the rest of the conversation. Going into the office wasn't an option for her. It wasn't an option for two of her co-workers, who took care of special needs children. As one of the longer tenured employees, would they make an exception for her? She doubted. The city was a major signing. If they required all of their employees to adapt to a hybrid environment, the company would make that happen.

Shortly after the announcement, the meeting came to a close. Before Sienna could think about getting up to stretch, her team lead called. She took a deep breath and pressed the join button. Sadness covered Cecily's dark complexion. They'd worked at the hospital together; she in billing and Sienna in the ER. Cecily left while Sienna was out on bereavement. It was Cecily who encouraged Sienna to pursue coding and medical billing when she wanted to leave nursing for her sanity.

"I am so sorry you didn't find this out from me," Cecily started. "I met with leadership minutes before the team meeting started."

Sienna saw the sincerity in her friend's eyes. "I know you would have said something earlier if you'd known. So, are they really asking everyone to come back to the office?"

"I'm afraid so. They are trying to make it so it's still sixty percent remote, but the city made that a requirement. You know they wouldn't turn down money like that. It's a five-year deal."

"I guess. What does that mean for me and those who aren't able to be on site?" Sienna knew what it meant, but she needed to hear it from her.

Cecily sighed. "It means that if you can't or are unwilling to work on-site by the middle of next month, then they will let you go."

Sienna closed her eyes and took a deep breath. On paper, she didn't need to work for a few years. Between what was left over from the sale of her house, Dylan's life insurance and the survivor's social security checks she and Kai received, she was more than okay. Everything was in savings and a college fund for Kai. Her paycheck is what they lived off of. But Sienna enjoyed working and loved what she did.

"Are they offering any sort of compensation to those who aren't able to be on site?"

"I'm not sure, but I plan on asking when leadership meets again on Monday. They want to give people the weekend to come to grips with what's happening."

"They know people are going to leave."

Cecily nodded. "They do. My guess is that, depending on the number of people threatening to leave or turn in their resignation, they will offer a financial incentive."

No amount of money could get Sienna to move back to Philly. "Well, tell whoever you need to that I will submit my resignation on Monday. I'll stay until they implement the change."

"Will do. I will tap some of my resources and see if I can find a fully remote company for you, but I'm sure you could find a job locally. Do you still need to be remote?"

Cecily knew of Sienna's anxiety, and the question was out of concern. It was one she would need to think about. Did she need to be remote? Could she find a small medical practice in town? What about Kai's after-school care? He was too young to be on his own, but what options were there?

Sienna shrugged. "I don't know. I know I can't get back into nursing. It's something I would need to think about this weekend."

"That makes sense. Don't submit your resignation until you hear from me on Monday. I want to see what information I can get from the next meeting. If you have to leave, know that I will give you a glowing reference."

Sienna smiled. "Thank you, friend. I'd better let you go so you can reach out to everyone else."

"Not something I'm looking forward to." Cecily leaned closer to the camera. "Don't limit yourself if you have to look for other employment. I can see the difference the move has had on you. You're more open, and that glow you had when I first met you is back."

Sienna swallowed the lump in her throat and could only nod. Hearing that people could see glimpses of her old self meant that she'd made the right decision in moving. She forced a thank you out and ended the call.

What would she do? Would national online job boards even list anything for Oak Mountain? Stark Valley, perhaps. One thing Sienna learned in her short time in Oak Mountain is…everything depends on who you know.

Luckily, she knew the right people.

After logging off for the day, Sienna pulled out her phone and sent Noah a text.

> *Sienna: Instead of going out, how about a nice romantic dinner and movie in? I'll bring the Chinese food.*

After her conversation with Cecily, Sienna focused on finishing her work. It was hard when side chats with her two teammates with special needs children expressed their feelings towards the matter. Like Sienna, they knew companies that offered work-from-home for medical billing, but the pay was less, with no benefits. That wasn't an option. She didn't share her conversation with Cecily. They finally agreed to touch base first thing Monday morning to see what everyone had decided.

Since Kai planned to go to the movies with Maya and Vince. It would also give her time to talk openly about her job without her son worrying. She also didn't want Noah to panic and hadn't told him about the meeting. That was a face-to-face conversation.

Besides, a little romance wouldn't hurt either. His response was instant.

> *Noah: You had me at romantic. I'll supply the whiskey and dessert.*

Sienna couldn't stop the smile.

> *Sienna: You had me at whiskey. See you around 6.*

Garlic, onions, and sesame seed oil drifted from the bag resting on Sienna's passenger seat. It took every ounce of willpower not to delve into the bag of spring and egg rolls on the drive to Hawkins Ridge. She did, however, pop a few fried wontons.

The sun was just below the mountain ridge as Sienna turned onto the property. She waved to the workers leaving for the day. She made her way through the gate for the residences and turned on the path to the goat barn and Noah's home. A sense of calm washed over her. No matter what happened, she and Kai would be okay. If she had to commute to Stark Valley for a job, so be it. She'd invest in meditation music for the thirty-minute drive, but Sienna felt confident she could handle it.

Bringing her car to a stop behind Noah's truck, she took a deep breath and giggled when her stomach growled. Noah was strolling towards her car by the time she climbed out. A blinding smile on his face.

"Hey, beautiful."

Sienna ran her hand over her wild, natural spirals before glancing down at her outfit. She took a little time deciding on an outfit that was comfortable but nice. They may be staying in, but she wanted to impress. Deciding on a pair of jeans and a dressy red sweater, it made her feel good he liked it. "Thank you."

He gave her a quick kiss on the tip of her nose. "Even though Kai isn't eating with us, did you get him egg rolls?"

She grinned and opened the passenger door. "I would never hear the end of it had I not. He'd probably call his grandparents and say I was holding out on him." Next to popcorn shrimp, egg rolls were her son's favorite.

"Well, we can't have that." Noah snagged the bag from her grasp and took her hand with his free one. "Josie said she'll have the cats available for you and Kai to see after breakfast. She said they have new toys, litter boxes, and scratching posts if you decide on one."

Noah mentioned to Josie the day after their chili dinner her interest in adopting a cat. The matriarch of the Beckett family was beside herself with joy. She called and offered for them to visit during the week, but she wanted her and Kai to have the weekend to bond and get the cat settled. Giving it all the attention it needed. Including introducing it to Scooter.

"Now that we don't have to worry about keeping my mother hopped up on Benadryl, he's excited. I'll make sure he thanks Josie."

"She's happy that there's another cat person. Don't be surprised if she hits you up for fostering."

Sienna shook her head and stepped into his home. "Between Kai and me, they would probably be foster fails and a guarantee my mother would never step foot in my home again."

The two laughed as they set the food on the coffee table. Noah had taken time to light a few candles around the room. Seeing the quality whiskey in an ice bucket in the middle of the table brought a smile to her face.

"You're pulling out all the stops," she teased nodding towards the drink.

"Wait until you see dessert." He held out his hand and guided her towards the kitchen. When he opened the refrigerator door, a tray of bite-size cheesecakes with varying toppings greeted her. If she wasn't falling for him before, she definitely was now. She stood on her tip toes and pressed a kiss to his lips.

"It's perfect."

"I'm glad. Now let's eat before your stomach revolts."

As if on cue, her stomach let out another roar causing heat to rise to her cheeks. Noah handed her plates and forks while he grabbed the glasses and bottles of water. They made small talk about their day as they unpacked the bag. She wanted to get the conversation about her job out of the way first so they could enjoy the evening. Meadow chose that time to jump from her perch and pressed her head against Sienna's leg. She reached down and gave her a scratch under her chin. She would need to make sure any cat she adopted got along with Meadow. It was something Sienna would think about the next day. She had something on her mind and wanted to talk before the games started.

Noah poured two fingers of the amber liquid into the rock glass and handed one to her. She was staying with Maya, so she didn't have to worry about limiting her alcohol. Once they settled onto the couch and Meadow was whiskers deep in the salmon bites Sienna bought for her, she jumped into what was on her mind.

"They made an announcement at work today. Starting in the middle of next month, they are moving to a hybrid work environment."

Noah dropped the spring roll he was going to bite. Normally, she would have laughed, but it was a serious subject.

"What does that mean?"

She could see the concern on his face when he asked the question.

"That means I need to find another job." She stopped him from saying anything with a finger. He took a bite of his roll and motioned for her to continue. "My team lead is going to see if they will make exceptions, but it's doubtful. Since they are based out of Philly, I don't see them having a satellite office here or in Stark Valley. So, I'll stick around until they fully implement the change. I am hoping to have a new job lined up by then."

"You know I'll help you with bills until you find something. Denise would also work with you on rent."

Sienna smiled. They hadn't discussed finances because there hadn't been a need to until then. "I'm okay. I have plenty in savings and really don't need to rush into finding something for a few years if I want."

"Okay." Noah plucked a shrimp from his stir fry and set it on a napkin for Meadow. "How are you feeling about this?"

Sienna chewed her Szechuan chicken as she looked deep inside herself. She'd had a few hours to let the announcement sink in. She enjoyed working and loved what she did. However, there was a small part that felt a little relief at having a little time off between jobs. She didn't have to take the first thing that came along.

Sienna wiped her mouth and shifted slightly to face him more. "I'm a little sad because I love my job and the people I work with. Angry because there are some who aren't capable of going into the office. A little relieved because I have experience and could find another job in coding."

"Are there other companies like your current one that are one hundred percent remote?"

"There are, but few are legit. Most medical practices and hospitals like billing to be done on site, or they offer hybrid."

Noah nodded and took a swig of his beer before speaking. "Have you thought about going back into an office? Are you ready? You have a community that would ask around for you. You know that, right?"

Sienna slid closer and rested her hand on his. "Thank you. I know if I need help, I can ask. Cecily, my team lead and the one who helped me get the job, asked me the same question. If I were still back home, the answer would be no. I'm better with crowds and noise, but I don't know if I will ever be one hundred percent." She sighed and picked up her beer. "I think I would be okay here, or maybe at a small practice in Stark Valley. I also have to figure out Kai and school with a new job."

Since her son started school, he never used the after-school programs. Before moving, her parents would pick him up while she studied for her coding exams or worked. With his school a five-minute drive away, she could pick him up during her afternoon break. A new job meant finding care for him. She couldn't ask Maya, Vince, or even Noah. As quiet and seemingly safe as Oak Mountain was, having her nine-year-old son walk home or stay by himself for a few hours guaranteed anxiety attacks.

Noah rested his hand on hers, drawing her attention. "I saw you start to go down a rabbit hole mentally. Before you do that, let's take a step back. The first goal is finding you a new job. Josie and Denise are your sources of information. Why don't you talk to her when you look at cats tomorrow? If you want to continue doing what you're doing, they are the people you need to talk to."

Sienna nodded, releasing the breath she didn't realize she was holding. Noah motioned for her to eat while he spoke.

"As far as Kai is concerned. The school has wonderful programs, but he can get a ride here with Fiona. One of us always picks her up from school. Elementary gets out at the same time as the middle school kids. It's just a different pickup line. Going to the other side of the building to get Kai would take an extra minute. Heck, if you pay Fiona a couple of bucks, I'm sure she would babysit, or between Maya, Vince, and me, we would take care of him until you got off work."

"Huh." Sienna tossed the idea in her mind while she chewed. She'd seen the Becketts picking up Fiona when she went to get Kai. They always waved, but she never stopped because of the time constraint. Over the past two months, she's gotten to know the Beckett family, and they've been nothing but kind. She'd offer payment for picking him up, but her gut told her they wouldn't take a dime.

First, she had to find a job.

Sienna leaned forward and gave him a soft peck. "Thank you. For listening, your support, and just everything."

"You don't need to thank me. I love you, Sienna. I want a future with you and Kai. There was no way I'd let you handle everything on your own. I got you."

She blinked back tears and gave a trembling smile. "I love you, too."

Noah cupped her cheek and kissed her within an inch of reality. His full lips were soft against hers. For a moment, it was just the two of them. Then Meadow made herself known and placed a paw on their joined lips. They snickered as they pulled apart. The tail of a shrimp dangled from her mouth.

Finding love when she moved to Oak Mountain wasn't a priority. Rediscovering herself and building a bond with her son was. While doing that, she found a tribe that accepted and cared for her—and one she cared for as well. Maybe it was time for her to look for an on-site job. With the love of these people, she could do anything.

Chapter 18

Activity buzzed around the property as workers went about their morning chores. Sienna took a clarifying breath as she stood on Maya's porch. Today was the day she would be a cat mom.

While they prepared and ate breakfast, Sienna told her family about the meeting at work. Kai immediately worried they were moving back to Philadelphia. Sienna quickly assured him there was nothing for them in Philly. Kai calmed down and enjoyed the pancakes Vince had made.

Maya went into big sister mode, confirming what Noah said the night before that Kai would be cared for after school. Since Maya focused on paperwork for the last two hours of the day, he could stay in the office with her and do his homework. It eased Sienna's mind so she could concentrate on finding her next employer. Her family agreed Josie would be the person to talk to. She was the one who told Maya about Denise and the apartment. Noah offered to go with her and Kai to look at the cats and support her when she brought up the job.

"Are you sure you don't want us to go with you?" Maya said as she closed the screen door behind her. "Vince and I can put the trip to Stark Valley back an hour or two."

Sienna shook her head. Josie was like a mother to Noah, and she wanted to get to know her better. At the same time, asking the woman for help with job leads was nerve wracking. "I appreciate the offer, but I need to do this on my own."

"I know. Don't be nervous. Josie is a very down-to-earth person. She'll set you up with a cat and tap her resources. She'll have a few names for you to contact by the end of next week."

Sienna hoped so. Now that one of her worries was solved, she found herself getting a little excited about taking the next step on her journey.

"Mom, I helped feed the goats!" Kai yelled as he ran up the walkway. "It was so cool."

A few steps behind him, Noah laughed. "He's a natural. He didn't give too much and helped change the water." Noah rested his hands on Kai's shoulders. "He was the perfect help."

Her son preened, and she swore he puffed out his chest. Pride washed over her. "Good job, baby. I know they appreciated the help. Did you wash your hands? You don't want to smell like goats around the cats."

Sienna didn't know if the felines would pick up on the scent and steer clear of him. She didn't want him to feel bad if a cat didn't take to him. Noah walked past Kai and kissed her cheek.

"He wore gloves, and I made sure he washed up to his elbows in the barn sink."

So it was a valid concern, she thought. They waved goodbye to Maya and strolled across the street. The cat sanctuary was an addition to Josie and Thomas Beckett's home. It housed those who would spend the rest of their days on the property. The spacious remodeled room led to a screened-in area for the cats to sun themselves on warm days. From what Noah explained, they kept the cats for adoption, including the kittens in one bedroom and the other bedroom was for pregnant and new mothers.

They stepped onto the walkway to the Becketts' home, and Sienna pulled Kai to a stop. She smiled at Noah before crouching in front of her son.

"Listen to Mrs. Beckett if she gives you directions on how to approach the cats. We're in no rush, so we'll take our time."

Kai ran his hands across his shirt. "We should have gone home and gotten Scooter. He should have a say."

Noah turned his head to hide a smile. Sienna shook her head. "I am sure he will be okay with whatever cat we decide."

Noah and Jace stopped by her place early that morning to feed and change Scooter's water on their way to drop off the egg delivery for the diner. She had no intention of having them lug around Scooter for possible mauling by a cat.

Sienna rose to her feet just as the front door opened. Josie Beckett was an attractive, voluptuous older woman. Tall, standing a few inches above Sienna's five foot six, her long gray hair styled in a low ponytail.

"Good morning. How are you three this morning?" Josie said in greeting.

Noah rested his hand on the small of Sienna's back and motioned for her to go first. "We're okay."

"I helped with the goats this morning," Kai announced before holding out his hand for a shake. Josie wrapped her arms around him instead.

"A handshake was fine when we first met. We hug family." To prove her point, she pulled Sienna in for a quick hug. "Did you help with the goats, too?"

Sienna stepped back and flashed a grin. "I was on chicken duty."

"I think the chickens are worse than the goats sometimes," Josie quipped. Noah gave her a half hug and kissed her cheeks. "Come in. Can I get you anything to drink? I have freshly brewed tea and leftover coffee cake from breakfast."

Kai pleaded with his eyes. It sounded yummy, but she wanted to wait until they sat down and talked. Sienna still didn't know how to bring up needing Josie's help. Maya said to just be straightforward. Considering she only interacted with her when she visited the property, she wanted to ease into it. Noah must have sensed her hesitation and grasped her hand.

"Why don't we have the snack after we look at the cats? Sienna needs to talk to you, Josie, if you have time."

Concern showed in her eyes. She gave a nod and patted Sienna's arm. "Of course. Follow me. We have five kittens, their mother and a senior cat. All rescued together. We think the senior is the grandmother."

Like most of the homes Sienna had seen on the property, Josie's home was an open floor plan. They walked through the living and dining rooms until they reached a hallway to the left before stepping into the kitchen. Josie stopped at the first closed door on the left. Across from it was a glass door that looked into the bright sanctuary. Cats lazed in hammocks, napped on cat trees or played with toys. Sienna could see herself spending time cuddling and laughing with the rambunctious group.

"Have you thought more about moving the senior to the sanctuary?" Noah asked. He linked his pinky with hers.

"I think so." Josie nodded, following Sienna's gaze. "Most of the cats there are older and rescued from shelters. People pass them over for younger ones. Most don't want the heartache of having a pet for only a couple of years before they pass. A nine-year-old cat can still give love for another five to ten years if it's healthy."

"I'm considered a senior?" Kai asked, humor in his eyes.

Sienna ruffled his hair. "In cat years, yes. In human years, you still have an eight o'clock bedtime."

Everyone chuckled, lightening the mood. Josie opened the door for the adoptable cats and motioned them in. "They've been spayed or neutered. Logan has given them all a clean bill of health. Anyone you choose, bring them here for check-ups or emergencies."

The morning sun filtered in through the window and onto the five-tier massive wire enclosure. The door was tall enough for a human to enter and open for the adult cats to move in and out. On the lower level was a soft playpen for the kittens. The enclosure took up half of the space and gave more than enough room and freedom for the cats.

"The calico on the middle hammock is the grandmother. Fiona named her Lacy. Midnight is the black cat on the top level and the mother." Josie ambled over to the playpen. Two of the kittens were sleeping; the other three meowed their hello. "Four girls and a boy."

Sienna leaned forward and sighed. Fluffy balls of fur clambered to reach Kai. His joyful giggles filled the room. A soft nudge brushed against Sienna's arm. Midnight hopped down from her perch to move closer to the kittens. The new mother rubbed her head against Sienna, who returned the need for affection with long strokes down her back.

"Seems someone likes you," Josie quipped.

"Meadow took to her also," Noah added.

Sienna smiled and continued to rub the cat. Kai gravitated towards the gray kitten with white spots. "Can I take her out?"

"Of course." Josie moved closer and pointed to a wicker basket. "Why don't you pick out a toy and I'll set her on the mat."

Kai hurried to the basket and selected a stick with a ribbon and jingle bell. Josie carefully lifted two kittens. Sienna felt it was to make sure there was a connection with the right cat. Once Kai made himself comfortable, Josie placed the two kittens between his legs. Both took to playing with her son. Midnight hopped down to the floor and weaved her way through Sienna's legs while keeping an eye on her babies.

"I need to give the cats in the sanctuary their breakfast." Josie turned to Sienna. "Do you want to help?"

"I'll watch them," Noah offered. "Maybe Meadow would like a friend?"

This was their way of letting her and Josie talk. Sienna appreciated the gesture and kissed Noah's cheek. It surprised her when Midnight followed them out of the room.

"Should she be out?" Sienna asked, motioning to the black cat. Josie nodded.

"She follows me when I come into the kitchen. She doesn't go into the sanctuary. I'm not sure why." Josie reached into a mini fridge and pulled out a round container. "Can you grab that bag of kibble from the cabinet? Then you can tell me what's wrong."

Sienna was used to her family caring about her. People she'd only known for a few months were something she was getting used to. She lifted the bag onto the counter while Josie set out stainless steel bowls.

"I don't know if anything is wrong per se, but something happened yesterday." Sienna went into detail about her meeting, including her private conversation with Cecily, while she scooped kibble on top of the soft food Josie placed in the bowls. When she finished, the older woman returned the soft food to the fridge and returned with a small piece of chicken for Midnight.

"Are you leaving Oak Mountain?"

Noah saw Josie as a second mother, so her question didn't surprise Sienna. She quickly shook her head. "Oak Mountain is my home. My folks are renting their home and moving to Puerto Rico to be closer to my mother's side of the family. There's nothing for me back in Philly."

The hint of a smile told her she had answered correctly. Josie spoke as she placed the bowls on a tray. "Oak Mountain isn't known for having work from home positions."

Sienna agreed. "I noticed that when I checked the national job boards. More openings for labor and farmhands."

"If you see an ad for those positions, that means they've exhausted all the local contacts. Before we hired your sister and Vince, we went that route." Josie pressed a button with her hip and the door to the sanctuary opened. Sienna scurried behind her before the door closed. "Word of mouth, who you know, and the local papers are how people find jobs here."

"What about people who aren't qualified for a job? Do they get it because of who they know?" Sienna didn't know how she felt about that.

Josie cooed to all the cats who greeted her and set the bowls down in various locations before answering. "There are a few who have jobs they shouldn't have. People in my generation and even as young as yours won't recommend someone because they'll be putting their reputation on the line. In my case, if I suggest someone and they don't work out, they question the quality of my produce or the work here at Hawkins Ridge."

"So you aren't going to risk your reputation for someone you know isn't qualified." That made sense. There were several of her teammates she wouldn't recommend for a coding job, and some she would. "What about when you told Maya about the apartment for me? You didn't know me."

"True, but Maya told me *why* you were moving here. You were a single mother with a job that would follow you. You weren't a risk."

That made Sienna feel better about the apartment. What about the job? "Do you know where I can look for a coding and billing position?"

Josie handed her a broom while she shook out the padded mats under the litter boxes. "I know people who work at the hospital and the medical park. But they most likely won't be remote positions."

Sienna nodded and swept. "I figured. Noah asked if I was okay working in an office again. I am. Commuting to Stark Valley may push a little on my anxiety. My biggest problem I had was with Kai. Noah said that when Fiona is picked up, Kai could be as well."

She knew Noah would do what he could for Kai, but she wasn't sure if he could speak for everyone. The brothers may run the day-to-day activities of Hawkins Ridge, but everyone recognized Josie as the person with the final say.

Josie nodded. "Logan and Naomi do what they can to pick her up, but their patients may not allow it. Myself, Thomas, and Owen are usually next in line. I can honestly say picking up Kai won't be an issue."

"Thank you."

The two worked in silence, cleaning the floors, switching out the covers on the hammocks and replacing the beds. When they filled the fountains with fresh water, Josie spoke.

"I love Noah as one of my own."

Sienna stopped scratching a tripod tuxedo cat and looked at Josie. "Noah thinks the same of you."

"I know I asked earlier if you were leaving Oak Mountain. What if there aren't any jobs right away? What then?" Josie held her gaze. "Will you run?"

Maya was right—Josie is a straightforward person. The question didn't bother her. Everyone loved Noah. She loved him. Even if Noah wasn't in her life, she would still stay. It wasn't a lie when she said nothing was back home for her. Going back to Philly would be a leap backwards in her mental healing. She couldn't do that to herself or Kai.

Sienna leaned against the wall and shoved her hands into her pockets. She sighed but never shifted her eyes from the older woman. It was time to speak to her woman to woman.

"The only way I would run is if it was for the welfare of my son. Considering how much my son loves it here, I don't see that happening." She reached for the same tuxedo cat and ran her fingers down its spine. "I am not sure if Noah or Maya has told you, but I suffer from anxiety. After the death of my husband, I couldn't handle the ER and nursing any longer. It's how I became a coder and biller. The noise and congestion are triggers. It helped me hold on to my grief longer than I should and not be fully there for my son.

"I have savings and am in a position where I don't need to work for a bit," Sienna continued. "But I also know that if that is the case, I need to do something or else risk getting lost in my head. Maybe that means volunteering to help Denise at the flower shop. Help Maya and Vince here. Who knows?" She shrugged. "But I can assure you and everyone else that cares about Noah, because I know that is the reason you asked." Sienna gave a saucy wink, causing Josie to laugh. "I'm here to stay. Robin leaving instead of talking to him was wrong. I love him, and the last thing I want to do is hurt him."

Josie studied her for a beat before pulling her in for a hug. They embraced for a moment before the older woman took a step back. "You can always help me here at the sanctuary."

"I may take you up on that."

"I'll get Thomas to grab the bowls," Josie said, motioning Sienna towards the door. "Let's go see if Kai has chosen a kitten. Have you considered two cats?"

Midnight curled in the hallway and stretched when Sienna stepped out of the room. She scooped the cat up and rubbed her cheek against the soft fur. Maybe they could get two. Laughter drew her attention to the other room. Noah and Kai had all the kittens on the floor playing with them. Her son still focused on the gray spotted kitten and knew that was his pick.

Noah rose to his feet and met Sienna's eyes, Squeezing her hand. An unspoken question of whether she was okay. She gave him a smile and a quick nod before turning her attention to Kai.

"Have you decided?"

Kai's light brown eyes beamed with happiness. He pointed to the gray kitten. Not a surprise. "Do you think Scooter will like her?"

"Scooter?" Josie lifted the other kittens and set them in their playpen.

"His box turtle," Noah answered. "I'm sure he will love her."

"What are you going to name her?" Sienna still held the black cat and figured she was coming with them.

Kai held the kitten in front of his face and stared into its eyes. The adults each held back a smile. "How about Roxi?"

"I think that's perfect," Josie said, taking the kitten from him. "Let me give her a good wipe down. What about Midnight?"

Sienna looked at the cat curled in her arms. "You mean Onyx? Yeah, she's coming home with us, too."

"You're a softy," Noah teased, making them laugh.

"Why don't I clean up both?" She handed the kitten to Noah and took Onyx, formerly known as Midnight. "In the meantime, text me your contact information and email your resume when you get home. I'll make some calls this weekend."

"I have access to the drive on my phone and can email it now."

Josie rattled off her email address and disappeared with the cats down the hall, Kai and Noah on her heels. Sienna didn't want to get her hopes up that she'd have another job before the switch with her current one occurred, but it would be nice.

A smile graced her lips as she sent her resume. This was her new tribe. A new love and a bright future. Which now included two cats and a turtle.

Chapter 19

Noah reached across the console and linked his fingers with Sienna. Anything to get her to stop tapping a beat on the lid covering the salad. He understood she was nervous; they were meeting his mother for an early dinner after all, but they'd had meals with his mother before. A quick glance in the rearview mirror explained her nerves.

Bev was meeting Kai for the first time.

Or it could be that his mother found out about Sienna's job situation in less than thirty-six hours. He didn't know whether Josie or his father told her, but he had to admit, his mother knew people. If it helped her find another job and stay in Oak Mountain, Noah didn't have a problem letting the world know.

He admitted that when she mentioned her job shifting to a hybrid schedule, he panicked. Memories of Robin leaving flashed through his mind, but he believed Sienna when she assured him she wasn't going anywhere. He overheard her conversation with Josie when they were preparing food for the cats. She was adamant that she wouldn't run. Sienna then told him about their conversation in the sanctuary that night at her place. She wasn't afraid to let his second mother know she loved him and didn't have plans to leave. Noah hated he had that fear, but he did.

He loved Sienna more than he thought was possible in such a short amount of time. With Robin, it took a year to get to where they would say they loved each other. After two months with Sienna, he was ready to put a ring on her finger.

"I didn't know Josie and your mother still talked," Sienna said as she glanced out the window.

"They grew up together. My mother is a year younger, but my grandfather helped with the horses at Hawkins Ridge back when it was a horse farm with a few chickens and vegetables."

"I like your mother, but I don't see her mucking the barns."

Noah snorted and took the exit for the Stark Valley city limits. "My mother will work in a garden, but she is not farm material."

"But she's okay with you working at Hawkins Ridge."

Noah sighed. "She didn't have a choice. Josie's father had all of us boys out there helping. He called me a natural at growing things. When I found there was such a thing as agriculture business, I hopped on it. It made my parents happy because of the business side, and I got to learn the growing side."

Sienna shifted in her seat. "She has to be proud of what you've accomplished." Noah nodded.

"She is. Like every parent, they want their children to be happy. She sees I am."

The music in the truck filled the air for a few minutes while he maneuvered toward the newer community on the outskirts of the town. When Noah's stepsisters moved to the DC area, his mother and Malcolm didn't see the need to keep a house. They sold their home and bought a condo overlooking a golf course. It wasn't Noah's cup of tea, but they were social empty nesters.

"So you think the cats are going to be okay?" Kai piped up from the back.

"They'll be fine, and we won't be gone long," Sienna answered. Onyx and Roxi were in Sienna's office while they were away. They placed a bed in every room, but Roxi's portable playpen was in the office. They would have full run of the place, but since they'd only been there for a little over a day, they wanted the two together unsupervised.

Noah pulled the visitor placard from the console cubby and hooked it off the mirror.

"I know you said your parents live on a golf course. For some reason, I just couldn't picture it until now." Sienna let out a whistle as they waved to the security guard. "I am sure we underdressed."

Everyone in the truck dressed in jeans. Kai wore a nice polo shirt. Sienna opted for a red tunic, and Noah chose a simple white collared shirt. In his eyes, they dressed appropriately.

"We're fine." Noah pulled the truck into the parking lot of a four-story building. Expert maintained grounds highlighted a stone fountain surrounded by spiral topiaries. Decorative benches sat under oak trees. A chain-link fence surrounded a covered pool.

"Can we use the pool next summer?" Kai asked as he took Sienna's hand.

"Maya said there's a pool closer to home. I think that's where we will be going."

Noah punched a code into the box next to the front door. He held it for them when it swung open. "Your mother's right. People that go to this pool are over fifty-five. They aren't the Marco Polo type of crowd."

"Are you and Mom over fifty-five?" Kai asked, sincerity glowing in his eyes.

Noah looked at Sienna and chuckled. "We aren't quite there yet."

"Auntie will be that old before we will." Sienna looked around the elegant yet casual lobby. "I get why my mother and yours hit it off. I could see my parents living here."

Noah pressed the elevator call button. "You asked about my mother being okay with my career path. Were your parents okay with Maya pursuing ranch management?"

"My mother was more than my dad. Mom's family has horses and farms, so she was used to it. Dad was a city guy who was the first to go to college. I had uncles in the military, but they made careers out of it. Dad wanted something more." They stepped into the lift, and Sienna finished once the doors closed. "Since Maya and I were tomboys, we loved going to stay with my grandpa and grandma in Puerto Rico because we could get dirty. Maya was in her element."

"I can see that."

The door opened onto the top level. Noah guided them to the left and stopped at the door close to the elevator. He shook his head when Sienna fussed with Kai's hair to which the young boy swatted his mother's hands away. Noah leaned down and pressed a kiss on her cheek.

"He looks fine. They will love him."

"Everyone loves me, Mom," Kai replied with a cheeky grin.

Sienna rolled her eyes, but Noah could see the love and pride on her face. He took a deep breath and pressed the bell.

Sienna practiced her yoga breathing. She couldn't answer why her nerves were running a marathon. She was a little nervous about Bev and Malcolm meeting Kai, but it wasn't enough to make her feel out of her element.

The two times she and Noah had lunch with Bev, it was in a restaurant and usually because they were in the area doing something for the property. Noah felt obligated to call his mother to see if she was available for a quick bite. This was different.

When Bev called Sienna, she still wondered how the woman got her number. She said she wanted to talk about her job situation and invited them for dinner. Sienna explained that on Sunday nights, she and Kai try to have a quiet evening so they could prepare for the work and school week. Bev planned for them to eat at four. Sienna appreciated the woman's tenacious attitude.

Before Sienna could exhale another breath, the door flew open and Bev greeted them with a perfected hostess smile. Sporting an expensive lounge outfit, the woman looked flawless.

"Welcome! I'm so glad you could make it."

"Seems like we didn't have a choice." Noah hugged his mother. "How did you get Sienna's number, anyway?"

"Her mother," Bev replied, like it was normal. "She texted me earlier in the week to tell me about a sale at this wonderful site we both shop. She gave me Sienna's number in case of emergency. When Josie called to put out feelers for opportunities, I felt it was an emergency."

"It really wasn't," Sienna quipped, but gave Bev a hug. Her manners overrode her natural response. "But thank you for keeping your ears open for anything."

"Please. I made calls." Bev turned to Kai and crouched in front of him. "You must be Kai. I'm Noah's mother, Mrs. Johnson. You can call me Mrs. Bev."

"At least she didn't say to call her grandmother," Noah whispered in Sienna's ear, causing her to choke on a laugh. Malcolm chose that moment to stroll down the hall. Dressed in a pair of track pants and a long sleeve tee, he looked relaxed.

"Noah. Sienna. I'm glad you could make it." Malcolm gave Sienna a side hug. "This must be Kai. Nice to meet you, young man."

Kai shook his hand. "Nice to meet you, sir."

"Oh, he is just precious. I remember when you were that little, son." Bev patted Noah's arm before reaching for the salad. "Let me take that. What can we get you to drink?"

Sienna stopped herself from asking for a whiskey neat. "Water or tea is fine."

They followed Bev into the spacious living and dining room. A large sliding glass door led to a balcony with a view of the golf course and mountains. The neutral beige and brown overstuffed couch and matching loveseat popped with splashes of vibrant red and buttery yellow accent pieces. Despite the air Bev projected, the room held a comfortable and lived-in vibe.

"We can head to the dining room. I just pulled the salmon from the oven." Malcolm motioned for them to sit at the six-person cherry wood table with cushioned high-back chairs. It fed into the open kitchen, displaying modern stainless-steel appliances and gray granite countertops.

"Is there anything I can do to help?" Naomi asked.

"Nope. You and Kai sit. Noah and I will have this plated and on the table in minutes. In the meantime, tell me what's going on with your job." Bev picked up a platter and handed it to her son. "Josie said something about the company changing operating structure."

Sienna nodded and thanked Malcolm for the two glasses of iced tea. He thoughtfully placed Kai's in a juice glass. As she waited for the meal, she explained her meeting and the company's decision. By the time she finished, Bev and Noah strolled in with the salmon and roasted potatoes on a serving tray and her salad in a large wooden bowl. Noah quickly fetched a few dressings and set the bottles on the table. For a few minutes, everyone worked on making their plates and complimenting on the succulent flavors. Malcolm set his utensils down and picked up his wine glass.

"You were a nurse at one point. Have you thought about going back into the field?"

Sienna shook her head. She didn't know if Noah had told his parents about why she left nursing. A quick look in his direction and a slight head shake told her he hadn't. It wasn't something she was embarrassed about, and she told Kai once he was older. She took a sip of her tea before answering.

"No. I don't have a desire to return to nursing. When Kai's father was shot, they brought him into the ER while I was working. Obviously, I wasn't allowed to work on him, but I stayed in the area and watched him die. It was hard for me to go back into the ER after my bereavement leave since our ER handled a lot of violent victims." Sienna took a moment and centered herself when Kai rested his head on her arm. She kissed the crown of his head and finished.

"That moment led to crippling anxiety, and I found I wasn't fully there for my son and relied a lot on my parents. A former co-worker at the time suggested I get into coding and billing. Since I was familiar with the ICD codes, it wasn't too hard of a jump."

Bev gave Sienna's hand a squeeze. "I'm sorry. We didn't know."

She appreciated Bev's sincerity and patted her hand. "I'm better now, but my nursing career is over. I enjoy what I do, and it allows me to be there for my son."

Malcolm gave a nod. "You have your priorities straight."

"You do," Bev agreed. "Earlier I mentioned I'd made some calls. We have friends in the medical field. Believe it or not, there aren't that many coders in rural areas."

That didn't surprise Sienna. Larger cities have a shortage, and most coders rarely leave a job once they find a position they love. Offering a hybrid schedule may lure some coders from in-office positions to fill the upcoming openings. Malcolm continued Bev's point.

"We know Josie has also reached out to people in Oak Mountain. Are you willing to commute to Stark Valley if something comes up?"

Sienna swallowed her moist salmon and nodded. "I had concerns about after-school care for Kai, but Noah and Josie assured me I had nothing to worry about."

"I can help Noah take care of things," Kai added, before shoving a piece of potato into his mouth. Bev's soft smile at her son's statement warmed her heart.

"Noah tells me how you always volunteer to help. Shows you're a big boy and a testament to your mother."

Sienna glanced at Noah to confirm Bev's statement and blushed when he sheepishly shrugged. Man, did she love him. She turned her attention back to Bev before she went completely gooey. Turns out she was observing their interaction. The wink Bev tossed her had her ducking her head.

"You both are adorable, but on to serious things." Bev picked the wine bottle from the ice chest and topped off her glass. "Ideally, I know you'd prefer to stay in Oak Mountain, but it's good to know that you're willing to commute."

"I'm a realist with job opportunities in smaller towns. I don't have the desire to start a stay-at-home business, so commuting is something I've accepted. Stark Valley and Philadelphia are different as night and day. Commuting to a town of roughly sixty thousand is better than dealing with the traffic of one point five million."

Malcolm nodded as he forked a potato wedge. "When I moved here from Baltimore, I thought I was moving to the country. People here complain about traffic, but I just laughed at them. Nothing like rush hour around Baltimore."

Sienna chuckled. She'd visited the Charm City a few times. Malcolm was not wrong.

"Is working at Hawkins Ridge with your sister something you've considered?" Bev asked. Sienna took a sip of her tea before responding.

"I like helping here and there but that's Maya's thing. She's always wanted a career working outdoors or ranches."

"That's how Noah was. My father was a talented trainer and helped several of the farms in town. Though he was retired by the time Noah came along, he would take him out to Hawkins Ridge when he visited Josie's father. Between the two older men and the Beckett boys, Noah just fell in love working on the property."

Sienna nodded. "That's how it was with Maya. My family in Puerto Rico has a ranch and Maya was there every summer. I stuck with my grandma helping to care for the family."

"And your parents were okay with your sister pursuing that career? It was hard for me with Noah because I wanted him to have a business. Another reason I'm proud of him doing the blog. But I knew that stopping him from pursuing his passion would put a wedge in our relationship. That was the last thing I wanted at the time."

Sienna suspected she was talking about her marriage to Owen ending around the time Noah began applying to colleges.

"He is still successful and happy," Sienna pointed out.

Bev ran her hand down her son's forearm. "He is and that's the most important thing. I'm proud of the man he's become."

Noah leaned over and kissed his mother's cheek. It was a touching moment and soon the conversation turned to lighter topics while they finished the rest of the meal. Sienna's nerves eased to where she could enjoy spending time with Noah's family. They reminded her of her parents. It made sense that her mother gravitated towards Bev. She would have to talk to Flora about passing her number willy-nilly, but she appreciated her doing it if it led to another position.

After an hour, it was time to call it an evening. Sienna didn't want to leave Onyx and Roxi alone for too long, and Kai would need to take his bath. They said their goodbyes, with Bev promising to contact Sienna by the middle of the week. Noah linked his fingers with hers and made their way to his truck.

"I like your parents," Kai said as he clutched the container holding his extra piece of pie.

"They like you too," Noah replied. "Mom doesn't just pass out pie to just anyone."

"It was good pie. Everything was great." Sienna rubbed her thumb across the back of his hand. "Thank you for not letting me freak out about tonight."

Noah pressed the fob to unlock the doors and stopped at the passenger side. Kai scrambled into the back seat. He slipped his fingers under her chin and smiled.

"We're in this together. Partners. You calmed me when I met your folks. Now, you can see everyone wanting to help you. That's what I love about family. Blood and found."

"I love you."

Noah pressed a kiss to her forehead. "I love you too."

"I love you both," Kai shouted from inside the truck.

Sienna shook her head and let Noah help her climb inside. He closed the door and jogged around to the driver's side. She exhaled a breath of contentment. This was her life now.

She couldn't be happier.

Chapter 20

"Have you received any requests for interviews?" Flora's voice boomed from her phone as Sienna pressed the submit button on a claim she'd just finished coding.

"It's only been four days since I talked and emailed my resume to Josie. Even back home, that would be quick. I'm not expecting to hear anything for at least another week. Besides, I agreed to finish out the month." Sienna shook her head and pulled up the next medical report in her queue. "I need to run, Mom. I'll keep you posted."

She disconnected the call and took a deep breath. Flora was in full mother mode and worried Sienna wouldn't find another position. She tried not to take in her mother's fears. Sienna was okay with taking a break if needed. Noah, Maya and Josie all offered her time on the property if she wanted. Between the late fall harvest and helping to care for the animals, they would find something to keep Sienna busy.

Josie and Bev had reached out to her as promised, letting her know they'd given her resume to their contacts. Sienna thanked them both and started thinking of a way to show her appreciation. Something she would have to ask Noah when he came for dinner. It was Spaghetti Wednesday, after all.

As expected, of the fifteen coders, five submitted their resignations on Monday. The company agreed to provide a severance package of one month's pay provided they stay until month's end. Since she and Kai still received health insurance from the Philadelphia Police Association, that wasn't a concern of hers. As Josie and Bev reminded her, coders in the area stayed with employers. Sienna didn't rely solely on the two women and checked the local paper daily, and the community boards at the feed store and co-op.

Onyx chose that time to jump onto her lap and purred. Roxi laid sprawled on the small cat bed in the office after having a filling breakfast. Sienna absently stroked the shiny fur as she read over the office note. Some may think coding was mind-numbing, but she found it rewarding. Onyx adjusted herself so Sienna could type just as the doorbell for the street-level front door rang. The cat dug her claws into Sienna's thighs when she jumped down and sashayed out of the room.

She sighed and figured it was someone thinking it was an entrance to another store. She padded to the intercom by her private door and pressed the talk button.

"Hello?"

"Sienna? It's Caden Beckett. I was wondering if we could talk for a minute?"

Of all the Beckett brothers, the reserved middle brother was her favorite. She didn't have a clue what he wanted, though.

"Sure. Let me buzz you up."

He spoke before she could press the entrance button. "Actually, can you come down? Too many eyes, and the last thing we need is tongues wagging with me going up to your place in the middle of the day."

Sienna laughed because it was probably true. "Give me a minute to put some shoes on and let my Lead know I'm away from the computer."

She hurried and did what she had to do before jogging down the stairs, closing the door in Onyx's face. The last thing she wanted was for the cat to slip out the main door and run into traffic. When Sienna pushed the door open, she spotted Caden leaning against his truck. His therapy dog Scout, sitting by his feet. He pushed off the truck when he saw her. Sienna gave Scout some loving before turning her attention to the man.

"What's up? Are Maya and Noah okay?" She hoped the concern extended to Vince as well.

Caden shoved his hands in his pockets. "Yes. At least they were when I left the property this morning." He waved to Denise, who was looking at them through the flower shop window. He tilted his head. "That's what I mean. See the woman in the Buick across the street?"

Sienna nodded. The older woman was digging through a purse. Caden continued.

"When I pulled up, she was getting out of her car. She's been going through that bag this entire time and trying not to look to see why I'm just standing here. She's part of my mother's garden club." He motioned his head towards a bench in front of the bakery where two older men sat. "They know my father. I'm not trying to get cross-examined when I get home."

Sienna bit her lip to keep from laughing. Caden was ex-military and good at making observations. She thought the woman across the street was funny because her bag wasn't large.

"So what's up?"

"Mom and Noah were telling me about your job thing. I work with an organization that counsels people with mental illnesses. My therapy animal program is going to work closely with them. Anyway, about three months ago, the Centers for Medicare and Medicaid certified them as an approved provider. So now they can bill them for counseling. The director has her assistant doing it now, but she's leaving, and they want someone who knows what they're doing." Caden pulled out a business card and handed it to her. "Funding is through the county. I told the director about you this morning when I was there for my session. With over half of their patients on either or both programs, they want someone with experience. She wants you to email your resume. It's not some fancy doctor's office or hospital and the pay may not be as much, but..." He shrugged, letting the sentence go unfinished.

If Sienna didn't think they would be the talk of the town, she'd hug Caden. This was something she would want to do for a cause she supported. Caden was familiar with her anxiety issues and wondered if that was part of why he felt she would be good for the job. Either way, when she went back upstairs, she would email the person right away.

Instead of doing what felt natural, she clutched the card to her chest. "Thank you. This is something I would love to do if they give me a chance. I would hug you, but I don't think the woman across the street could handle it."

Caden barked out a laugh. "Probably not. You're welcome. I hope it works out. It's an amazing organization and helped me a great deal with the grant applications for the animal therapy program." He tapped his thigh, and Scout stood. "I'd better let you get back. Let me know if you need anything or a reference."

Warmth coursed through her as she blinked back tears. "I will."

She watched him open the door for Scout before climbing inside. Sienna waited until he started the engine before heading inside, giving Denise a wave of her own. She made a mental note to text Noah so he wouldn't hear of any fake nefarious actions between her and Caden.

Onyx met her at the front door. Sienna scooped her up and rubbed her face against the soft fur.

"Keep your paws crossed."

Old-school music blared from the sound bar connected to Sienna's TV. She and Kai danced in the middle of the floor between the dining and living areas. Because of their energy, Onyx came down with a case of the zoomies and ran around throughout the apartment. Poor Roxi tried to chase her mother but stumbled a few times. Sienna embraced moments like this.

As planned, Sienna emailed Caden's contact after letting her Lead know she was back at her computer. Twenty minutes later, Maggie Ellis, his contact, called, and spoke for fifteen minutes before setting up a formal interview. The conversation was promising, and she couldn't wait to tell Noah.

She chuckled, thinking of Noah's reaction when she texted with the potential for rumors. He responded with shock face emojis and stated: the town needed some excitement. Sienna thought Caden might disagree. It didn't matter to her. His visit held promise, and she wouldn't let busybodies get to her.

After spinning and dipping Kai for the end of the song, she fell back onto the couch to catch her breath. Roxi used her pant leg to scamper up to her lap. She wondered whether Josie or Noah had clippers. As if conjuring the man, Noah knocked before pushing the door open. His wide smile was on full display.

"You're having a party without me?" he asked while toeing off his sneakers.

"Mommy's in a good mood. We were dancing, and the cats were running around." Kai gave Noah a fist bump. "Are you going to dance with us?"

"If your mother's spaghetti is as good as usual, I probably will in order to fight my food coma." He leaned down and kissed Sienna's cheek. "Hey, beautiful."

"Hey yourself." She set Roxi on the floor and stood. She snagged the remote and lowered the volume. "The food is ready. I just have to heat the garlic bread."

"Let me do that while you tell me why you're in a good mood. Did you hear from someone?"

"Why don't you feed Scooter, then wash up?" she said to Kai. "I'll take care of the cats."

"Okay." Kai grabbed the container of veggies and fruit from the fridge and ran to his room as Roxi scampered after him. Onyx knew what time it was and followed Sienna. She spoke while she grabbed the fresh food and organic kibble Josie gave her for the cats.

"I heard from the woman Caden told me about."

Noah yanked a paper towel from the roll and dried his hands. "That was fast."

She nodded. "I thought so, too. Anyway, she explained that the person doing the billing was also her assistant. She wants to separate the duties because her assistant will be responsible for more in the coming months. Since this is sort of new to them, Maggie — that's the woman's name — wants someone with experience." Sienna placed the bowl in the holder and leaned against the counter. "The best part, it's hybrid. Three days in the office, two days from home. She wants me there when they have counseling sessions in case people need to supply insurance information. Since they're working with Caden, they are trusting his recommendation. I have an interview next week. They're willing to wait until I finish the month at the current job."

Noah closed the oven door before pulling her in for a hug. "I'm so happy for you. They're going to love you."

"Thanks. I also told her about my battle with anxiety, and she knows my therapist. I wanted to be honest."

He stepped back, but kept his hands on her hips. "That was a good call. I met Maggie when we went to her to review the grant proposal we created. She's passionate about mental health. Her father and brother battled PTSD. Both sadly took their lives because they weren't getting the help they needed."

"She mentioned mental health was a passion for her because of family members. I'll let her bring it up." Sienna placed the small bowl for Roxi when she followed Kai into the kitchen. "I will need to do a dry run to their office."

"We can go this weekend. It's just outside of downtown. Josie talked to everyone, so picking Kai up won't be a problem. Fiona offered to go to that side of the building and wait with him."

"I'm not a baby," Kai pouted, crossing his arms. Noah squatted in front of him and rested his hands on her son's small shoulders.

"No one said you were, Little Man. But it may make it easier for everyone to pick you both up at one spot. You're going to help everyone when you're finished with homework, so don't think we see you as a baby."

"Will I get paid?" Kai's smile was devilish and caused them to laugh. Sienna shook her head.

"We'll look into raising your allowance."

"Cool. Thanks, Mom."

Sienna wouldn't expect anyone to give Kai money if he helped around the property. If he helped, she didn't mind increasing his allowance from five to ten dollars. He used it for books on sale at the library or for a new item to put in Scooter's habitat. She tried to instill money management in the way her parents had with her and Maya.

"The bread's almost done. Can you take the napkins to the table for us? We'll bring the food over." Noah handed him a stack and watched him run off. Roxi tried to keep up. He turned to her and stepped closer. "I hope you don't mind what I said about not being a baby."

Sienna shook her head just as the timer went off. "Not at all. Thank you. I would have said the same thing. I thought once he went to middle school, he could take the bus if I couldn't give him rides, but nine is still just a little young when he's never ridden the bus before."

"Fiona did volunteer. It's just cutting across the playground. You've seen the teachers outside around the building."

It's what impressed Sienna when she picked him up. Oak Mountain might not have the crime of large cities, but they didn't take a chance with the children.

"I will have to thank her the next time I see her."

They quickly plated the meal, and she let him carry the plates while she took over the salad and bread. She loved how she and Noah worked together preparing meals. Sienna didn't know the level of intimacy it would bring to their relationship. With Dylan, their schedules usually meant her leaving a plate in the fridge for him or her doing all the cooking while he rested. Maybe it was age or just a level of respect. Either way, it was an activity she looked forward to with a man she loved deeply.

Chapter 21

Noah leaned against the front of his four-wheeler, watching the tree excavators remove the stumps and roots of the thirty trees cut down during the week. Once this was complete, they could have the contractors lay the pipes for sewage and gas. They wired the entire property for electricity years ago. It was the next step in building the therapy animal project.

When they met with the planner, he suggested three modules or pre-fab buildings connected instead of one building surrounded by tiny homes. It would take up less space and be easier to expand if needed. The larger of the modules would house four suites for clients to stay while they worked with the dogs. A lounge, game room with vending machines would be in the middle building. The free-roam kennel would occupy the last building. Caden wanted only ten dogs. They agreed to a tiny home for the manager, but most of the remaining five acres would be for training, dog runs, and a picnic area for the guests.

Noah glanced at the enormous stack of wood off to the side. There were plans to cut them into firewood and grind into chips once the harvest of the in-ground crops was done next week. It was something Sienna wanted to help with once she returned home.

It was a little over a week since she told him about the position at Western County Resources and Counseling. Maggie hired Sienna on the spot after the interview. She still had to pass the background and reference checks, but neither saw it being a problem. Given the timing involved with ending her old job and starting a new one, she and Maya moved up their plans to help Flora and Gerald clean their childhood home and left three days ago. Vince babysat Kai, but Noah took him to school for the two days. It gave them a chance to bond, and Noah fell even more in love with the boy. Sienna worried about Onyx and Roxi staying with Vince, but they took it in stride because Kai was with them. Noah couldn't wait until she came home that afternoon.

The sound of another four-wheeler pulled Noah from his thoughts and had him looking over his shoulder. Caden pulled up beside him and killed the engine. He climbed off and matched Noah's stance.

"They're making substantial progress. I thought some of those trees would take all day to uproot."

Noah nodded. "Me too. Have you seen Vince and Kai?"

"Kai is at the main house helping Mom take care of the twins while Logan, Naomi, and Fiona went out for lunch. Vince was helping cut the wire for the chicken coop."

"Did they need help?"

Caden shook his head as he pulled a water bottle from a saddlebag. "I asked before I headed out here, and he said they had it. I should let you know. Kai said he wanted a brother or sister when he was helping Mom get the bottles together."

Noah stared at his friend. He and Sienna hadn't talked about children. His initial thought of adopting was before he met the vibrant woman. Now that he had Kai in his life, did he want to add a little one to the mix? Did Sienna even want more children? How would he even bring up the subject?

"I haven't even brought up children to Sienna," Noah said, pulling his own bottle out. "I'm still trying to gauge whether she wants to get married again."

"Are you thinking about asking?"

He shrugged. "I've been tossing the idea around. That's why I'm doubting more children. If I did, I'd ask around New Year's, but the wedding would be after Jace and Claire's."

They set their wedding date for March twentieth, the first day of spring. Noah didn't want to take anything from them, and his gut told him Sienna would want to wait until school was out. Of course, he was jumping the gun. First, he had to see if she was open to getting married again. Was he?

"I think you should," Caden said. "I like Sienna. There's something about her that's different from Naomi and Claire. Don't get me wrong, I love my sisters-in-law. It's just Sienna—"

"Understands mental health," Noah supplied. Caden smiled.

"I guess that's it."

"Is that why you recommended her for the job?"

"It was." Caden took a sip of his water and watched the workers. Noah recognized his friend putting together his thoughts and stayed quiet. After a moment, Caden continued, "Sienna oozes empathy. It could be why she became a nurse. It's natural to her. The people she will have to deal with need that. They need that smile or a simple hug. She could have strung Maggie along to see if Mom or Bev came up with something paying more. From what I understand, Sienna said yes immediately."

Noah smiled, remembering the phone call when she finished the interview. He could feel the excitement and happiness through the phone. She said she regretted her commitment to finish out the month with her current employer. Just another thing he loved about her. Her maturity and loyalty. Most people would have just said screw it, knowing the result with her current employer wouldn't change. But that wasn't who she was.

"I think even if she had to be in the office every day, she still would have taken it. I agree, though. Sienna loves to help. I'm sure that's where Kai gets it from."

Caden laughed. "That kid has some serious work ethic. I thought he was just faking it to get something or got bored with a chore after a few minutes. Seeing Maya and Sienna, that goes back to their parents."

Noah agreed. "I think you're right. They lived with the parents for a couple of years. Sienna said her mother and father helped raise Kai when she was lost in her grief. I've been with them when she's asked him to help her with something. He doesn't complain, but just gets up and does it."

"That may change when he gets to be a teenager."

"I hope not." Noah kept his fingers crossed. "Oh, I got asked to do an interview. A farming magazine."

Caden turned. "Really? Are you going to do it?"

His friend's surprise didn't bother him. Jace was the face of Hawkins Ridge, something everyone eagerly agreed to. However, this was about his blog, which had over two thousand subscribers in less than a month. The article was also about the new generation of black farmers.

"Yes, I'm going to do it. They want to talk about the resurgence of farmers of color. I was going to see if Harold could sit in on it. You know, talk about how it was in the sixties and seventies."

Harold was Naomi's stepfather, and his son was the one that recommended Vince and Maya. Caden nodded.

"That's an excellent idea. Even if they decide against it, you interview him and release it when the article featuring you is out."

"I was thinking the same thing. You know, if I tell my mother, she's going to try an act like my agent."

Caden choked on his water. "I can totally see Bev making that suggestion. She'll think it's the start of bigger things."

"Yep. That's why I have no intention of telling her until the article comes out."

"She's going to ride that guilt train until her last breath."

It was Noah's turn to choke on his laughter. "Depending on when it comes out, I'll have to give her other good news so she can focus on that."

To those on the outside, it seemed Noah didn't care for his mother, but that wasn't the case. He loved his mother and chose to live with her when his parents divorced. Bev wanted the best for her son, and didn't want him to settle for less. She was protective of him. Noah loved her for that.

"Will that good news be a marriage proposal?" Caden teased.

"Only if the interview comes out around the end of the year and Sienna says yes."

Noah mentally crossed his fingers.

"I can't believe you're getting your own house." Sienna glanced out the window as they sped down Interstate seventy. "I see a lot of shopping in our future."

Maya spared a glance at her sister and smiled.

Bev called Maya thirty minutes before they got on the road to head home. She said the buyer accepted the offer she and Vince had put in three days ago. It was a three-bedroom house close to the feed store and sat on an acre of land. It would give them enough room to add an addition for their parents to stay when they came to visit. Maya quickly tagged the pieces of furniture not going with their parents to Puerto Rico. Her parents said they would come with movers to help move Maya and Vince, then head to visit the family. Sienna offered to give up the end tables in the back of the truck if her sister needed them.

The trip home had been an eye-opener for Sienna. She realized she didn't miss the constant hustle and bustle of city life. Sure, she made up for lost time, eating a month's worth of beef in three cheesesteaks over three days, and she and Maya even stopped by their favorite tattoo artist for new ink: a peace symbol behind Maya's ear and a black cat on Sienna's shoulder. Beyond that, the city would always hold fond memories, but she had moved on, and it felt good to finally admit that. The noise got to her slightly, but she used meditation and tai chi to help with the increase in anxiety. Sienna was proud of how she handled everything, but like Maya, she was ready to go home.

And Oak Mountain was home. She missed Kai, the pets, and Noah.

"I can't believe we're getting our own place." Maya bounced in the driver's seat. "Almost twenty years of marriage and we're getting something that is ours."

"Are you glad you waited to buy?" Sienna asked. The ranches Maya and Vince managed always provided housing. Her sister nodded as she took the exit for the county highway that would take them home.

"The last place in Kentucky was as close to feeling like home as any other place. However, something told us it wouldn't be our final stop. I'm glad we listened to our gut."

"And you'll be five minutes closer to me."

"For now, at least."

Sienna scowled playfully. "Can we not talk about moving in with Noah?"

"We could, but where would be the fun in that?" Maya pinched Sienna's hand when she tried to pluck her thigh. The two laughed but stopped for safety reasons. "Okay then, let's talk about the new job. What exactly will you be doing?"

Sienna beamed. She thanked the stars for Caden. She hadn't had time to get excited about the job. Maggie Ellis was passionate about mental health. The woman roughly ten years older than Sienna, she too, was of mixed race, taking more of her African American color than her Caucasian side. Maggie was slender, stylish, with a dry humor and a personable attitude. Her family moved to Stark Valley ten years ago to be closer to her husband's mother, who was battling breast cancer. When the county hired her to spearhead the rehab program for the spike in veterans moving to the area, Maggie jumped at the chance.

Sienna shifted in her seat slightly. "Besides coding and billing claims, I'll help clients find and apply for resources. It's another reason I'm going into the office. For now, I'm doing the billing when I'm home so I can concentrate."

"That sounds like something right up your alley. Is it a significant decrease in pay?"

Sienna shook her head. "About eighty dollars a check less. The good thing is that I'll be a county employee and get the same benefits. I'll compare health insurances and may drop the coverage we have with the police association. I guess it will be the end of my connection back home."

Maya reached over and squeezed her hand. "It may be for the best. You're starting a future with Noah."

"I know." Sienna sighed and looked out the window. Leaves decorated the forest ground as the mighty oaks and pines prepared for winter. "Do you think it's too soon to think about a future with Noah? I mean, we haven't talked about marriage, but he comes for dinner almost every weeknight. You know we rotate on weekends depending on what we're doing. It was different dating Dylan. We were young and focused on starting our careers."

"That right there is why it's different. You were both young and just starting careers with crazy hours. Do you think it's going too fast with Noah? Do you want to slow it down?"

"I don't. It feels like a natural progression."

"Then that's all that matters." Maya pointed a finger. "Don't let anyone tell you otherwise. Wait, has someone said something?"

Sienna chuckled at her sister's protective tone. "No. Just thinking, really. Being back in Philly helped me realize how much I love Oak Mountain. They could use a good cheesesteak place, but the burger joint sorta makes up for it."

"Girl, that burger place is our Monday go-to place. You know they added delivery, right?"

"They're on the next block from where I live. Why would I want them to deliver?"

"I don't know," Maya said. "Just making sure you're aware."

"I wonder about you."

Maya chuckled, shaking her head. The exit for Oak Mountain came into view. Butterflies danced in Sienna's stomach. She sent a text to Noah and Vince; they were ten minutes away. She needed a hug from her guys.

"We are going to put in an application to become foster parents in January," Maya said out of the blue. "It's the first step in the adoption of a child in the system. Just so you know, they will probably talk to you."

Sienna snapped her gaze to her sister. "We've been on the road for almost four hours. Minutes from home, you decide to drop that little nugget of news? We're going to need time to discuss."

"We have three months. Plenty of time to discuss."

"Whatever." Sienna crossed her arms before letting a smile grace her lips. "Kai will be happy to have a cousin."

Maya's smile was blinding. "He'll have to teach him or her the ropes."

"You don't care if it's a boy or a girl?"

Her sister blew out a breath and turned onto the road that would lead them to Hawkins Ridge. "It doesn't. I have a fear they'd send a girly girl. Mascara is the extent of my daily makeup. Tinted lip gloss for when I go out. I'd have to watch videos online to fully understand was a smokey look is."

Sienna cackled. She wore more makeup than Maya, but not by much. As a nurse, she sweated through her makeup after the first two hours, so she just stopped using it. Now, she would put on eyeliner and lipstick if going somewhere with Noah. She doubts it would change with her new job.

"It doesn't matter who they send, you'll make an amazing mother."

Maya sniffed. "Thanks."

Minutes later, they pulled into the property. The few Sunday workers milled around, tossing waves in their direction. Maya hoped Kai was up for sandwiches because cooking wasn't in the cards when they got home. They turned the bend, drove through the open gate leading to the houses, and laughed. Noah, Kai, and Vince stood in the middle of the road, holding signs welcoming them home. The handwriting said it was Kai's idea.

The guys jogged out of the way to allow Maya to park the truck. Each significant other ran to the doors for hugs.

"I missed you, Mommy." Kai wrapped his slender arms around her hips. "Scooter and the cats missed you, too."

Sienna wrapped her arms around him and kissed the top of his head. "I missed you too, Little Man." Noah took a step closer and pressed his lips to hers. "I enjoy coming home to that."

"We'll have to see what we can do about that, beautiful."

Sienna didn't want to read too much into his statement, but it sounded nice. She stepped out of the group embrace and reached for her crossbody purse. "I need to move the two boxes I brought home into my car, grab the pets, and then we're heading home."

"We got the boxes," Vince said from the back of the truck. "You take care of everything else."

Sienna didn't have to be told twice. She handed her keys to Noah and turned Kai towards the house.

"I already got dinner covered when we took Scooter home this morning," Noah said. "I have everything to make hot sandwiches and salad for us. You can just focus on resting."

Sienna stopped in her tracks and flung her arms around his neck. "Thank you. I love you."

"I love you, too. Now, I'm sure the cats are eager to go home."

Sienna hurried Kai along to make sure he had everything packed. He told her about what he did during the days she was gone, while she gave Onyx and Roxi the love they craved. After setting them into their carrier, and making sure Kai didn't forget anything, they were back outside in less than ten minutes. Sienna missed her apartment and bed and couldn't wait to unwind.

"I'll be right behind you," Noah commented as she set the cats in the back seat. "Leave the back door unlocked and I'll get the boxes on my way up."

"You don't have to do all this."

"I want to. You'd do the same for me."

He was right, she would. After another kiss and a wave to Maya and Vince, Sienna started the car and headed home.

Chapter 22

Sienna clicked on the submit button and tossed her reading glasses onto her new desk. Her eyes burned from overuse, but she couldn't be happier.

It was the end of her first week at her new job. She couldn't believe she still had thirty minutes left before she made the commute home. She spent the week completing paperwork, taking compliance courses, working with the IT department on her new laptop, and learning about her new position. During the first three weeks in the office, she wouldn't go to her hybrid schedule until the week of Thanksgiving. Sienna was okay with that. Maggie wanted the clients to get to know her. So far, that meant sitting in on two sessions.

After the dry run to the office before the interview three weeks ago, Sienna was no longer worried about the commute. The building was on the edge of Stark Valley before going into downtown. Caden explained the county chose the location because, like her and him, some clients struggled with being in congestion and crowded spaces. Having them navigate traffic would defeat the purpose of the support groups. Instead, they provided transportation to the tranquil setting. A building surrounded by trees with a tiny pond, with calming music piped into the session rooms.

Her start time allowed Sienna to take Kai to school. She enjoyed their morning routine and was thankful she could keep it. Noah worked it so that he picked up Kai and Fiona each day that week. She added every Beckett to Kai's authorized pick-up list with the school. Noah even offered to bring Kai to her place once she was home, so she wouldn't have to stop past the property. Noah was thoughtful like that.

In the three weeks since she'd returned from Philly, she and Noah had become closer. She didn't think it was possible, but they had. They've taken to having dinner together every day. Once they put Kai to bed, they would spend an extra hour talking about any and everything. Just getting to know one another. She learned he hated blue cheese dressing, mint chocolate chip ice cream, and cottage cheese. He broke his hand when he and Jace jumped out of a second-story window at age eight. He even shared losing a dare in college and had to wax his legs.

When it was Sienna's turn to share, she told him about placing a bunch of ants in Maya's shampoo as revenge because her sister had placed a worm in her hair. Also, she was a cheerleader for a week before getting into a fight with one of her teammates because Sienna refused to wear pink shorts under her skirt. Her latest admission was getting drunk at Maya's wedding. Her grandmother covered for her when she became sick after giving the toast. Another reason she limits her wine consumption to once a year.

Sienna smiled, remembering their conversation from the night before as she pulled up her work email. Noah asked if she could see herself living on the Hawkins Ridge property. Honestly, she hadn't thought about it since Maya had mentioned it during the festival. Now that the official question was out there, could she see herself?

Yes. Yes, she could.

Sienna loved everything about her apartment. The location, the size, and her balcony. But Noah's home was perfect. She'd add some more color to the space, but overall, it was a home they could grow old in. It was still something further down the road.

A quick knock on her doorjamb of her office brought Sienna out of her musings. Maggie flashed a one-hundred-watt smile and took a seat in Sienna's guest chair.

"Are you busy? I just plopped myself down and didn't even ask."

Sienna chuckled and waved her hand dismissively. "I'm free. I just finished the last compliance training and just pulled up my email."

"Good. How was your first week? Do you think you'll need anything? You should have received the login for the online coding site."

"I did and made sure it worked. As far as needing anything…" She glanced around her office. "I should be okay. If I need anything, I'll let you know."

Maggie crossed her legs and leaned forward. "I need you to be honest. Is this something you think you'll enjoy doing? It's different from what you're used to, I know. We just want to be sure you'll like it."

Sienna applauded the woman's straightforwardness. It was one thing she liked about her manager. She also understood where the concern was coming from. This position was relatively new to the program. The setup and duties differed from most coding and billing positions. Maggie recognized that. However, Sienna liked that it was different. They asked Sienna for her opinion on ways to streamline the process. So far, she couldn't be happier.

Sienna gave a sincere, warm smile and rested her forearms on the desk. "You know why I switched careers, but I missed helping people. I knew going back to nursing wasn't an option. This allows me the best of both worlds. Working with counselors and caseworkers to get people the help they need is rewarding."

Maggie nodded. "I feel the same way. I had to fight with the county that this would work. Then I showed statistics and costs from my previous job, and they gave it a two-year trial. Almost ten years later, they see the success."

"You should be proud of that."

"Oh, I am. That's why I want people willing to commit to making this work." Maggie held up her hand when Sienna went to protest. "I'm not saying you're not. But people are used to things being a certain way. Some I interviewed didn't understand the position required more than just billing. They weren't used to interacting with patients."

"They're used to speaking with providers, and some offices have staff just for insurance and self-pay issues."

"Exactly. I knew you would get it."

"I do, and I understand why you asked." Sienna glanced out her office window to gather her thoughts. "We touched a little on why I moved to Oak Mountain and my anxiety. Switching careers gave me what I needed when I needed it. This job is the final piece in making this area home. My previous position still had me tied to Philly. Not physically, but mentally. It reminded me of why I was no longer a nurse. I'm ready to move on from the past. Everything I've learned this week and the group sessions I've observed tell me I've finally found what I was looking for."

Maggie studied her for a beat, then smiled. "I'm glad we can be that for you. Now, why don't you cut out a little early? You said you have a party to get to."

Sienna glanced at her computer clock. It was only ten minutes early, but she'd take it.

"Thank you. Have a wonderful weekend."

The community center was having a 'costume optional' party for the elementary school kids. Halloween was in two days, but someone booked the center for the next day, and they didn't want to interfere with those who chose to go trick-or treating on Sunday. The town arranged for the grocery store to make meat subs, veggie sandwiches and gluten-free pinwheels. The citizens would bring side dishes and desserts. Sienna figured she wouldn't have time to make anything and was supplying snack-size bags of chips.

It was what she loved about Oak Mountain. That sense of community and inclusion. The holiday was not for everyone, and they respected that. Kai said his three friends weren't dressing up, so he wasn't. She respected her son's decision.

Sienna packed up her desk and sent Noah a text before walking out the door. He would bring Kai home. They would have an hour before they had to leave, giving her some quality time with her two guys.

She couldn't think of a better way to end an exciting week.

"Do you think Mom will be too tired to go?" Kai asked from his spot in the backseat. He swung his legs and glanced out the window. Noah met his gaze in the rearview mirror.

"Even if your mother was too tired, she would still go. Of course, she wouldn't say if she was or wasn't. That's not who she is."

"I know. It's weird not having her home all the time."

Noah pulled in front of their apartment and killed the engine. He turned in his seat, stopping Kai from climbing out. Was he upset Sienna was working outside the home? If he was, should Noah say something? And if it truly bothered Kai, would Sienna consider quitting?

"Are you okay with your mom's new job?"

Kai shrugged. "I guess. It's weird not coming home after school."

Noah didn't know his place with the conversation. He wasn't Kai's father or stepfather...at least not yet. It touched him that Kai felt comfortable to share his feelings with him. He had an obligation to Sienna to tell her what they talked about, but he didn't want to kill the trust he and Kai were building.

"I can see that. You're used to it. Do you like coming to the property?" If he didn't, he was sure they could come up with a solution.

"I like seeing the animals and you, Auntie, and Uncle Vince. Ms. Josie always sneaks me snacks." The cheeky grin told him that was the best part.

"Ms. Josie used to give me snacks too when I visited after school. You know, once your mom finishes training, she will work for home for two days."

"Will she be able to pick me up?"

Noah nodded. "If she can't pick you up, someone else will and just drop you off at home."

Kai contemplated the idea. "I like that. I like waiting with Fiona. Some of my friends have a crush on her."

Noah barked out a laugh and motioned for Kai to exit. He couldn't wait to tell Logan, his thirteen-year-old daughter, had a few nine-year-olds sniffing around her.

"Do you have a crush on her?" Noah was nosey. Sue him.

"She's pretty, but she's…"

Noah opened the main door and ushered Kai inside. He would let the boy figure if he wanted to share. They walked up the stairwell in silence until they reached the front door. Stepping inside, Kai finished his thought.

"I don't want a big deal made."

Noah held up his hands before reaching down and giving Onyx and the growing Roxi a scratch. "No one is going to make a big deal."

Kai studied him for a moment. "There's a girl in my class. Her desk is next to mine. I think she's prettier than Fiona."

Noah wanted to fist bump the boy, but didn't want to embarrass him. He would tell Sienna.

"Will the girl be there tonight?"

Kai shrugged. "I don't know. Maybe."

"I remember the first girl I thought was cute. She used to always ask if I wanted her milk. I'd say no, of course but for a few weeks, she would stop by my table and offer." Noah chuckled at the memory. "When she asked me to her birthday party, I used some of my allowance to buy her three candy necklaces."

Kai's eyes were wide. "Did she like it?"

"She did and give me a peck on the cheek. But in a week, she was asking another boy if he wanted her milk."

"Were you mad?"

Noah shook his head. "Nah. Another girl in my class asked me to push her on the swing during recess so I got over it."

Kai scuffed his foot against the floor not meeting Noah's eyes. "Do you think I should give her a present?"

He didn't know what to say but he wanted to keep it casual and open. "Maybe not a present, but offer her a cookie if she's there tonight."

The boy nodded in agreement. "Can I have a snack?"

"I thought you said Josie gave you a snack."

"It was half an apple. She ate the other half."

Noah chuckled and handed Kai his backpack. "Why don't you change, and I'll see about cutting up some cheese. There will be plenty of food there tonight."

Kai darted towards his room with Roxi on his heels. Onyx rubbed against Noah's jeans before hopping up on the window seat, which looked over the kitchen. He washed his hands and then pulled the block of cheddar cheese when the front door opened. Onyx hopped down and weaved herself through Sienna's legs. Noah stepped closer and kissed her temple.

"Welcome home, beautiful. I was just cutting up some cheese for Little Man. How was your day?"

Sienna kicked off her loafers and lifted Onyx. She rubbed her cheek against the cat's soft fur for a moment. Noah noticed the cat had become her support animal. He gave her time and went back into the kitchen. Sienna padded in a few moments later.

"Sorry, there was more traffic than I expected."

Noah handed her a beer and the plate that held a mound of cheese cubes. She popped a couple into her mouth and followed it with a swig of beer.

"No need to apologize. It's going to take time to get used to the commute." Noah leaned against the counter and flipped the cap off his bottle. "Kai is changing. He should be—"

"Mom!" Kai launched himself at her, causing Sienna to laugh. "Is it okay if I have a snack? Noah made some cheese."

"That's fine. I already had a couple of bites. Why don't you two finish that? I'm going to freshen up and change." Sienna dropped a few cubes onto a paper towel and grabbed her beer and purse.

Noah watched her disappear into her bedroom, closing the door after Onyx entered. He waited until Kai settled onto a stool before placing the plate of cheese and a sleeve of wheat crackers in front of him.

"I was thinking we should do something for your mom after the party," Noah said. He grabbed a handful of cubes and twirled them in his large palm. "Maybe watch one of her shows together when we get home."

"What about my bedtime?"

Noah forgot about that. The party was only two hours and ended at eight. Kai had an eight-thirty bedtime on the weekends. He chewed while he thought of options.

"Well, how about we make her breakfast in the morning?"

Kai nodded. "We can make pancakes and scrambled eggs. Do we have to go anywhere tomorrow?"

Noah mentally ran through his schedule for the next day. He planned to work on a few blog posts, but that was something he could put off until Sunday. Unless Sienna had something planned with Maya, maybe they could just have a day at home or do something together as a family.

Family. That was something Noah could get behind.

Noah moved the empty plate to the sink and twisted the top on the wrapper for the crackers.

"I think you're onto something. Unless your mom wants to go somewhere, we'll plan to just hang out tomorrow. Maybe play games or watch movies." He was sure his father would pick up Meadow and bring her to his place for the day. "Let's feed the cats and Scooter, then get ready to go."

Sienna strolled out just as Noah was dishing servings into the bowls. Kai focused on tearing a few leaves of spinach to mix with the pellets and thawed blueberries already in the bowl. Noah's appreciative gaze roamed her body. She'd changed into a pair of jeans and a rust sweater. She placed her black sneakers by the door.

"You guys didn't need to do this. I was going to take care of it." Sienna gave them each a kiss on the cheek.

"We wanted you to relax." Noah set the bowls in the holders and brushed his hands against his thighs. "Do you have anything planned for tomorrow?"

She tilted her head in thought, then gave a small shake. "Housework. I figured we would talk about plans later."

"Great. Kai and I were talking. How about a quiet day here? We can help with the housework. Watch a couple of movies. Maybe make *arroz con gandules* for dinner."

"And pancakes for breakfast," Kai added.

She looked between them and let a slow grin form. "That sounds like a perfect day. Thank you both for that."

Kai stepped off his kid-size step stool and carefully lifted Scooter's bowl. "You're welcome."

Sienna wrapped her arms around Noah's waist and rested her head on his chest. "Did I look that rundown when I came home?"

Noah chuckled and kissed the top of her head. "Not rundown, but tired. It's your first week working outside the home in five years. It's normal." Noah considered mentioning his conversation with Kai, but opted to wait until the next day. This was her time.

Sienna stepped out of the embrace but linked her pinky with his. "Maggie asked if she thought I would like the job since it's not a typical coding and billing position."

"What did you say?"

"I explained that it was something I wanted to do. Coding and billing was a way for me to deal with everything because it allowed me to work from home. Interacting with the clients taps into the reason I went into nursing. I get to help people."

Noah nodded. "I see that. That's who you are."

"Thanks." Sienna tossed her bottle into the recycling bin. "I may need you near me tonight."

After adjusting to something new for the past few days, her request didn't surprise him. He leaned forward and held her gaze.

"I got you."

And he did.

Chapter 23

"Did you save me some *arroz con gandules*? I'm telling Mom if you didn't," Maya whined on the other end of the phone. Sienna rolled her eyes.

"You know how to make it. Why should I save you some?"

"Because you love me," Maya deadpanned.

"Then I guess it's a good thing I saved some for you and Vince. I'll send it with Noah."

"Thank you, Cleo." Her sister's sing-song tone had Sienna laughing.

Talking to her sister was a great way to end a wonderful day. Sienna couldn't have asked for anything else. Except maybe for a serving of the raspberry shortcake Noah was in the kitchen dishing out.

When Noah suggested having a day at her place last night, she wanted to jump for joy. It wasn't a bad first week. She loved everything about the job. The commute would take time to get used to. Sienna found a calming music station on her satellite radio. It helped when traffic increased slightly. Knowing commuting five days a week was temporary helped a lot.

"So you signed all the papers?" Sienna asked, returning to the conversation.

"Yep, we'll move in two weeks. Dad said they'll have the movers deliver the furniture a week before Thanksgiving."

"We can still have Thanksgiving here, so you don't have that pressure." They planned on celebrating the holidays together since the folks would be in Puerto Rico until after the new year. With Maya's new home, her relationship with Noah, holiday plans were subject to change.

"I think that's best," Maya agreed. "What about Noah? Is he having it with Owen or his mother?"

The man in question strolled in carrying a tray with servings of the shortcake and two rock glasses of premium whiskey. He gave a winning smile and set the tray on the coffee table.

"I think it's still too early for that, but I'll ask. Give Vince a hug for me."

"So it's like that? Choosing a snuggle over your big sister?" Maya joked.

"Yep, because you would do the same thing. Love ya. Talk to you tomorrow." Sienna pressed the end button and tossed her phone onto the seat next to her.

"What are you going to talk to me about?" Noah handed her a saucer and fork.

"If you're doing Thanksgiving with Owen or Bev."

"Dad for sure. Mom and Malcolm are going to visit his family in Baltimore. Other than my stepsisters, I don't have a relationship with that side of the family." Noah shrugged and picked up his own serving. "I guess because I was an adult, there wasn't a need to. Even with Malcolm's daughters, we limit our time to saying hi and sending gifts. We don't hang out."

"Why don't you, Owen, and Sam come here? It was just going to be the four of us, and there's plenty of room."

"I planned on asking you what you were doing, but was going to wait until November first." Noah chuckled when Sienna tried to tickle his side. "We can talk more, the closer it gets. I know Dad is going to want to handle most of the cooking. He loves cooking."

"If he cooks, we'll pay for the food. I'll call tomorrow to invite him and Sam." Sienna took a bite of the flaky and sweet dessert. The raspberry still had a bit of tartness, despite the natural sugar syrup. "Did you can the fruit?"

"I helped. Cleaning several pounds of raspberries is hard work."

Sienna patted his leg. "How much did you taste?"

"You know me well."

The two laughed and enjoyed a few bites in silence. Kai went to bed half an hour ago. Sienna felt he needed the day just as much as she had. It was a change for both of them, and they would need to work out a new routine. Importantly, she needed to make sure they made time to stay connected. That was why she still wanted to drop him off at school.

Roxi padded from Kai's room to the bed her mother was curled up in. Sienna watched as the kitten made itself comfortable against Onyx's stomach.

"I would have adopted the unconfirmed grandmother if Josie hadn't said she would be part of the sanctuary." Sienna gave a last look before picking up her glass. "I like the setup she has for them."

Noah agreed. "Josie loves cats. Thomas just gives her free rein in making sure they're happy as long as it's not in their bedroom."

"Twenty plus cats trying to share a bed with you could kill the romance," Sienna joked.

"You mentioned introducing Meadow to your cats. I think bringing her here is the best move. She's used to my fostering other cats. Onyx, more than Roxi, will need to be able to retreat to her safe spaces."

"You're just a cat whisperer, aren't you?"

Noah tickled her side. "You weren't supposed to find out my secret identity."

"Your secret is safe with me."

Sienna leaned against him and rested her head on his shoulder. She closed her eyes, inhaling his rich woodsy cologne, and let the soothing jazz music relax her.

She opened her eyes when Noah cleared his throat and placed his half-eaten dessert on the coffee table. "I wanted to talk to you about something."

"Okay. Sounds serious."

"Not serious like you're thinking, but it's a conversation I had with Kai yesterday when we pulled up. I wanted to wait until we had time. You were too tired when we came home from the party."

Sienna was ashamed to admit she fell asleep on the couch about two minutes into the movie Noah had started last night. She shifted to face him and clutched her glass. The condensation grounded her. She motioned for him to start.

"Kai mentioned he missed coming home after school. I asked if he didn't like Hawkins Ridge. He said he does, but this week has been busy. So he's spent more time with Josie than with me, Maya, or Vince." A sly smile crept onto his face. "He said he likes waiting with Fiona because his friends have a crush on her."

Sienna snorted. "I can see that. That girl is going to keep Logan and her uncles on their toes." Fiona considered Noah an uncle, and vice versa. She felt sorry for the first guy she'll bring home. "Kai has always come home after school since day one. I thought he wouldn't mind hanging out on the property for an hour or two."

Noah took her hand and gave it a reassuring squeeze. "You both had a big change this week. In the end, it's good for both of you. I reminded him it was only temporary."

"Thank you. Is that why you wanted to spend the day away from Hawkins Ridge?"

"Pretty much. I know you both needed to take a break from the property."

"But that's your home. And we like going there."

A warm smile lit up his face. "I hope you both will see it as your home one day, but that won't solve the current issue."

Sienna wanted that too, but he's right. Now they needed to make Kai feel secure while he adjusted. In a year or two, he'd be old enough to stay by himself. Now, it would do more harm than good.

"I don't know what to do to assure him it's okay."

"I actually have an idea." Noah set his drink on the table and took her other hand. "Hear me out. Until you go to the hybrid schedule, what if I brought Kai here on the days you will normally work from home? The other days, he can hang out at my house if Maya is busy. I'd be with him the whole time. I can work on paperwork or write articles. This way, he can get used to the new situation."

Sienna didn't think she could love him any more than she did. Some men would tell Kai to grow up and deal with the change. Not Noah. He recognized Kai needed time to adjust to changes. Just like his mother. It made the day they spent together hanging out at home, watching movies and playing games more special.

"You would do that? What about work? You said it was busy this week. Won't they need you? You know, that means you'd have to pick him up every day. Are you okay with that?"

"Breathe, beautiful." Sienna did as instructed and took a few calming breaths. She nodded when her heart rate returned to normal and Noah continued.

"First, of course, I would stay with Kai. I would do anything for you and your son. They finished laying the pipes, which is why it was busy this week. I didn't need to be there and supervise, but I knew Caden had a sick stable hand, so he filled in. If I had known Kai was nervous, I wouldn't have been on site and stayed with him." He ran a finger down her cheek. She fought the shudder that ran up her spine. "And yes, I am okay with picking him up every day. You and Kai are my future. I love you both. Being with Kai until you come home isn't a chore; it's an honor. You trust me with the safety and well-being of your son. That's something I don't take lightly. I'll stick to whatever rules you have and make sure Kai does the same. This is all on you. If you decide against it, I'll respect that, and we'll continue with what we're doing until your regular schedule takes effect."

"I think I should tell you to breathe now," Sienna quipped, then sobered. "That is a lot for you to take on. The last thing I want is for the Becketts to resent me or Kai for taking you away from your responsibilities."

"Part owner, remember. Besides, it's for what, another two weeks? Then you'll be working from home for two days."

"Huh." Sienna hadn't thought about it that way.

"Also, the Becketts adore you and Kai. They know taking care of him is important to you…and me."

Warmth flooded Sienna's heart. She leaned forward and pressed her lips to his. Sienna wanted to deepen the kiss, but they were still talking. She sat back and nodded.

"I think that's a great idea, but I want to get Kai's okay first. He needs to be on board with everything."

"Agreed. We can talk at breakfast."

They were quiet for a moment. Sienna reflected on the conversation. She smiled and brought the glass to her lips.

"You're mine and Kai's future, as well." She took a sip and met his gaze. "So much has changed since I moved here. All for the best. Kai has blossomed so much I don't even recognize the shy boy from Philly. There was a time I thought my grief would stop me from ever finding love again. Let alone finding a career where I could still help others. I'm thankful Maya pushed me to move."

Noah gently placed a kiss on her forehead and smiled. "I'm thankful to your sister, too. Not just for what she and Vince have done to Hawkins Ridge, but for bringing you and Kai into my life. Like you, I never thought I would find someone to love again, especially with someone born and raised in a large city. I'm glad I didn't listen to my brain and took a chance."

"I'm glad we *both* took a chance."

Onyx chose that moment to jump onto the couch and cuddle on her lap. Roxi made an attempt, but her legs were too short. Noah scooped up the little fluff ball and let her get comfortable on a throw pillow. Noah grabbed the remote and pulled up a streaming service to select a movie.

Sienna didn't know what the future held for her and Noah, but it looked promising. She and Kai left Philly for a new start. She found acceptance, healing, and love. Sienna looked forward to finding what the rest of her life in Oak Mountain would bring.

Epilogue

Two Months Later…

"Do you think we're making too much food?" Sienna asked, glancing at her friends and family, either stirring something in a mixing bowl, chopping ingredients for a recipe or preparing drinks for the crew.

It was New Year's Eve and Sienna, Noah, Kai, Owen, and Sam all gathered at Maya and Vince's new home to help ring in the new year. The ranch style home was spacious, and unlike the open floor plans most of them had, this older home had dedicated rooms. A half wall separated from the living room from the ample kitchen. It would allow them to socialize while keeping any mess from the view of their guests. Sienna could be happier for her and Vince. They also had their first interview to become foster parents in two weeks, with a home visit a week later. Everyone planned to help paint the next day.

First they planned to spend the morning preparing the appetizers and snacks they would enjoy waiting for midnight.

"Are you excited about being on TV?" Maya directed the question to Noah. She was showing Kai how to recognize the small shells in the containers of crab meat.

Noah rolled his eyes. "It's PBS and a video call."

He may downplay the opportunity, but Sienna was proud of Noah. The interview he did for the magazine led to a Midwest PBS station picking up the story. They felt his and Harold's knowledge could benefit new farmers looking for information on how to start.

"PBS or not, it's exposure," Owen said. "Your blog is taking off."

"And Hawkins Ridge is also benefiting from it," Vince added. "We've seen an increase in orders for the goat milk products."

"Which means more goats for Kai to name," Sienna joked.

"I already started thinking of some," Kai said before sneaking a piece of the succulent meat into his mouth.

Maya shook her head at her son. Kai jumped at the idea of breaking up his after-school time between home and Hawkins Ridge. Sienna thought she would feel weird about Noah being in her home while she wasn't there. That was unfounded. His being there when she came home was natural. Noah took care of dinner. Since she worked from home on Wednesdays, they still had spaghetti.

"Have you met the contact person for the animal program yet?" Sam asked and he separated the pastry sheets for the crab puffs.

Sienna nodded. "Her name is Blair Emerson. The new executive assistant recommended her. They met while working together at a clinic. She'll start at the end of January. The cool thing is she has her own support animal. A shepherd mix."

"That will give her a connection to the clients signing up for the program," Noah commented.

Sienna carefully dumped the spinach from the final harvest they froze onto a set of paper towels to drain the excess water. She had a great recipe for a spinach artichoke dip she couldn't wait to dig into later. The group continued to talk about what they wanted in the new year while listening to music and preparing the appetizers.

Six months ago, Sienna was contemplating Maya's offer to move to Oak Mountain. Now, she found work to be more fulfilling than she expected. Interacting with the clients and sitting in on a few group sessions helped with her own healing. It satisfied her desire to care for others and gave her tips she could share with Noah. The couple included Kai in their tai chi meditation on the weekends. It brought them closer as a family.

Even Meadow and Onyx took to each other. They gradually introduced them over four visits, including one at Noah's. With a blizzard forecasted for the following week, they planned to hunker down at Noah's, giving Onyx and Roxi their first overnight visit.

"Should we wake up Kai?" Owen asked from his spot on Maya's sectional. "He wanted to ring in the new year."

Sienna strolled in from the kitchen, carrying two bottles of champagne. "If our shouting at midnight doesn't wake him, we'll give him his sparkling grape juice in the morning." Kai wanted to make it to midnight, but barely made it to ten o'clock.

She set the bottles in the ice bucket before popping a chocolate covered strawberry into her mouth. Noah tugged her onto the seat beside him and kissed her temple. "I don't want you too far when midnight strikes."

"Afraid you're going to miss a kiss?"

"Something like that."

She studied him for a second before dismissing the comment. Maya gave her a wide smile causing Sienna to roll her eyes. Her sister was acting weird all day. She made a mental note to corner her in the kitchen later to get it out of her.

"Time for the champagne." Sam pointed to the counter on the TV.

They popped the corks, filled the flutes and quickly rose to their feet. Everyone joined in counting down the final ten seconds. After yelling 'Happy New Year,' Sienna turned to kiss Noah and found him on bended knee.

"What's happening?"

"I think you have a clue, beautiful."

She looked at her teary-eyed sister. Vince had his arm wrapped around her. His own eyes were misty. She turned her focus back to the man who held her hand.

"Sienna. First, your father and Kai gave their blessings." Everyone chuckled before turning serious. "I never thought I would find love again. After my first marriage, work and family were my priorities. Then, out of nowhere, this beautiful woman with an adorable son strolled into my life, and I knew it would never be the same. You've given me a second chance at love and happiness. You've healed my heart and soul." He took the box that Owen handed him and flipped it open. A stunning diamond flanked by a ruby on each side sparkled in the light. "Sienna Marie Parker, will you do me the honor of sharing the rest of your life with me?"

Tears flowed freely down her cheeks as she nodded. "Yes."

Cheers and congratulations erupted as Noah slid the ring on her finger and pulled her in for a kiss. Maya pulled her from the embrace and smothered her in the way only a big sister could.

"Did you do it?" Kai's voice interrupted the celebration. Her son, still rubbing his eyes, strolled towards the group. Sienna picked up her son and gave him a hug.

"You kept a secret from Mommy."

Kai's smile was blinding. "I had to. It's a guy thing."

Everyone broke out in laughter as Noah wrapped his arms around her and Kai.

Sienna came to Oak Mountain to start over. A fresh start after a tragedy in her life. Finding a new career and love wasn't part of the plan.

But life has a way of rewriting even the best-laid plans.

The End

Afterword

Thank you for reading Rescuing Sienna's Heart. This is the third book of the Hawkins Ridge Animal Sanctuary series. Each brother will have their own chance at finding their forever love.

Mental health is a subject important to me. At no time do I mean for this piece of fiction to diagnose nor offer a solution for those suffering from anxiety. My purpose was to show you that you are not alone. Counseling and talking to someone are the best solutions. If you don't know where to start, contact the National Menal Health Hotline (United States) 866-903-3787.

The Asher House, an organization based in Oregon, partially inspired the idea of the sanctuary. What Lee Asher and his staff are doing is amazing. If you have not seen their videos on YouTube or social media and you love animals, check them out.

I have a soft spot for all animals, and I'm embarrassed by the rabbit hole I go down watching animal videos on Instagram. If you are interested in sharing your home with a furry friend, please visit your local shelter. So many dogs, cats and a variety of other friends are desperately looking for homes. If you don't have the space, consider volunteering your time. They are always looking for people to take the animals on walks or simply just sit with them. Too busy? Consider donating food, blankets or toys. Something to let the underpaid and overworked staff know they are not alone in their love of animals.

Yes, I am a baseball fan. I've only written one book that takes place outside of baseball season. I promise I'll incorporate football soon.

Want to keep up with what's going on in the series and be the first to see cover reveals and sneak snippets? Sign up for my monthly newsletter. or follow me on Instagram at @rubyjameswrites.

Also by

Point Harbor Sweet Romance
From Illustrating To Love
Maybe More Than Friends
Ronan's Queen
Seasoned New Beginnings
Point Harbor Box Set
Hawkins Ridge Animal Rescue—Sweet and Clean
Small-Town Romance
Sheltering Naomi
Claires' Forever Love
Rescuing Sienna's Heart
Blair's Sanctuary (Caden and Blair-Spring 2026)

Acknowledgements

There are so many I want to thank. First, my husband, Paul. I wouldn't be able to follow my dream without your love and encouragement. I am thankful every day for agreeing to meet you for that glass of wine 2 decades ago. You are my second chance at love.

To Becky, you have been a cheerleader since day one, and I am forever thankful for your friendship. I am still waiting to hit the lottery so we can buy the small island, set up our sanctuary and stop adulting.

My friend Dawn. There may be gaps in texts, but we always know who to reach out to when we need that encouraging voice. Thank you for your service to our country and your friendship.

To my mother. thank you for teaching me how to be a strong black woman. You are the muse for several mothers, grandmothers and aunts in my stories. I wouldn't know how to love and be myself if it weren't for you. I miss you every day.

To my father, thank you for letting me be me and encouraging me to follow my heart. I miss you.

My LERA (Land of Enchantment Romance Authors) group. Present and past members have been nothing but encouraging. All of this, every book, is because my group of fellow writers talked me off the ledge when I wanted to give up. You've all made me a better writer. Thank you.

Melody Jeffries, my cover artist and friend. Your smiling face will always pop into my mind whenever I hear the Friends theme song. Your artistic vision for my covers is appreciated. Continue to have faith.

My new editor, Ramona Mihidi. Thank you for improving my voice instead of changing it. I am thankful I found you when I was close to giving up on my writing dreams. I am looking forward to growing as a writer with your support.

To my ARC team. Thank you for being my first 'fans.' It means more than I could ever express.

Most importantly, thank you to <u>every</u> reader who has purchased or borrowed one of my books. I am thankful for helping me make my dream a reality,

About the Author

Ruby James is the pen name of a midlife woman living in the beautiful state of New Mexico. Born and raised in Washington, DC, she moved to the Land of Enchantment in 2006. Ruby is the 2022 Leslie Esdaile Aspiring Author winner and released her award-winning debut novella in September 2022.

Ruby's books feature plus-sized heroines and cinnamon roll heroes who appreciate strong women. Family, both blood and found, is at the center of every story she writes. Diversity is also key in her writing, as she believes every reader deserves to see a representation of someone they know, and she strives to include a presentation of our wonderful human race.

In her spare time, Ruby can be found with a book, listening to music, getting her daily dose of completing an online jigsaw puzzle or Monopoly Go, and learning random things on YouTube with her husband. During baseball season, there's almost always a game on, hopefully featuring the Orioles or Nationals. She also has the twenty-four-hour job of serving her cat, Random.